In the tradition of Jennifer Weiner's *In Her Shoes* and Cara Lockwood's *I Do (But I Don't)*, Eileen Rendahl's captivating novels meld humor and heart!

BE SURE TO READ EILEEN RENDAHL'S

Balancing in High Heels

"With hot action and hilarious antics, Rendahl crafts an enjoyable tale of starting over that will appeal to fans of both romance and crime fiction."

—*Booklist*

"Humorous, but Rendahl's latest has plenty of depth. . . . A book about finding your purpose in life."

—*Romantic Times*

Do Me, Do My Roots

"Heartwarming and hilarious, and the characters jump off the page."

—*Romantic Times*

"Moving. . . . An engaging relationship drama . . . [with] a wonderful cast."

—Thebestreviews.com

"Simply a winner. . . . Hilarious. . . . It makes me wish I had sisters."

—*Old Book Barn Gazette*

"A warm and touching novel."

—*Booklist*

UN-BRIDALED IS ALSO AVAILABLE AS AN eBOOK

Also by Eileen Rendahl

Do Me, Do My Roots
Balancing in High Heels

In One Year and Out the Other: A New Year's Story Collection
with Cara Lockwood, et al.

Un-Bridaled

Eileen Rendahl

doWn tOwn press

New York London Toronto Sydney

An *Original* Publication of POCKET BOOKS

DOWNTOWN PRESS, published by Pocket Books
1230 Avenue of the Americas
New York, NY 10020

Library of Congress Cataloging-in-Publication Data

Rendahl, Eileen.
    Un-bridaled / by Eileen Rendahl.—1st Downtown Press trade pbk. ed.
      p. cm.
    ISBN-13: 978-1-4165-0749-9 (pbk.)
    ISBN-10: 1-4165-0749-3 (pbk.)
    1. Brides—Fiction. I. Title.

PS3618.E5745U53 2006
813'.6—dc22   2005057950

First Downtown Press trade paperback edition March 2006

10 9 8 7 6 5 4 3 2 1

DOWNTOWN PRESS and colophon are
trademarks of Simon & Schuster, Inc.

Manufactured in the United States of America

Designed by Jaime Putorti

For information regarding special discounts for bulk purchases,
please contact Simon & Schuster Special Sales at 1-800-456-6798
or business@simonandschuster.com

ACKNOWLEDGMENTS

Writing can be lonely. Sitting in my kitchen in my jammies with a coffee cup the size of a soup bowl and a cat in my lap day after day is wonderful, but sometimes a little short on human interaction. I am wildly grateful to the people who are willing to put up with me, such as:

- My agent, Pam Ahearn, who fights the good fight for me and assures me that I am not high maintenance.
- My editor, Micki Nuding, who often seems to understand what my books are about better than I do.
- My fiancé, Andy, who shares my tiny home office with me and knows when not to complain about me still being in my jammies at three o'clock in the afternoon and also knows when to announce that I need to put on a pair of shoes that are neither my Asics nor my Uggs and get out of the damn house.
- My children, Ted and Alex, my two old souls who give my life so much meaning and so much joy.
- My wonderful friends who take me out bicycling, running, swimming, quilting, coffee-drinking, wine-swilling, and other fabulous activities.

Very special thanks to Julie Guida for the cake story and the wedding food.

For my mother who, for once, doesn't have a character based on her.

Un-Bridaled

CHAPTER ONE

Chloe's Guide for the Runaway Bride

Sure, you can run out of the wedding days, or even
weeks, before the actual event. You can spark a nationwide manhunt (womanhunt?) and cause giant bug-eyed
photos of yourself to be plastered on billboards by pretending to have been abducted. But why put everyone to
that kind of trouble? Be considerate. Run out on your
groom right there in front of everybody, and let someone
else alert the media.

"It is traditional, at this point in a Jewish wedding ceremony,
for the bride and groom to share a glass of wine and then
smash the glass." The rabbi smiled at Mark and me.

This was it. The final moment. We'd smash the glass, kiss.
Then, *presto finito*, *abracadabra*, *ta da!* I'd be Mrs. Mark
Hutchinson. My stomach flipped.

I looked up at Mark. He smiled back at me and gave my
hand a squeeze of encouragement. I took a big deep breath. He
hadn't wanted to smash the glass. I was glad he was being nice
about it now, because Mark could really cop an attitude when
he had to do something he didn't want to. I hadn't insisted on
much, but this was important to me—the smashed glass thing

and being under my grandfather's prayer shawl. I'm pretty sure I got the glass and the *chuppah* by agreeing to an extra half hour with the passive-aggressive photographer, having Mark's sister Kendra (who has never warmed up to me) as a bridesmaid, and most horrific of all, by agreeing to let his mother throw me a truly excruciating bridal shower where she served fruit punch. I couldn't even get drunk as a way to cope with it.

Mark took a sip of the wine and then handed the glass to me. I knocked it back. It's not like Manischewitz Blackberry is a vintage you want to savor. The guests giggled and I blushed. Mark shook his head but he was still smiling, so he couldn't have been annoyed with me. He hadn't gotten that tight-lipped look that signaled incoming thunderstorms.

The rabbi took the glass and wrapped it in a linen napkin. "Now that the couple has shared the sweetness of the wine, they will break the glass, showing that they will also share in any sorrow that comes their way." He put the wrapped glass by Mark's foot.

Mark raised his foot and brought it down hard. But instead of the resounding pop of shattering glass, there was a kind of *fftt* noise as the glass shot out of the napkin and flew across the room, bounced off a wall, and rolled for a few feet before coming to rest, whole and unbroken.

No one made a sound. Not a gasp or a peep broke the silence. Mark wasn't smiling anymore. Not even a teeny bit. His lips had started to tighten. I was *so* going to pay for this, and it was going to be a lot harder than spending an afternoon with Mark's female relatives without booze.

If I ran over and stomped on the glass myself, would that somehow undermine Mark's masculinity? It wouldn't be the first time he'd accused me of that.

Maybe I should wrap it back up and let him try again. Or would that somehow be patronizing?

The bottom of my stomach dropped like when you're in an elevator in a really tall building. I couldn't breathe. My heart pounded and the room swayed. The rabbi's big shaggy eyebrows rose like caterpillars doing backbends. Clarissa, my best friend and maid of honor, mouthed "Uh oh" at me. Jennifer, my half-sister and bridesmaid, hadn't noticed yet. She was waving at her son, Troy, who sat on his father's lap in the first row. Kendra, the bridesmaid-cicle I'd added as payment for the *chuppah* and the glass, smirked. To tell the truth, I've never exactly warmed up to her, either.

Then, a little voice inside my head said, "Run."

I am not prone to hearing voices. I am a steady, serious person with a logical, scientific approach to life. I do not have prophetic dreams, see visions, consult Tarot cards, or think the universe is trying to send me messages.

Yet one little voice says *Run!* and I picked up my skirts and ran like the devil himself was on my tail.

Faces blurred as I flew past them and raced down the ramp to the next floor.

I'd left my purse in the ladies' room, so I ducked in and grabbed it. Footsteps and voices were coming down the ramp behind me, and visions of braying dogs and searchlights filled my mind. Villagers with pitchforks and torches would be right behind them. They were getting closer!

I dashed out the door and jumped into my pickup truck. Gravel spit from under the tires as I reversed my red Frontier out of my parking space, and I sped by the Opera House as a small group of wedding guests burst out the door. A shout went up and someone pointed in my direction. I'd been spotted! Of course, I was hard to miss with my veil sailing behind me like a bizarre bridal freedom flag. I floored the truck and fishtailed through the intersection of Railroad and Main, heading for Interstate 505 south.

My heart pounded as if I'd just run a six-minute mile. The inside of the truck was an oven, and the blow-dryer breeze whipped in like a sirocco. My hair, however, did not move. It had so much gunk in it that it could probably withstand a hurricane. The rest of me shook like a leaf.

I was almost to Vacaville before my hands stopped shaking. I pulled into the Outlet Mall and saw a Starbucks; just the sight of that green awning made my heart stop racing and my breathing slow. An oasis of quiet and calm with espresso and baked goods awaited me. I could get a mocha if I wanted. I didn't have to worry about fitting into my wedding dress anymore, did I? I could eat muffins until I popped every button.

The veil, the Belgian lace, the tulle, and the dyed-to-match shoes naturally did not go unnoticed, which cut down considerably on the quiet and calm thing.

"Congratulations," the clerk said with a sappy sweet smile as she took my order for a grande.

"Excuse me?" I said.

"Your wedding. It's today, I take it," she said, smiling. "Congratulations."

"Yeah, today," I mumbled, which was not technically lying. My wedding *was* today—"was" being the operative word.

I grabbed my coffee and my low-fat cranberry scone (I can only throw so much calorie caution to the wind at one time) and made my way through the crowd that I swear had doubled since I had come in. Each person murmured congratulations or best wishes as I went past them. Their hands reached out to pat me or touch my dress. One woman actually pulled a tissue from her purse and dabbed her eyes with it.

What would happen if they found out I was a fraud? Would they turn ugly if they knew I was a runaway bride? Would they grab seed pearls and bits of lace off me? Would I end up like cousin Sebastian in *Suddenly, Last Summer*, consumed by a rabid pack of coffee-crazed wedding well-wishers?

I stumbled out onto the sidewalk into a blaze of June sunlight. Two cars honked at me as they went by.

Clearly, my first order of business was a change of clothing.

It wasn't just the unwanted attention. The stays from the long-line bra dug into me every time I took a deep breath. The shoes pinched. The hose itched, and the off-the-shoulder neckline kept me from raising my arms high enough to make a sharp left turn effectively in the Frontier. How could anybody expect this to be the happiest day of somebody's life when they also forced you to wear underwear that prohibited blood circulation and oxygen intake? Luckily the Outlet Mall boasted a Gap, a Levi's store, a Vanity Fair outlet, and fifty other stores.

But when I walked into the Gap, everyone turned to look at me. Then, seemingly as one, they walked toward me. It was like a cross between a jeans commercial and a zombie movie. I fled back to the truck as fast as my dyed-to-match shoes would take me.

I had plenty of clothes at the little house in Davis that Mark and I shared, but what if he was there? My favorite stretch denim jeans were folded over the chair in the ladies room in the Winters Opera House, but I couldn't go there, either. What if all the guests were still there, frozen in space and time with their eyes wide and their mouths like little round o's?

Worse yet, maybe only Mark was still there. Poor Mark. Poor smart, sensible Mark, whose fiancée started hearing voices at a most inopportune moment. Was he still standing at the altar, waiting for me to come to my senses?

I pulled off the highway and into the gravel parking lot of the Green Creek Saloon, a one-story white building with a green roof and green trim. The Frontier looked right at home

between a Ford 150 and two Harleys. No one would even notice I was there, unless they looked inside the truck and saw me
done up like Wedding Barbie.

I rested my head against the steering wheel. The points of the
comb that held my veil in place dug into my scalp. I needed a
cold drink, a shower, a pair of jeans, some flip-flops, and a pair
of country-girl underpants to replace my lacy white thong. The
thong had seemed sexy and enticing this morning, but had now
ridden up so high I wasn't sure it was ever coming out.

I looked up and the Green Creek's neon OPEN sign flickered
at me. At least I could get the cold drink.

I shouldered past the HELP WANTED sign on the dusty door
and into the dimly lit interior. The floor was linoleum until it
met the industrial-grade green carpeting. The bar looked like
plywood. The smell of mildewed dishrags dominated, with a
whiff of urine underneath. The tight-faced redhead (absolutely
not natural) behind the bar looked me over and asked, "Going
to or running from?"

I sat down on one of the barstools. "Running from."

She poured a shot of Jack Daniels, pulled a draft beer, and
plunked them down in front of me. I contemplated them for a
second, then knocked back the Jack and chased it with the beer.

I nearly fell off the stool.

Once the room stopped spinning, I asked, "What would you
have given me if I was going to?"

"Brandy old-fashioned sweet. Brandy is a restorative, and the
sugar would give you some energy. If you're running from, well,
you already did the hard part. You can put your feet up now."

I nodded, making my veil flop back and forth. I ripped it off
my head and smacked it down on the bar, feeling bold. "I think
I'd like another."

Til (according to the name tag on the tight-fitting sleeveless cowboy shirt with pearl-covered snaps up the front that barely contained her prodigious assets in that area) poured and pulled again. She slid them to me and leaned over the bar. "So why'd you do it?" she whispered conspiratorially.

"Hmmmm?" I said, wiping a dribble of Jack Daniels off my chin.

"Why'd you run? Did you catch him with one of the bridesmaids, trying to prove he was really the best man?" She winked.

I shook my head. "No."

Til's brows pulled down in a scowl. "He hit you? Smack you around?"

"No. Nothing like that. No."

"Then what? Did you find out he really didn't have a job, that he was broke? Did he lie to you about his family? What happened?"

I sighed. "The glass didn't break."

Til straightened up. "What?"

"At the end of a Jewish wedding, the bride and groom share a glass of wine and then smash the glass. It symbolizes that they'll share in both the sweetness and sorrow that might come. When he stamped on the glass, it didn't break."

"And you ran?"

"It seemed like a bad omen."

"Maybe it just meant that you wouldn't have any sorrow. Maybe it meant there would only be sweetness," Til said.

I stared at her. "That never occurred to me," I said, and then I ran to the bathroom and threw up.

I rinsed my mouth out at the grimy sink and contemplated my choices. There weren't many. Say what you will about my brother, Rafe, he always has my back. Whether it was monitoring Dad at the rehearsal dinner without me asking, or knowing whether I'd want cocoa or whiskey in any situation, Rafe was always there for me.

I fished my cell phone out of my purse. It bleeped at me about the twenty-seven calls I'd missed, and I scrolled through the list. The first fifteen were from Mark's cell phone. Four from my mother, two from Rafe, one from my father, two from my half-sister Jennifer, one from my friend Clarissa, one from my grandmother, and one from Mark's mother, Shelby.

I called Rafe's cell.

"Where are you?" I asked when he answered.

He laughed. "I'm at the park pushing Troy on the swings. But I think everybody's way more interested in where *you* are."

"What happened?"

"Uh, you ran out of your own wedding, leaving your husband-to-be standing under the canopy all by himself with an unbroken wineglass," Rafe said. "I'm surprised you've forgotten. I found it quite memorable."

I pinched the bridge of my nose between my thumb and forefinger, hoping to stop my headache before it spread. "I know that part. What happened after I left?"

"Much milling about and gnashing of teeth. We then progressed to tearing of sackcloth and smearing of ashes. Then Mark's parents took him home. Gran took Jennifer back to her place to put her feet up after they'd packaged up all the reception food, and Lily tagged along with them. Cara, Jackson, Dad, and The Charm went back to their hotel to go swimming, and I brought young Troy here to the park."

The Charm is our stepmother. Before she and Dad got married, everyone kept saying "Third time's the charm!" and Rafe and I couldn't help ourselves. We christened her The Charm then, and now, twelve years later, we can't seem to stop. Cara and Jackson are their kids, Rafe's and my littlest half-sister and half-brother. Jennifer is our mother's daughter from her second and present marriage, and if you're not confused yet, you're not paying attention.

"So there's no one at the Opera House?" I asked.

"Nope," he said cheerily. "Locked and deserted."

I chewed my lip. "I don't suppose anybody thought to grab my stuff."

Rafe snorted. "Are you kidding? Jennifer and Mark had a tug-of-war over your jeans until Dad made a Solomon-like comment about cutting them in half."

"And . . . ?" I prompted.

"And Mark was still trying to look reasonable about everything, while Jennifer doesn't give a shit what anyone thinks right now, so she's got your clothes at Gran's. I don't think Mark realized how irrational pregnant women can be. Or how strong." There was a pause and then Rafe said, "Hey, buddy, put that down. Trust me, it's not food."

"Excuse me?"

"Troy's eating wood chips."

Troy, our nephew, is Jennifer's little boy. He's three and considering the whole-grain, unsweetened, no-preservative stuff Jennifer feeds him, the wood chips probably tasted better than his breakfast cereal.

"So who all is at Gran's house?" I asked.

"Let's see. I told you that she took Jennifer there. David trooped along in his role as Dutiful Husband, so, not to be outdone, Lily is playing Supportive Mom and Stuart has reprised his role as Stalwart Dad." He paused. "I think that's it."

My stomach rolled. I could maybe face Gran. Possibly Jennifer. But Lily and Stuart, my mother and stepfather? Definitely not. And all of them together? Maybe not for years.

"Rafe?" I asked, my voice quavery.

"Chloe?" he imitated back at me, all quavery and whiny.

"Rafe, I need a favor. I need my clothes."

"So go get 'em." He chuckled, the rat bastard.

"I can't face all those people yet. I feel so stupid. I took you to the emergency room and didn't tell anyone that time you put your butt through the plate glass window, and when you got your head stuck in the gate over at the Little League field, I was the one who found the janitor with the key to the pad-lock." And countless other emergencies after which Rafe had looked at me and said that it had seemed like a good idea at the time. I choked back an unexpected rush of tears. "Please, Rafe. Help me."

Rafe paused. In all fairness, he didn't enjoy hanging out with Lily and Stuart any more than I did. "I'll get your clothes. I think Troy's had his fill of the park anyway. He's gnawing on a twig now."

"Thanks, Rafe," I snuffled.

"Forget about it. By the way . . ."

"Yes?"

"Just for the record, I'm not sure that what you did today was all that stupid."

Cold comfort, coming from a guy who had once gotten his head stuck in a gate.

I was on my third Diet Coke when Til said, "Bless my soul, I do believe I'm all shook up."

I knew it was Rafe without even turning around. That has been pretty much the universal female reaction to Rafe since he went through puberty. He's tall, broad-shouldered, and has soulful brown eyes. That's not all, though. There's just some-thing about Rafe; he exudes something that attracts women. I cannot count the number of girls who befriended me in high school in hopes of being invited to my house to hang out with Rafe, or the number of Lily's friends who had had to be discouraged from trying the Mrs. Robinson thing.

A paper bag plunked down on the bar in front of me. I peered inside it. Yes, yes, yes! My jeans. I hugged the bag to my chest.

"You're welcome," Rafe said as he slid onto the barstool next to mine.

Til sidled up, all fluttering eyelashes and an extra snap on that cowboy shirt undone. "Can I get you something?"

I nearly gagged, but a big grin spread across Rafe's face. "A beer." He glanced over at my empty glass. "What's she having?"

"Diet Coke," Til replied, sounding disgusted.

Rafe nodded. "Good choice. If you gave her booze right now, she'd probably toss her cookies."

"That's exactly what happened!" Til leaned over the bar, her breasts so plumped up they were nearly falling out of her shirt. "I gave her whiskey with a beer chaser and she ralphed everything up."

"Hmmm." Rafe rubbed his hand over his chin, which was clean-shaven for once. He generally sported stubble. "She threw up when they got engaged, too."

"You're kidding!"

I wanted to sink into the floor.

Rafe laughed. "Yeah. He did that thing where he had the waiter hide the ring in her dessert. The whole place was watching while he got down on one knee. He proposed. She said yes. Everybody cheered. Then she ran into the bathroom and blew chunks."

"I'm going to change," I announced, not that anybody noticed.

"She hates surprises," Rafe told Til as I left.

In the bathroom, I shoved my wedding dress into the grocery bag and my pantyhose into the garbage can. Mark's mother had loved shopping for that dress—unlike my own mother, who was much more concerned with shopping for her own. Lily had even asked me if I minded if she wore white as well. She looks fabulous in white. She has this dusky skin and thick black hair that sings when she wears a white dress. I inherited that from her, and I get mistaken for a Latina more often than people think I'm Jewish.

Shelby had loved all the wedding planning. I guess *someone* had to. I know every little girl is supposed to grow up dreaming of the day when she walks down the aisle, but maybe watching your parents do it repeatedly takes the magic out of it. (Twice for my mother and three times for my father. Though in all fairness, I was only there for one of my mother's weddings and two of my father's.) Or maybe I'm simply not much of a romantic. Or maybe it's because crowded social situations make me feel all itchy, like I'm about to break out in hives.

We hadn't even gotten my engagement ring sized before Shelby Hutchinson had compiled a list of caterers and venues. So I stocked up on hydrocortisone cream and played along, despite feeling like I was trapped and couldn't catch a breath.

I contemplated heaving the wedding dress into the garbage along with the pantyhose, but couldn't quite do it.

I don't know what Rafe was saying to Til when I went back out to the bar, but judging by her flushed cheeks, bright eyes, and trilling laugh, it was unspeakably witty. She might as well have thrown herself down on the bar and yelled, "Take me."

Til looked from him to me, and then back again. "Are you two twins?"

"Of the Irish variety," Rafe replied.

We're eleven months apart, proof of the fact that breastfeeding isn't always the most effective form of birth control. People have been asking the twin question since we were toddlers.

"You sound just like Dad when you say stuff like that," I said, then immediately wished I could suck the words back in when Rafe looked like I'd slapped him. Dad is not exactly Rafe's role model.

"I didn't have to come here," he pointed out. "I could have left you to the tender mercies of Lily and Stuart."

"You wouldn't," I said. Rafe and I had always been allies. Against Lily. Against Dad. Against Stuart and Sara and The Charm (well, we usually didn't need to ally ourselves against her) and pretty much the whole world.

"You really want to push me and find out?" he said, taking a sip of beer and not looking at me.

I put my head back down on the bar. "No. I'm sorry. I'm not myself today."

Rafe snorted. "You can say that again."

A chirping noise emanated from my bag.

"Your phone's beeping," Rafe informed me.

"Messages," I said, looking up. "Mainly from Mark."

Rafe's eyebrows went up. "What did he have to say about your hasty exit?"

"I don't know. I didn't listen to them."

"Want me to listen and summarize for you?" Rafe offered.

I nodded, then dialed my message number, put in the password and passed the phone to Rafe. He took it and started listening.

He held up one finger. "Mark wants to know if you're okay."

Well, that was nice. Considering what I'd just done.

Rafe held up two fingers. "He still wants to know if you're all right, but now he also wants to know where you are."

He held up a third finger. "He really, really wants to know where you are."

Rafe added a fourth finger. "Mark would also like to know when you're coming back." Full hand raised. "Mark would like you to come back right now." Back to one finger. "Mark is demanding that you come back immediately and explain yourself." Two fingers. "He'd like you to pick up the phone." Three fingers. "No actual message on that one." Four fingers. "Nothing there, either." Full hand. "This is your last chance." Back to one finger again. "This is really, really your last chance." Two fingers. "He can't believe you're doing this to him and to his mother." Three fingers. "Don't bother coming back." Four fingers. "He's going home and he'd prefer you not be there." Full hand. Rafe winced and shook his head. "I'm not repeating that one."

He worked his way through the rest of the messages. "Dad thinks it's funny. Gran wants to know if you need help. I want to know if you need help. Jennifer says that you can stay with her and David and that Dad—ours, not hers—is an ass. Though I think you could lump Stuart in with that without getting much argument from either of us. Clarissa wants to know if she can burn the bridesmaid dress and you should call her when you feel like it. Lily thinks you should go to Gran's, and I didn't know that Shelby Hutchinson even knew those words."

I put my head back down on the bar. "Turn it off before anyone can call again."

Rafe powered down the phone. "So what now, pussycat?"

"I honestly don't know. I don't even know where I'm going to sleep tonight," I muttered into my arms.

"You can stay with me," he offered.

Rafe rents a little house that he shares with two male roommates. They have one bathroom. I use the McDonald's bathroom down the street when they have parties there. No way am

I going to stay there. "Thanks, but I'd like to stay someplace where the shower doesn't host alternate life forms."

"Hey, if the mold doesn't talk, it's not an interesting morning," Rafe replied. "Wanna take Jennifer up on her offer?"

Visions of my younger half-sister, glowing with her second pregnancy while being doted on by her husband in their tasteful tract home, flashed before my closed eyes. "Not really. I want someplace quiet. Someplace calm. Someplace safe."

I sat up and looked at Rafe. "Gran's," we said in unison.

"Well, I don't see their car," I said. Rafe and I stood at the gate at the bottom of Gran's driveway. "If Stuart parked his BMW under the almond tree for shade, they're gone. But if he parked it on the other side of the house to be closer to the door, they could still be in there waiting for me." In ambush. "Can't you remember where they parked?" I pleaded.

"I'm sorry, Chloe." Rafe sounded defensive. "You didn't tell me that parking diagrams would be part of today's quiz."

"Just try to think. I can't face Lily right now, and I can't even bear the thought of Stuart." Just because I'd run out of my own wedding doesn't mean today should be different from all other days.

"I *am* thinking. I just don't remember."

"And you wonder why they call it dope?" I murmured under my breath.

"What was that?"

"Nothing. Let's just go." If my mother and stepfather were there, I'd turn on my blistered heel and walk back out.

Stuart's car wasn't there. Jennifer's was gone, as well. I heaved a sigh of relief. I'd clearly blown "acting normal," which Jennifer constantly hissed at us to do whenever her husband, David, was around. Which was pretty much all the time, since he was crazy about her.

Gran was out in her garden, turning off the fountain. She stood up and turned, her white hair a snowy cotton candy puff against the blue sky. She was all neat and tidy in a flowered pastel shirt tied at her waist and blue capri pants. She took one look at me and opened her arms. "Chloe."

I launched myself into her embrace and burst into tears.

CHAPTER TWO

Chloe's Guide for the Runaway Bride

Your engagement and wedding rings symbolize the hopes and dreams you had for your relationship. The diamond in your engagement ring is virtually indestructible, like you expected your relationship to be. The circular band is like the eternity you planned to spend together. Return it ASAP. Who needs that crap hanging around as a nasty reminder of what you've thrown away?

"But Gran, this is the craziest thing I've ever done. I'm the normal one, remember? I've never even been institutionalized." I clung to my grandmother as if she was literally my lifeline.

"Hey," Rafe broke in. "I was never institutionalized. You're talking about Mom and Jennifer."

"And Dad and you," I said into Gran's shoulder. Mom has done two stints in rehab and, based on what I saw at the rehearsal dinner, is probably due for a third. Luckily, it's still fashionable. Dad had a manic-depressive phase between Sara and The Charm that necessitated special hospital rest. Jennifer refused to eat when she started junior high and got down to seventy-three pounds, and had to be hospitalized to be tube fed.

And then there was Rafe. "Remember when you kept running away in ninth grade, to try and get to Kelly McMahon after her family moved away and Stuart got so fed up he had you declared incorrigible? What do you call that?"

"A youthful indiscretion from the depths of a fractured heart," Rafe said huffily, but I could see he was fighting back a grin. Oh, he remembered Kelly McMahon all right. He remembered her just fine.

"Yeah, well, you fractured your heart right into a detention facility, as I recall."

"For a weekend." Rafe played at indignation. "And as I recall, they dumped you and Jen here with Gran and went to Napa for the weekend. I think it was a babysitting arrangement."

Gran stroked my hair. "No one's going to lock you up for walking out of your wedding."

But they might for hearing voices. Probably best to keep that little detail to myself. After all, it only said one word. "Maybe they should. What was I thinking, Gran? He's a great guy, smart and good-looking. What sane person would walk out on a guy like that?"

"Maybe a person who knew in her heart that the smart, good-looking guy wasn't the right one for her." Gran patted my back and then said, "Raphael, stop making those disgusting gestures."

My chin started to wobble. "Couldn't I have figured that out before I walked down the aisle?"

"Apparently not, dear." Gran gave me another hug, then started toward the house. "It's done now, anyway. Would you like a lemonade? How about miniature pizza margherita or a scone with asiago cheese? Or some lovely salmon? We have quite a few leftovers from the reception. You must be starving. How about you, Rafe? Are you hungry?"

As we followed her up the stairs and into the house, Rafe kicked at a corner where the old linoleum was coming up. "You should get this fixed before someone trips on it and sues your butt off, Gran."

"Time was, people would have said someone might trip on it and break their neck, and would have been more worried about that," Gran said, pulling Tupperware from the refrigerator.

"Yeah," Rafe said with great seriousness. "And a dollar meant something, and children knew how to respect their elders and . . ."

"Yes, I know," she said, still pulling piles of containers out of the refrigerator. In a couple seconds, the Tupperware tower would be taller than she was. "Times have changed and I have to change with them. Would you like the job of fixing the linoleum before someone breaks their neck and sues your old grandmother's butt?"

Rafe thought for a minute. "I have some time next week. Maybe we could go Monday and pick out what you want."

"I like this linoleum. The pattern doesn't show dirt," I said.

"It's probably thirty years old and they might not make it anymore," Rafe warned. "It's just linoleum, Chloe. Not your legacy."

I was tempted to disagree with him.

"Chloe, dear," Gran said, surveying the structure she'd created on the counter. "You need to call your mother. She's concerned about you."

Lily concerned about me? That doesn't exactly fit my mother's personality profile. She might be concerned about her pearl earrings which I was wearing (my "something borrowed"); she'd inherited those from my great aunt Laura. "Do I have to, Gran? I don't think I can talk to her yet."

Gran's lips went a little thin. "She's your mother, dear. Of course you have to talk to her."

"She's not going to help, you know."

"Well, she'll want to know your plans. Chloe. I guess we all will."

I wanted to know them, too. "Can I stay here, Gran?"

"Of course you can. You know you can always stay here with me." Gran paused. "Or . . ."

"Or what?"

"Well, would you consider doing me a favor? I could really use some help at Aunt Laura's bungalow."

Aunt Laura had been Gran's older sister. She choked on a Jolly Rancher in 1962 and died before I was born, so I never met her. She had lived in a little California bungalow less than a mile from Gran's house, which she left to Gran when she died. Gran had had a steady stream of tenants in the bungalow for as long as I could remember.

"Sure, what kind of help?"

"I told you I'm remodeling, didn't I?"

"Of course. You also know that I have to repeat that righty-tighty rhyme to put in a screw."

Gran started scooping salmon onto plates. "I don't need you to do the work, dear. I want someone to keep an eye on things and supervise. You know, make sure they're painting the walls the right color and not putting the cabinets in upside down."

"Is this like when you let me 'help' you make Thanksgiving dinner when I was seven? Are you just humoring me?"

"No, I'd never make that mistake again. Those were the worst yams anyone ever ate." She grinned and plopped a spoonful of pesto pasta primavera next to the salmon.

"You shouldn't have expected me to be able to double a recipe properly. We hadn't even done fractions yet."

"You *wanted* to dump in that whole bag of brown sugar, my dear. But let's get back to Aunt Laura's. Every day I have to go up there to check on things and frankly, I'm getting a bit tired."

Gran tired? Gran was never tired. Lily got "tired." "Tired" was one of our many euphemisms for hung over, possibly our favorite one. "Feeling under the weather" came in a close second. When Lily got "tired," she used to pack Rafe and me off to Gran's, who was never tired *or* "tired."

On the other hand, Aunt Laura's bungalow could be the answer to my problem, and if it really would be a help to Gran at the same time, I could live with that. It would be a place to stay—rent-free—and an easy commute to work.

"Before I go up there, I'm going to have to go into Davis. I have to go to Mark's."

Rafe cocked his head to one side. "I know you didn't hear his actual message, Chloe, but he was pretty clear about not wanting to see you."

Knowing Mark when he was mad, I could just imagine what the message had been. I also knew one other thing. "He has Jesse."

"You're going to have to get out soon, Chloe, or one of the neighbors is going to call the police," Rafe said from the backseat of my truck.

"No one's going to call the police, Rafe. Until earlier today, I lived here, remember? They're used to seeing my truck."

"But not with three people sitting in it and watching a house, dear," Gran said, patting my arm. "Rafe's right. We shouldn't sit here anymore. Would you like me to go in with you?"

Yes. I wanted her to deal with the whole thing, but I knew

that wasn't the right way to handle it. "Thanks, Gran, but I'll do it."

Years ago, Gran had found Jesse wandering the back roads around her house. He'd been dirty and hungry and had a nasty gash on his leg. Gran was one of the only people he'd let near him, and she'd spent a small fortune on hamburger trying to lure him into her car. She has a soft spot for shepherds. I think it's something about their faces that gets her. But Gran hadn't needed a dog, especially not a big dog that needed a lot of exercise, so I'd ended up with Jesse. "What will you name him?" she'd asked.

I hadn't thought for more than a second. The name just popped into my head as I looked into his big brown eyes. "He looks like a Jesse to me."

"Jesse?" she'd said. "Why Jesse? He looks more like a Bongo to me."

"Bongo? Where did Bongo come from?" I'd laughed.

"CNN. He's that Irish boy with the band who's so political."

"You mean Bono?"

"Bono, Bongo. What's the difference?" Gran had sniffed a little. "Where did Jesse come from?"

I couldn't tell her; I just knew that was his name. She'd dropped it eventually.

I now unstuck myself from my sweaty seat and got out of the truck. Rafe slid out from the backseat behind me.

"I'll walk you up to the door," he said, "so Mark knows you're not alone."

I shot him a look. "Mark's not violent, Rafe."

"Not physically," he said.

"What's that supposed to mean?"

"Let's just get Jesse and your toothbrush and get out of here."

I nodded, swallowed hard, and rang the doorbell.

I'd never stared at this door before and waited for it to open; the whole thing gave me a creepy sense of déjà vu.

Dad had moved a few times while we were kids. Many times, Rafe and I had stood in front of a front door that we'd been told was ours, but felt we had to wait for someone to answer. Lily or Gran would be waiting in a car at the curb while Rafe and I stood and waited for Dad or Sara or The Charm or any of a series of girlfriends in between to answer the door. Our door. To our house. Sort of. But not really. Like every place we lived.

We'd come back to Lily's after a few weeks at Dad's, and feel just the same way whether she'd moved while we were gone or not.

I'd just turned to say something to Rafe about it, to see if he felt it, too, when the door was flung open. I took a deep breath and turned to face Mark.

Except it wasn't Mark.

It was Vicky Montoya.

I went to graduate school with Vicky. She wasn't a super close friend, just someone I met for coffee occasionally. Someone who'd be on the guest list for big events. Not someone I expected to find opening my door after my un-wedding.

Vicky launched herself at me, wrapped her arms around me and wailed, "Oh, Chloe, I'm so sorry. I just had to do something to help."

Okay, this is part of why Vicky and I aren't closer. She emotes too much. *Waaayyyy* too much. I'm inherently suspicious of laughter that trips off the lips too easily and tears that spring like projectiles out of eyes. I'm also not crazy about unnecessary touching. Vicky is one of those people whose hands are constantly on you when she's talking to you. It's like she doesn't think your ears are activated until she gets hold of your arm.

"Uh, thanks," I said, wondering why answering a door to which I had a key was so helpful, and required this much hugging.

"Mark looked so devastated after you . . . well, you know . . . uh . . . left."

That was a charitable way to describe ditching a man at the altar. Vicky had an annoying way of refusing to dish about fellow graduate students, faculty, or staff. She was forever making up reasons and excuses for the idiotic things they did.

"So I asked him what I could do and he asked me to come pack up your things." Vicky released me and and bit her lip. "I hope that was okay. I thought it might help you, too. You know, so you wouldn't have to spend too much time here."

Mark emerged from the bedroom right then with a large cardboard box in his arms. He dropped it on the floor next to two other boxes and my big suitcase. "Chloe," he said, his tone flat and uninflected. He had on a pair of faded jeans and a plain blue T-shirt that he filled out just right. Mark works out and it shows.

My heart thumped. He was so handsome, blond and Adonis-like. I'll never forget the day he walked into Chromonology, the biotech firm where I work. Every woman he walked by nearly swooned. In all fairness, there are not a lot of hunky plant pathologists out there. Our eye candy possibilities were usually limited to the UPS guys, so Mark wasn't exactly running in a strong field. But still . . .

Sales at the local department stores soared during the weeks Mark spent doing consulting work at Chromonology. Every female (and a few of the males) updated their wardrobes and started wearing makeup. Several people got new haircuts and more than a few got the first manicures and pedicures of their lives. All in all, Mark's presence upped the attractiveness of the Chromonology staff considerably. When he asked me out—me, just a lowly research assistant—I felt like Cinderella being asked to dance at the ball by the prince.

Jesse and Aziza bolted in from the kitchen. Jesse shouldered Aziza aside and gave her a little bite on the neck to boot, in his zeal to make sure that he was the first dog to get to me. I knelt down and Jesse raced to me, his body turned almost sideways from wagging his tail so hard. He licked my face as thoroughly as if it had been covered with beef gravy.

"That dog has the worst case of sibling rivalry I have ever seen in an animal," Rafe said to Vicky.

Vicky made a noncommittal noise and crossed her arms as if she was cold, which I suppose was possible since the air-conditioning had been cranked up. This had the salutary effect of plumping her large breasts up in her sleeveless white eyelet top. I have been Rafe's sister my whole life and it still amazes me how many women flaunt their breasts at him with almost no encouragement whatsoever. Rafe never complains about this or makes an attempt to discourage it. Right now, I was grateful that it had distracted him from my dog.

The rivalry thing wasn't Jesse's fault; Aziza was a pest. A needy, whiny nuisance. "It's not sibling rivalry. It's pack mentality. He's asserting that he's the alpha dog," I said.

Mark threw his hands in the air. "God forbid you should say something bad about Chloe's dog. Leave her fiancé standing at the altar and you don't have to say a word, but don't you dare say anything bad about Jesse."

I couldn't bring myself to look up at Mark. Jesse made a *harrumphing* noise and wagged his tail so hard it banged on the floor like a judge's gavel, which I suppose should have said that I was guilty, but somehow didn't. "I'm sorry, Mark," I said quietly.

"Well, then that makes it all okay, Chloe. You're sorry. That's super."

I didn't know what else to say, so I kept my head down and my mouth shut—skills I've perfected during years of practice with Dad and Stuart, and the best way to keep Mark's anger from escalating.

After an awkward pause, Mark went on. "Well, you're not as sorry as I am. I'm sorry that I ever laid eyes on you. Now take your stuff and your goddamn dogs and go."

That did make me look up. "Dogs?" I asked. Aziza was Mark's dog.

"Yes, dogs. Take Aziza, too."

Mark had adopted Aziza a couple of months ago, not long after I moved in. He'd thought another dog would give Jesse a playmate, something to dilute what Mark felt was an overclose bond with me.

Mark said I anthropomorphized Jesse too much, but he was just as guilty of it as I was. He was always complaining that Jesse was jealous of him. I mean, so what if Jesse horked up part of a dead squirrel in Mark's favorite loafers? Stuff like that happens with dogs. You can't take it personally.

"You want me to take your dog?" I stood up to face Mark.

"I only got her because of you. Now you're gone. I don't want her, either." He crossed his arms across his broad chest.

I looked down at Aziza, who had been trying to wiggle between Jesse and me, her stump of a tail quivering. "Mark, you made a commitment when you took that dog in."

"Yeah, well, you made a commitment when you put that ring on." Mark gestured with his chin toward my left hand.

Okay, he had a point. I slid the ring off my finger and held it out to him. He extended his hand, palm up. I dropped the ring in. He closed his hand into a fist and crossed his arms again. "Good-bye, Chloe," he said, then turned on his heel and marched back toward our bedroom.

Well, not my bedroom anymore. It was even less my bedroom than the one my dad had turned into a ceramics studio for one of his girlfriends when I was in eighth grade. "Come on, Rafe," I said softly. "Let's load this stuff into the truck and go."

"I tried to make sure I got all your clothes and your, you know, uh, personal stuff from the bathroom," Vicky confided as we carried the boxes and suitcase out to the truck, where Gran was waiting. "I didn't know about the books and things. I'm sure you can come back to get them when Mark, uh, you know, calms down."

I wasn't entirely sure that Mark would ever, uh, you know, calm down, but Vicky's full lips were already trembling and her eyes were tearing up. Rather than be hit by a flood of Vicky tears, I kept that thought to myself.

"You're taking Aziza, too?" Gran asked as I ushered both dogs into the truck.

"Mark kind of insisted. Do you know anybody who might take her?" Gran lived far enough out in the country that a lot of her neighbors had multiple dogs; it's a farm thing.

"I'll ask," she said and gave me an encouraging smile.

I got in the truck and rolled my eyes as Rafe said a lingering good-bye to Vicky. "I can't believe you're flirting at a time like this," I told him when he finally climbed in.

"I was not flirting," Rafe protested, earning himself a snort from Gran. "I was being polite."

"You'll be 'being polite' to the morticians as they close your casket, if they're female," I said with disgust.

In the rearview mirror, I saw a slow smile spread across my brother's handsome face. "Man, I hope so."

Aziza licked his cheek and we drove off. As I rounded the corner, I saw a police officer on a motorcycle pull onto the street from the other direction. I guess I really didn't belong there anymore.

"How torn up is Aunt Laura's place?" I asked Gran the next morning, while eating a lightly grilled fruit kabob from our vast selection of reception leftovers and a piece of toast. Sun poured into Gran's kitchen, but it wasn't really hot yet. Jesse slept on my feet under the kitchen table.

"Not very, yet," said Gran. "Are you going in to work today? Or can we go up and have a look around and figure out what you need to move in?"

"I'm not going in to Chromonology today." Jesse shifted under the table and Aziza whined at the sliding glass door to come in.

Gran turned from the counter and opened the door for Aziza. "Did you call?"

"Mm hmm." I'd gotten Dennis's voice mail and left a message. Since he'd been at the un-wedding, he'd know I wasn't likely to be leaving on my honeymoon today. Aziza put her paw up on my lap and whined a little for my food. I brushed her away. "Get off, Aziza."

Gran shook her head. "How long were you taking off for the wedding?"

"Two months."

Gran's eyes widened. "That's a lot of time."

"Well, I wanted a week for the wedding and then two more for the honeymoon, and a few days after that to get settled. It was actually easier for Chromonology if I took two months off at that point because they could get an intern in to do my bench work while I was gone."

So now I had sixty days to think about why I'd taken the Crazy Exit off the Normal Highway. The boulder in my chest got a pound or two heavier. I shook my head. If thinking about thinking made me feel this bad, real thinking was going to be truly nasty. "I'd rather keep busy. I'll see if Dennis can find a project for me to work on. Besides, I blew most of my savings on the wedding. I doubt Mark will be willing to keep me in groceries right now."

Aziza set her nose on my lap again. I gave up, split the rest of my toast and gave half to her and half to Jesse, and got up to get dressed.

Before I could leave the kitchen, my cell phone started ringing with "Insane in the Brain." My mother. I almost didn't answer it, but Gran gave me that very expectant look and Jesse put his head to one side and woofed at me. "Fine," I muttered at both of them and hit the button.

"Hi." Keep it short, keep it simple, maybe I'll get out of this in one piece. The key to my mother is knowing how to manage her—and as soon as I figure out how to do that, I'll alert the media.

"Chloe, are you okay?"

"Fine. Thanks."

"Fine? That's it? After the performance you pulled yesterday, all you can say is 'fine'?"

I took a deep breath. "I'm at Gran's. I picked up my stuff from Mark's last night. A friend packed it for me. I've got Jesse, but Mark made me take Aziza, too."

"Has your father said anything yet?"

"No."

"Call if you need anything." A heavy sigh traveled over the airwaves. "Who is Aziza?"

Click. Buzz.

I smiled at Gran. "I'll go get ready to leave."

Someone not raised by Lily Gold Sachs Turcotte might think that exchange was strange. Of course, I wasn't really raised by her either.

My parents split up when I was six and Rafe was seven. My father was an assistant professor of sociology at CSU-Fresno. My mother happened to stop by to visit him during office hours, found him playing Hide the Thesis with two of his female graduate students, and promptly left him.

In a way, this was unfair. As near as I can tell, my father has always been completely honest about being a first-class lech. Over the years, I've found a certain amount of security in his predictability. If a young woman with particularly large breasts or a noticeably firm and round rear end should walk by in a restaurant, I know my father will stop in midsentence to watch her walk by. He's a tits and ass man. I don't want to count on this, but I know I can. He will tell you that he likes women. I think he likes them the way those guys who pay inordinate amounts of money to eat sushi off a naked woman like women: as serving trays to satiate their own appetites. Still, he is always consistent.

Lily, on the other hand, is a chameleon, turning personas on and off at her whim. I'd almost be okay if I could identify the whims that made her flick the switch, but my mother is a complete mystery to me.

When Rafe and I were born, she was Earth Mother Extraordinaire with occasional Jewish American Princess flights of fancy. We were both born with the help of a midwife in the Berkeley co-op where my parents lived while my dad did his graduate work, but Rafe's bris was catered by Jacoby and Sons Bagels and All Kosher Deli. She founded a La Leche League chapter, protested the Vietnam War, and burned her bra, but had a monthly appointment to get her hair and nails done. Dad got his Ph.D. and they moved to Fresno where the student seminars on Dad's erogenous zones took place, and Lily flew the co-op.

We lived in a variety of seedy apartments in West Sacramento with a succession of "uncles" during what Rafe and I refer to as our Poor White Trash phase. Then Stuart Turcotte showed up and we abruptly moved into my mother's Betty Crocker phase. No more tie-dye and half-smoked roaches in the ashtrays from the Earth Mother era; the thrift shop clothes, canned beer, and Twinkies were gone too. Fresh baked cookies and have-you-washed-behind-your-ears became the order of the day. Don't get me wrong, I am grateful to Stuart. I doubt the road we were on was leading anyplace any of us wanted to be— but it was an abrupt shift, and Rafe and I were often the gears that got ground.

Both the Earth Mother and the Poor White Trash phases featured a distinct *laissez-faire* attitude toward child-rearing. During the first phase, our instincts ruled. We were supposed to follow them. During the second phase, no one really cared what we followed or where it led us, as long as we didn't get in the way. We had no set bedtimes, took baths when we felt like getting wet, and discovered the joys of eating Pillsbury cookie dough straight out of the tube.

Then, all of a sudden, Rafe and I were supposed to keep our elbows off the table and take baths every night and do our homework the way the teacher wanted it and eat our brussels sprouts. And not be seen or heard. I learned quickly that there was such a thing as bad attention; Rafe never seemed to figure that out. It didn't help that we never knew if we'd come home from school to find Lily making pot roast for dinner or passed out in a recliner with an empty glass in her hand.

Then came Jennifer. Our baby. I was almost ten when she was born. She is my baby just as much as she is Lily's, maybe even more, since I took better care of her. I love that girl.

There have been several different Lilys in the intervening years. There was Tennis Lily, PTA Lily, Craft Lily . . . and let's not forget Twelve-Step Lily, who still makes periodic appearances. It's more like having a big Barbie than a mother since each comes with its own wardrobe and shoes.

Lily is currently in a Jane Fonda-ish phase of staving off the aging process with diet, exercise, and judicious application of the surgeon's knife. She debuted her new breasts at the rehearsal dinner for my wedding.

I looked at my own breasts now as I got dressed. Until recently, I'd felt they were okay. Maybe not quite as symmetrical as I would have liked, but perfectly fine. Now my mother's breasts were bigger, rounder, and higher than mine were. I pulled a tank top out of my suitcase, finished getting dressed, and Gran and I left for the bungalow with the dogs in tow.

At Aunt Laura's place, Gran pulled herself up the front porch stairs by the banister—or was that just my imagination? When she opened the front door, a wave of stale hot air greeted us. Jesse sniffed at it and growled. Aziza had settled herself under the plum tree and was having an ecstatic back wiggle in the grass.

"How long has it been since anyone's lived here, Gran?" I asked, peering inside. I hoped the place hadn't become a haven for squirrels or, worse yet, rats. Out here in the hills, those were definite possibilities. I refuse to discuss snakes. If I pretend they're not there, maybe they'll go away.

"It's been more than a year since Cynthia moved out," Gran said. Cynthia has been the last of Gran's renters. Usually it was some student at UC-Davis, but occasionally it was someone with a job in Vacaville. They provided a little extra income and paid for the property taxes on the bungalow. Gran looked around the living room. "It looks like more than a year's worth of dust, though."

It did. Jesse followed us in and sneezed. "I hadn't realized it had been that long. Couldn't you find anyone after her?"

We walked into the dining room. Dust coated the parquet floor and furred the baseboards. "I couldn't seem to get the energy up to interview people." Gran sighed.

We turned to the hallway and peered into the two bedrooms and bathroom. It was the same there—empty and dusty. We went back into the dining room and then into the kitchen. Gran looked around. "This kitchen is like a cell."

It *was* a little prisonlike. There was one window over the sink looking out toward the road. "It's a shame the window doesn't look out the other direction," I said. "Then you could see the hills."

Gran rapped the wall between the kitchen and the laundry room. "I thought Laura was crazy to put this wall up, but she said she wanted a separate laundry room. That it was more modern that way."

"You know, if you're serious about remodeling this place, you could take that wall out," I said.

"Do you think so?" Gran examined the wall.

"Sure. If Laura put it in, it isn't load-bearing. That would make the kitchen bigger and you'd have the view of the hills behind. I bet you'd spend a couple thousand to do it and it would add tens of thousands to the sale price." I rapped on the wall. It sounded hollow. Jesse sniffed at its base and whimpered a little.

Gran tapped her thumb against her lower lip. "I'll ask Etienne what he thinks."

"Etienne?"

"Etienne DeLaurier, the contractor," she said.

"Ooh la la," I said. "A French contractor? What exactly did he do to win the job, Gran?"

"Don't be fresh," Gran replied.

"Harrumph," Jesse harrumphed.

Gran laughed. "Come on, Chloe. Let's make a list of what you need. Put Pine-Sol and a mop on the top of the list."

I'd forgotten how exhausting cleaning with Gran could be. She didn't believe in "clean enough." It had to be really clean, shiny clean, eat-off-the-floor clean before she was satisfied.

"Really, Chloe," she said when I'd whined for the hundredth time that I was unlikely to get down on the floor to look under the cupboards, so why did we have to clean there. "If it's worth doing, it's worth doing right."

"Can't we just do it well?"

"Well enough for whom?" She wiped a skinny forearm across her forehead.

"For me?" I suggested. "Since I'm the one who's going to live here?"

She bent down and started scrubbing again. There's something very guilt-inducing about watching a seventy-eight-year-old woman scrub your kitchen floor for you on her hands and knees. I got back down and scrubbed.

We spent the rest of the day cleaning. Somewhere in there

The Charm called to see if I needed anything. She and Dad would be heading back to Santa Cruz and she wanted to check in before they left.

"Your father says to call if you need anything," she said.

"And tell her I'm glad she finally came to her senses," I heard Dad yell in the background. Dad didn't like Mark much, but it's not that significant. Dad doesn't like many people except himself. Besides, is it really a good sign when crazy people think you've come to your senses?

"Thanks, but I think I'll be okay." Calling on Dad when I needed something rarely produced the results I wanted. It's easier to strike him off the list from the start.

There was a pause and then The Charm said, "Even if you just want to talk, Chloe, please call."

I promised her I would and we hung up.

Clarissa called too, and I gave her the lowdown. I told her we'd get together soon and gave her permission to burn the bridesmaid's dress, but she was trying to think of a way to use it in a performance piece.

By four o'clock, the bungalow looked great. Spartan, but great. There were a few pieces of furniture that Gran always provided: a bed or two, a table and chairs, a sofa and an armchair, a few lamps. It wasn't fancy, but the empty blankness was restful. I hated to admit it, but the cleanliness was restful too. From now on, whatever dirt came in would be my dirt, not anyone else's. "You know, I think I could sleep here tonight," I said, looking around.

"You don't have to, dear. I don't want you to think that I'm giving you the bum's rush." One of the things I love about Gran is that she says things like "giving you the bum's rush." I get this mental picture of her strong-arming some Emmett Kelly clown out the door.

"I don't think you're giving me the bum's rush. I do think I need to have a new routine, and the sooner I start it, the better."

Gran smiled. "A very sane and sensible choice, Chloe."

If she only knew.

I didn't feel so sane or sensible in front of my boss's desk at Chromonology the next morning. It bothered me way more than I expected to find someone else at my place in the lab. Who was that person at my computer? And why was he using my coffee mug?

I had actually helped hire the shambling, six-foot-five-inch, long-haired, bearded intern who, frankly, could have used a shower. Deep down in my heart of hearts, I'd hoped that Dennis had sent Cody packing and would have my place waiting for me at the lab. It wasn't rational to expect that, nor was it likely. But, hey, rational wasn't exactly my shtick these days, now was it?

So it disappointed me when it hadn't happened and made me more than a little angry that someone was usurping my spot at the electron microscope. So angry, actually, that my chin wobbled as I spoke, and I hate chin wobbles.

"Uh, Dennis, in case you missed it, I'm not doing the wedding/honeymoon thing anymore. Any chance you could get that guy out of the lab and I could come back?"

Dennis looked uncomfortable. He twiddled his pen against his desk blotter. "Look, Chloe, you're a great employee. I could probably drum up a project that could get you back in, but it'll take a couple of weeks to get something going and then there's the matter of funding. . . ."

Chromonology was doing well, but it wasn't like they had money to burn. I knew that; I'd spent more than a few late nights finishing up grant requests to help keep Dennis's projects going.

I shook my head. "Forget it. Two months isn't that long."

I could see his spirits rise as I let him off the hook. He practically grew in his chair. "Sure, two months will go by in a flash. It'll give you time to think."

Out in the parking lot, I rested my head against the Frontier's steering wheel. Two months. What was I going to think about for two months?

CHAPTER THREE

Chloe's Guide for the Runaway Bride

Brides are traditionally carried over the threshold of their new home to symbolize their reluctance to leave their father's house. When you've run out of your own wedding and would rather poke a sharp stick into your eye than return to your father's home, go ahead and walk over that threshold yourself. Just remember that no one's there to catch you if you trip and fall.

This felt exactly like the first few days Rafe and I spent after being shuttled from one parent to another. We'd arrive and no one would seem to know quite what to do with us. Eventually someone would step in—Gran or Sara or The Charm or Stuart— and we'd have an agenda. Places to go and people to be. But the first few days were always a special little hell of confusion.

Don't expect some big revelation about how Rafe and I were beaten, abused, or molested because we weren't. There was kind of a benign neglect, especially at Dad's, but no one put cigarettes out on our feet or climbed into our beds late at night. Honestly, I don't think we mattered enough to anybody to inspire cruelty. Stuart was the closest to cruel we had, and as long as we stayed out of his way, he barely noticed us.

Who would step in to give me some direction now? I pulled over to the side of the road and called Clarissa.

"McMurphy, Slater, and Ramirez," she sang out.

Clarissa's a receptionist at a law firm by day and a painter of huge, surreally realistic paintings of enlarged vegetables and women's makeup by night. She's a first class flake, but she's also my best friend. We met in the bathroom of our dormitory freshman year. It had been eight in the morning. I had been brushing my teeth before leaving for my chemistry class. Clarissa was on her way in to vomit after her first night on hallucinogens. She'd told me that my aura was really pure and golden looking. I'd thanked her and then held her hair for her. Of such things are true friendship made. I can't think of another way to explain it, since we have almost nothing else in common.

"It's just me. You can drop the receptionist voice," I said.

"Chloe," she squealed. "Where are you?"

"Riding around in my truck."

"What are you doing tonight?" she demanded.

"I'm moved in to the bungalow. I guess I'll be there tonight." It's not like I had anyplace else to be.

"I'll be there right after work. Wait for me."

"Bring booze, but don't bring any food." Gran and I had transferred the majority of the reception leftovers to my refrigerator, along with several creative salmon dishes that she'd whipped up. I had salmon croquettes, salmon mousse, salmon tettrazini, and salmon loaf. Then, of course, I had salmon.

"Gotcha." She hung up.

Fine. A plan. Wait for Clarissa at the bungalow. Excellent.

At the bungalow, Gran had left a note on the kitchen table along with an article about the heart-healthy benefits of salmon. She and Etienne had been by and he agreed with me about the kitchen wall. He'd start knocking it out tomorrow and had already left his sledgehammer leaning against the wall.

The round white plastic kitchen clock ticked loudly in the silence. It was ten-thirty. Clarissa got off work at five, so the earliest she could get here was five-thirty. What was I supposed to do for seven hours?

I always felt better if I had a plan, so I made a list and worked my way down it. First, the post office for a change of address form. Luckily, I didn't get the same clerk who had taken my piles of wedding invitations six weeks ago. Then the phone company and utility company. I also stopped by the county clerk's office to see if I needed to cancel the marriage license, but as it turns out they expire after ninety days. I've purchased Twinkies with longer shelf lives.

I beat Clarissa to the bungalow by about ten minutes. She walked in and pulled two bottles of champagne out of a shopping bag while I started reheating the baked goat cheese and Parmesan-dusted fried ravioli.

Clarissa usually doesn't favor bubbly drinks, so I asked, "Why champagne?" The fruit kabob I was munching was a teensy bit slimy.

"In celebration," she said.

"What exactly are we celebrating? My lack of a husband, a home, and a job?"

The cork popped and champagne sprayed onto Clarissa's hand. She licked it off. "All three."

"Greeaaat," I said.

Aziza came scampering in and Clarissa looked over at me. "You brought her? What were you thinking?"

Clarissa isn't a dog person, but she makes an exception for Jesse. She claims he hasn't been a dog for very long, that he was clearly human in his last life and still is human in a lot of ways.

Jesse responds to this by talking like Scooby-Doo and doing Leonard Nimoy-ish things with his doggie eyebrows.

"Mark didn't want her," I said.

"And you did?" Clarissa asked.

I shook my head. "Not really, but what else could I do?"

Clarissa nibbled at a fruit kabob, made a face and put it down. "I dunno. Tell him to take care of his own dog."

Aziza snuffled around Clarissa's feet. She has a thing for Clarissa's toes. One time, when Clarissa fell asleep on my couch watching a video with me when Mark was out of town (Mark did not approve of my girlfriends "hanging around" for no real reason when he was there), Aziza had actually nibbled through Clarissa's socks. Clarissa had not been amused.

"I'm not going to give you anything, dog. If you had a brain in your head, you'd have figured that out by now."

Of course, if Aziza had a brain in her head, she wouldn't be Aziza. I watched her now with her one broken ear flopped over, following Clarissa around the kitchen, hoping for a scrap to fall. The dog was completely relentless. I couldn't believe I'd let Mark talk me into taking her.

Not that he'd really talked all that much; I suppose I'd let my guilt do most of the talking for him. Poor Aziza. She was like the "ours" kid of one of those blended families. There are the "his" kids from his first marriage and the "hers" kids from her first marriage and then the "ours" kid of the second marriage. Except what happened to the "ours" kid when that relationship busted up? Did it become the "nobody's" kid?

"So here's to your newly refound singleton status!" Clarissa cried, raising her champagne flute. Clarissa was not exactly Mark's biggest fan. Mark wasn't a big Clarissa booster either. Mark preferred softer women, women who expressed their opinions in quiet ways. Clarissa painted meticulously rendered six-foot lipsticks that were so phallic, they made your knees wobble.

The whole lesbian thing made Mark a little uncomfortable too. When Clarissa came out during our junior year, I thought she was a LUG, a Lesbian Until Graduation, and that she'd grow out of it. She hasn't. She may have been just trying it on to start with, but apparently lesbianism was like her favorite pair of fingerless fishnet gloves. It just fit.

"I'm not so sure my singleton status is something to celebrate." That didn't stop me from drinking the champagne, though. I like the way the bubbles go to my head.

Clarissa drained hers, too, and smacked her lips. "Well, at least I don't have to share you."

"There was plenty of me for both you and Mark."

"I knew that," Clarissa said. "I'm not sure he did."

Mark wasn't crazy about coming home and finding Clarissa in all her multiply-pierced and bizarrely dyed glory draped over his button-down tuxedo-style leather couch, so I went to her place when we wanted to hang out. Then he'd fret until I was home safe and sound, often calling two or three times during the evening to check on me.

"He's not checking on you," Clarissa would say, rolling her eyes with exasperation. "He's controlling you."

I'd laugh, because I knew he just wanted to make sure I was safe and sound. And I liked that. Who would make sure of it now?

I set down the champagne and tried to smile at Clarissa who, being the excellent friend that she is, saw the chin wobble and the blinky eyes and threw her arms around me.

"I'm so sorry, sweetheart. I'm just being selfish and thinking about me. So, girlfriend," Clarissa said, leaning forward. "Spill it. Why'd ya do it?"

I hesitated. "If I told you that I heard a voice telling me to run, would you think I was crazy?"

"Maybe, but not necessarily in a bad way." We took the champagne and the food into the living room. Clarissa kicked off her shoes and folded herself up tailor style in the recliner chair while I draped myself facedown on the scratchy couch. "You know, though, now that I'm thinking about it, there were signs."

"Signs of what? That I was getting delusional and would start hearing voices on my wedding day?" I asked.

"No. Signs that this wedding wasn't going to work out."

I took a bite of the salmon mousse my grandmother had made. It wasn't bad if you didn't mind your pudding a little fishy. "There were no signs."

"Chloe, you threw up when you got engaged. You broke out in a rash when you went wedding dress shopping. You sprained your wrist the day before you were supposed to address all your wedding invitations."

"Those weren't signs; those were life. There was something wrong with that fish. My skin is sensitive and all that lace irritated it, and everyone falls when they Rollerblade." On second thought, maybe I did mind my pudding being fishy. I took another big swallow of champagne to wash it down.

Clarissa said, "How about the fact that you didn't want to marry Mark in the first place?"

"What are you talking about?"

"I'm talking about the fact that Mark wheedled you into getting married. You would have been perfectly happy shacking up for a while; he was the one who wanted everything legal and permanent and binding. Very, very binding." Clarissa took another bite of bread and cheese.

I knew I hadn't been as enthusiastic as I'd seen other friends be about getting married, but I'd figured my family history had just made me mistrust the process. "My genetics are clearly catching up with me. I'm losing my mind. I've bought a one-way ticket for Nutsville, and I'm never coming back."

"Well, you certainly out-drama-queened the lot of 'em for once." Clarissa grinned as if I'd accomplished something truly grand.

"I did, didn't I?" I giggled. Jesse thumped his tail on the floor. "Did you see Shelby as I ran out? She looked like one of those red mouth fly traps with something caught on her trigger hairs."

Clarissa snorted. "I have no idea what you just said, but I know exactly what you meant. I thought she was going to burst a blood vessel when she overheard the videographer talking about sending a tape to America's Funniest Home Videos."

"Rafe said she drank so much scotch that she was slurring her words."

"Oh, and what words she slurred!" Clarissa trilled. "That woman can swear like a sailor when she's plowed. I almost liked her there at the end. Not that she warmed up any to me. She practically spat in my face as Mark and his dad carried her out of the Opera House."

"I don't think I'm going to have to worry about calling her Mom anymore." Shellay had asked me to call her "Mom" a few months before the wedding. I'd tried, but I don't really call any-one "Mom." My mother has been "Lily" to me since I was about thirteen. Dad's second wife never asked us to call her anything but Sara and The Charm was, well, The Charm. Maybe I was un-Mommable.

Clarissa stood up and kissed the top of my head. "Unlike you, I have to go to work in the morning so I'm going home now. I'll talk to you tomorrow. Okay?"

I gave her a hug and watched from the door as her headlights moved off into the night. The country quiet settled around me like cotton. I gathered the champagne flutes and plates and took them all into the kitchen. *Clean the kitchen before you go to bed. Go to sleep with a shiny sink and wake up in the pink,* Gran always said.

Everything neat and tidy. It had been one of the things that Mark liked about me. He said most women were pigs, that half the women he had dated were serious slobs, but not me. I never left my things lying around. I think it's the product of constantly being shuffled from house to house as a child by a set of adults who could barely keep track of their own belongings, much less mine.

I sat down at the kitchen table. I had nothing to do. I couldn't even watch mindless TV because the bungalow didn't get cable. I wondered how long it would take to get one of those satellite thingies set up and if they really did blow over the way those commercials said they did.

Then I started wondering why I was sitting here all alone, with nothing to do but stare at my hands folded neatly and tidily on the kitchen table, in the house of a woman who had died all alone.

I was supposed to be in Tahiti, drinking mai tais and screwing my new husband. Instead I was sponging off my grandmother without a job to go to in the morning.

And I didn't even know why I'd done it.

I looked over at the wall and the sledgehammer, then got up, picked up the sledgehammer, and gave the wall a tap. Dust and a little plaster shook loose. The hammer weighed more than I'd expected. I also hadn't expected it to feel so good in my hands. I swung it a little harder. It made a nice *thunk*ing noise and a good-sized dent in the wall. More dust shook loose, making me sneeze. I swung harder and really knocked some of it loose.

Then I was just swinging. Over and over and over, I lifted the sledgehammer and smashed it into the wall. I swung until my shoulder started to hurt and there was so much plaster dust in the air that my eyes streamed and my lungs burned.

Finally I backed away. At least half the wall was down. I dropped with a thud onto the kitchen chair, my breath coming in rasps. I let the hammer fall to the floor. Blisters covered my hands, and a few of them had popped. I hadn't even felt them as I was swinging the sledgehammer.

I walked over to the sink and started running water over my hands. The sting of the water on my blisters was a slap across the face, bringing me back to my senses. I leaned over the sink and started to weep.

When Jesse nudged the back of my legs, I sank to the floor and buried my face in his doggie neck. Aziza whined anxiously behind him. When I finally looked up, he gently licked the tears from my face.

Now that the dust had settled, I could see I hadn't knocked out anywhere near as much of the wall as I'd thought. Still, I'd done some damage. I rubbed my shoulder. It would be stiff in the morning. I went over to inspect the hole I'd made and peeked down between the wooden studs.

Tucked down inside was a light green metal box. I tried to reach it, but the space was too narrow and I couldn't get my arm through. Jesse began to pace back and forth behind me, yipping every now and then with excitement. I pulled my arm back. Maybe there was something down there besides the box. Something live, like a squirrel or a rat or (a shiver ran through me) a snake. I got the flashlight from over the stove and shone it down in. No critters.

By this time, Jesse was nearly hopping up and down with excitement, his front paws coming off the floor as if he wanted to look into the hole. "It's okay, big guy," I told him. "Just relax. It's only a box."

I tried to reach it again, but still couldn't quite get to it. Its edge remained tantalizing inches out of my grasp. I grabbed the sledgehammer again and gave one more big swing. Aziza barked. Jesse howled. The edge of the drywall pulled off in my hand and I reached in and pulled out the box.

I was afraid it would be locked and I'd have to pry it open, but the latch popped open under my fingers.

Inside was a mass of envelopes and papers, yellowed and brittle looking. In the corners where the stamps should be were wavy lines and the word FREE written above them. I pulled one out. It was addressed to Miss Laura Hirsch and postmarked Camp Wolters, Texas, April 7, 5 p.m., 1943. I took the letter out and read it.

Dear Laura,

How are you, sweetheart? Not as busy as I am, I hope. The reason why I didn't write was because they drill us the whole day, then pile things to do on us at night. When you have to clean rifles, polish shoes, wash, shave, and turn the lights off at nine o'clock, it doesn't leave much time for yourself. It will be the longest year I've ever put in.

I have some good news though. I was made squad leader yesterday. That means after five more months of having fun in the army, I'll be eligible for a corporal rating although I am not promising anything. Well, that is all the dirt so I will hang up my pencil and go wash out my underwear and socks.

Yours truly,
Jesse

Jesse? "Just like you, boy," I said and patted my dog's head. I looked at the envelope again. The return address read: Jesse Hernandez, Company C, Eighth Infantry, APO #4, Camp Wolters, Texas.

I pulled out another letter. This one was dated November 30, 1943, and came from Fort Jackson, South Carolina.

Dear Laura,

How's my little sweetheart doing? Full of goose and turkey, I suppose. I heard the family did all right in the bingo games this year. I didn't fare so well but it certainly didn't hurt me any. I weighed myself today after a hot bath and with all the dirt off I still weighed 186 pounds. We sure had a hell of a month.

The war games ended Friday afternoon at five o'clock and you should have heard the cheering then. We were certainly a happy bunch of fellows. We moved back to our bivouac area at Lando Saturday. We will stay here until Thursday then head back for Benning. Those hard cots will even feel good to us after sleeping on the cold hard ground for a month.

I don't know for sure when I will get my furlough but it don't make much difference. It will seem just as good to me at one time as another.

Did Jacob get his Thanksgiving bonus again this year? If so, I suppose you will have turkey again. (Ha Ha)

There isn't any news around here so I had better sign off for today. Say hello to Jacob and Naomi for me.

Good-bye with love,
Jesse

Jacob and Naomi—that would have been Gran and Granda. Whoever Jesse was, he knew my grandparents, too. Of course, as close as Gran and Aunt Laura had supposedly been, that wasn't surprising.

My Jesse paced around my feet, a noise somewhere between a whine and a growl erupting from him every few seconds. I took the flashlight and looked inside the wall again. "There's nothing there," I told him. "Settle down."

He harrumphed, but lay down with his head on his paws. His tail kept swishing back and forth and he kept looking up at me, his eyes anxious and his eyebrows pulled together. Is there anything worse than an anxious-looking dog? I patted him and Aziza came up, demanding her fair share. I patted her, too, but then she wiggled in too close to Jesse and he snapped at her, sending her scurrying away.

I shook my head at him and pulled out another letter. This one was dated December 7, 1943, and came from the Fourth Infantry Division Detachment, Amphibious Training Base, Fort Pierce, Florida.

Dear Laura,

Well it's about time that I am answering your letter. I don't know if my pen will hold up or not. The darn thing is sure acting up now. It gets spells like that.

Are we ever getting a workout down here. It's sort of fun though. We have something new and different every day. The amount of time that we spend in the water leads me to believe that I have been to sea more than most sailors. We are out more than the recruits at this camp. We train with these seven-man rubber boats. At first I didn't think that they could be tipped over but I sure underestimated the strength of the ocean. When the surf starts coming in with breakers twenty feet high it can tip most anything.

We had a six mile speed march today which we made in

fifty-eight minutes. That was only half of our troubles. We had to run the obstacle course after we finished the speed march. They have a dandy down here. I forgot to mention that we had two hours of log P.T. to start the morning off. Log Physical Training consists of a seven man crew doing all sorts of exercises with a tree trunk about ten inches in diameter and about fifteen feet long. It is very good for us. It isn't so hard after you pick up the knack of handling them and working together.

I am beginning to look like Charles Atlas—muscles sticking out all over me. Of course, I think it is just swelling because they are all sore.

Well, I could tell you a number of things about our training but it would probably bore you to death so I had better sign off for now. I will write again soon. Good-bye.

Love,

Jesse

The box was filled with envelopes; there were probably more than a hundred of them.

I reached in again and started reading.

CHAPTER FOUR

Chloe's Guide for the Runaway Bride

Don't pamper yourself in the days after your un-wedding. Keep busy. Try a home improvement project. It's not like you have to keep that manicure nice for anything.

I woke in a sea of envelopes to the sound of banging. I'd hauled Jesse's letters to bed with me and had fallen asleep reading them. The banging came from outside the house.

"Allo," a voice called from the front porch. "Eez anybody home?"

I rolled over to look at my travel alarm clock, and the tangle of sheets and blankets came with me. I'd gone to sleep with all the windows and the sliding glass door in the bedroom open to catch the available breezes, and now everything felt damp with dew. I shivered. Seven-fifteen a.m. What sadistic son of a bitch would be on my porch at seven-fifteen a.m.?

"I hope you are decent as I am coming een now," the voice called in a sing-song.

I wrapped my quilt around me and stumbled out of my bedroom. A creature with hair like a haystack and clothing covered with paint and dirt stood inside my living room. It looked at me and scratched its belly. A cigarette with an inch of precarious ash dangled from its lips.

"What . . . I mean, who are you?" I rasped.

"I am Etienne." He puffed up his chest. "Zee contractor."

This was ooh-la-la Etienne? Why do we think all French men are going to be handsome and suave? There are bound to be as many funny-looking, doofy French men as there are any other nationality. Still, I was disappointed. "Hey," I mumbled, and shuffled back to my bedroom, where I crawled back into my bed and pulled the quilt over my head.

About five minutes later, a huge thud echoed through the house. Clearly, Etienne had decided to get right to knocking out the wall. Jesse barked. Another thud. Another bark. I pulled my pillow over my head. *Thud. Bark.*

I sighed, gathered up the envelopes and letters, tucked them back into the green box, and went to take a shower. When I wandered into the kitchen, white dust filled the air. Etienne swung the hammer rhythmically.

"Hey," I said. "Shouldn't you be wearing a mask or something?"

He stopped swinging and gave a Gallic shrug. "Perhaps. I do not like how zey feel." He coughed, then opened up the kitchen door and spat out into the grass. "Perhaps I should wear one anyway, *non*?"

"Perhaps yes," I said.

"Thank you for getting the work started for me." He nodded his head toward the wall.

"It was my pleasure." Pleasure really wasn't the right word. Release, maybe, but not exactly pleasure.

Etienne grinned again. "Perhaps there was someone's face you imagined when you picked up the hammer?"

Oh, great. Etienne had clearly heard about my un-wedding. I gave my best Gallic shrug back. "Perhaps."

I backed out of the kitchen. Perhaps I should also consider

getting my breakfast someplace else. I put leashes on both the dogs and walked over to Gran's.

Her house was less than a mile if you took the back way. Which was accessible only by foot or four-wheel drive. Jesse resisted all squirrel-and-rabbit chasing temptations, for which I praised him lavishly. Aziza tangled herself in her own leash seven times.

Gran was still in her kitchen although she'd already had breakfast. She was sorting through plums, tossing the bruised and overripe ones aside.

"Hi, Gran, want some company?"

She smiled at me with that smile that always made me feel that she was delighted to see me and couldn't think of a place she'd rather be than with me.

I sat down at the kitchen table. "Who was Jesse Hernandez?"

Gran's hands paused in their sorting for a second. "Jesse who, dear?"

"Hernandez," I said. "I found a box of letters to Aunt Laura from a Jesse Hernandez inside the wall that Etienne is knocking out." I didn't see any reason to tell Gran that I'd gotten a head start on the demolition.

"Really? Letters to Laura from Jesse? They must be ancient."

"World War Two. I only read a few of them, but they all seem to be from while he's in army training and then in Europe. Who was he?"

"Oh," Gran sighed. "A friend of the family's. He worked with your granda at the store. Not exactly the most dependable of men."

"I think he might have been more than a friend to Aunt Laura. He calls her 'sweetheart' in his letters."

"Really?" Gran's eyebrows drew down. "Well, be that as it may, nothing came of it. He went away to war and never came back."

I gasped. "No!"

Gran sat back and looked at me.

"It's just his letters . . . they're so sweet. How sad."

"Where did you say you found them again, dear?"

"In the wall. The one Etienne is knocking out. In a green metal box tucked down between the wooden frame. Why do you suppose she put it there?"

Gran shrugged. "Who knows?" she said, but her brow stayed furrowed. "What does he write about?"

"Sometimes it's hard to piece together, because he's answering things she's asked in her letters. Plus, they're all out of order. I should probably read them chronologically."

Jesse's eyebrow went up and he grunted a little. Gran patted his head. "I suppose. Hard to know." She put a cup of coffee and three miniature quiches down in front of me.

"Did he have any relatives? Anybody who might want the letters?" I asked.

Gran bit her lip. "No. Not that I can think of. He didn't really belong to anyone. I'll get rid of them for you, if you'd like." She pushed the apricot preserves toward me. "So what are you going to do today, dear?"

What indeed? The day stretched in front of me like an abyss of pointlessness.

"Rafe is coming to rip up the linoleum. You could help him," Gran suggested.

"Sure. When will he be here?"

"Right now," a voice said from the door.

Tearing up linoleum is just about the stickiest, nastiest, dirtiest job out there. Servicing Porta-potties at rock concerts might be worse, but that's about it. Gran's entire linoleum floor was stuck down with some adhesive compound that neither love, money, mineral spirits, nor the special solvent that Rafe had bought at Home Depot could dissolve. All we could do, after clearing the furniture out, was cut and scrape and pull, and cut and scrape and pull some more.

We started in the corner where the linoleum was already coming up. Rafe pulled out a big X-Acto knife and cut some diagonal strips in the flooring. He used a scraper to pry up an end, and then he just pulled and scraped and pulled and scraped until he tore a hunk off. Then he started again.

"Where'd you learn to do this?" I asked. It's not like Dad ever did much manual labor, and Stuart felt he'd done something like this if he'd paid for someone else to do it.

"Internet."

"Greeaattt," I said, and grabbed my own X-Acto knife and went to my own corner. Within ten seconds, I'd broken a nail on my right hand. I sat back on my heels. "Ouch!"

Rafe sat back on his heels. "Chloe, if you're going to cry every time you break a nail, perhaps this project isn't for you."

"It's not just a nail. I paid thirty-five bucks for this manicure," I protested. I held my hands up with fingers splayed, nails toward Rafe, so he could appreciate the artistry of the French tip manicure I'd gotten for the wedding.

"Thirty-five dollars to get your nails done?" Rafe shook his head. "Why?"

"So they'd look good in the pictures of our rings," I said.

Rafe bent back over the linoleum. "Well at least the nails lasted longer than your marriage."

I threw a scraper at him.

"Stop bickering, children," Gran called from the living room.

Rafe turned on the radio to the classic rock station, stuck his tongue out at me, and got back to work.

At noon we were more than halfway through. Luckily, Gran's kitchen isn't all that big. She made us sandwiches with the leftover salmon.

"This is not nearly as much fun as I hoped it would be," I told Rafe as we devoured our sandwiches on Gran's porch. Knocking out the wall at Aunt Laura's had been cathartic. Here, all I had were some broken nails, a sore lower back, and the probable beginnings of pulmonary fibrosis from the dust. I couldn't help remembering that I was supposed to be lying on a beach with people bringing me drinks.

"First of all, you volunteered, and second of all, I don't recall advertising it as fun." Rafe took a long pull of his beer. "Although it definitely gives one the impetus to stay in school."

"You were thinking about quitting?" I was shocked. Rafe is the Poster Child for ESS (Eternal Student Syndrome). Every time he finishes a degree, it seems it was just the building block he needed for another one. He has one bachelor's degree, two master's degrees, and is working on a Ph.D. in anthropology. "Dad will be so upset."

"That's almost a reason to do it." Rafe smirked.

My father considers academia to be our family business. He's a professor. His father was a professor. He has an uncle who is a professor and an aunt who teaches at a nursing college. His frustration with my refusal to go on for my Ph.D. has reached nearly explosive heights from time to time, including one memorable dinner at which he literally stood up, pointed to the door with his finger, and cast me out. Dad has a bit of a melodramatic side. If he could smite, he totally would.

But that's not why I haven't gone back for the degree that would let me run in the backbiting hallways of academia. Okay, it's an added benefit, but it's not the real reason.

Mark and I had gone over it dozens of times. I made around

forty thousand dollars a year at my job at Chromonology, a job I sincerely love. It could take five years for me to get my Ph.D. I would be giving up my salary for those whole five years *plus* have to pay tuition, and at the end of it all, I *might* get a professorship that would pay sixty thousand a year. Then again, I might not. I might end up with the same job and have gone through all that for nothing. It just made no sense.

"So are you thinking of quitting?" I asked. Dad would hit high C, and I didn't want to be there when Rafe told him. Even if it wasn't directed at me, I got the shakes when he just yelled at anyone—Dad has a really big voice.

Rafe leaned back on the steps, absentmindedly scratching his flat stomach through his T-shirt. "Nah. Not really. It's just hard not to get disillusioned sometimes. I start wondering what it all means and thinking about how much more sense manual labor makes. How you'd actually see the products of your labor. How you'd have something to show for what you'd been doing all day."

"Then you spend a morning ripping up linoleum for Gran and the whole ivory tower thing seems much more appealing?"

Rafe raised his beer to me. "You betcha."

We returned inside, Rafe turned the radio back on, and we went back to work. There's something meditative about this kind of work. I went into a dreamlike zone where I was both aware of what I was doing and yet very separate from it. I experience the same thing sometimes when I'm running assays for Dennis at the lab, or making jam with Gran. It's repetitive, monotonous, mindless work and yet you have to pay attention. The second you don't, something can go terribly wrong. I came damn close to slicing my bare thigh with the X-Acto knife at about two o'clock that afternoon when we were almost done.

Rafe took the X-Acto from me. "That's it, you're benched. Go home and shower and I'll take you out for a beer."

"A beer? I spend the day breathing in poisonous dust and then nearly amputate my leg while helping you out, and all you offer to buy me is a beer?"

"A beer is the universal guy compensation for all help and good deeds. Got a problem with that?"

"I'm not a guy."

He smiled that obnoxiously charming smile and said, "You're my sister. Next best thing."

"Fine, but I want a burger, too."

Gran begged off, pleading fatigue, although I suspect she was just tired of listening to us bicker. I called Clarissa, who was looking to blow off some steam, so she agreed to meet us at the Green Creek.

"Hey, Rafe," she said an hour later as she slid onto the barstool and flipped her hair behind her. Even my lesbian friend flirts with him reflexively; he has that much sex appeal.

When Til came over to take our orders not only did she flirt with Rafe, damned if she didn't start sliding her pendant back and forth over its chain and across her cleavage with her head cocked to one side while Clarissa decided what kind of beer she'd have. Considering she only had the choice of Bud Light, Budweiser, or Miller High Life, it took an inordinately long time.

Clarissa leaned back on her barstool to watch Til walk away. "She's hot."

Rafe nodded. "You got that right."

"You've both got to be kidding me," I said.

"I am dead serious." Clarissa raised her glass to Rafe. He knocked his against hers.

"So clearly a career in home remodeling is not going to be your distraction for the next couple months," Clarissa said after once again nearly falling off her stool to watch Til's backside go by. "Any more ideas on what you're going to do?"

Rafe leaned forward on the bar. "Why does she have to do anything? Why can't she just hang?"

"Because we're talking about Chloe here. She doesn't just hang."

I washed down a big bite of burger with my beer. "I do too hang. I hang with you all the time."

Clarissa stuck out her hand and wobbled it in a so-so gesture. "You usually have an agenda. Like we're going to address wedding invitations while we watch a movie, or we're going to talk about why you ran out of your wedding while we're doing laundry or something."

"Laundry?" Rafe looked from one of us to the other. "You do laundry together?"

I shrugged. "Sure. It's hard for one person to make a full load. That way we spend some time together and we conserve water at the same time."

Clarissa clapped her hands. "See? An agenda. That's exactly what I mean."

"Fine, I don't hang well. Maybe I need to learn. Maybe that will be the lesson I take away from all this."

"That, and the fact that many Jewish couples put a lightbulb in the napkin," Clarissa said.

I stared at her. "You're kidding. Where did you learn that?"

She shrugged. "Internet."

I didn't last much longer. Being woken by a filthy crazy Frenchman in the predawn hours, then hard manual labor, had definitely taken their toll. By the end of my first beer, I was yawning. Two sips into the second one and my head was nodding.

"She needs to go home," Clarissa said to Rafe.

"That she does."

Normally, I don't like it when people discuss me as if I wasn't there, but today I found it oddly comforting. My friends and family were looking out for me. "You guys are the greatest," I said. My eyes welled up.

"Time to take her home," Clarissa said. "She's all sloppy drunk."

Clarissa's not big on sentimentality. It doesn't have much of a place in sexually-charged paintings of giant mascara brushes. Rafe said he would take me back to the bungalow and headed down the bar to settle our tab.

"You going home too?" I blearily asked Clarissa.

She shrugged, her eyes on Rafe and Til at the end of the bar. "In a bit. I might just hang for a while."

"Ah, hang." I nodded my head sagely. Then Rafe slid his arm around my waist and helped me from the barstool and out to his car. We had kind of a hard time angling me into his little MG. My legs had stiffened up after spending a day on my hands and knees, but Rafe eventually got me settled and belted in.

Winding along the twisting back roads in Rafe's little car was a little like being rocked in a swing, and I drifted off during the ten minute drive. I woke up as Rafe got back in the car after opening the gate. "Sorry," I mumbled. "I'll close it."

Rafe put his hand on my arm. "No, just sit still." He pulled through and got out to close the gate behind him.

"Do you want to see those letters I was telling you about? The ones to Aunt Laura from that Jesse guy?" I asked as I opened the door. My Jesse stood just inside, his mouth open in a smile and tail wagging. Aziza stood two steps behind him. She took a step forward and Jesse shot her a look over his shoulder. She retreated.

Rafe looked at his watch. "Maybe some other night. Okay?"

"You got a date or something?" I asked, thinking I'd made a joke.

He blushed. "Sort of. Til gets off work in an hour and I want to be there."

My stomach dropped. "Til? Are you serious?"

He shrugged. "As serious as I ever am."

"Oh, Rafe."

"What's wrong with Til?"

"The words 'cheap' and 'tawdry' leap to mind pretty quickly." I know, I know. Catty and childish. But I wanted my big brother to stay and look at letters with me, not go chasing after barmaids.

Rafe grinned. "Mmm. Cheap and tawdry. Two great tastes that taste great together."

I glared at him.

"Look, Chloe, I'm not talking about a lifetime commitment here. I'm just talking about spending a little quality time."

I made a face. "Yuck. Is that really what you call it?"

He shrugged. "Call it whatever you want, but it starts in less than an hour and I don't want to be late for it." He kissed my head and walked out the door. He is occasionally too much like Dad, whether he knows it or not.

I let the dogs out and sat down on the porch to wait while they made their nightly rounds. I leaned against the heavy banisters and watched Jesse patrol the perimeter of the property, stopping to pee strategically on various fence posts and marking them as his own. The delta breeze wafted through the valley and the air grew cool and sweet on my face, picking up the faint scents of grass and growing things from the countryside around me. When the dogs came back, it took a nearly inhuman amount of willpower to get myself up off the steps and back into the house.

I crawled into bed without even brushing my teeth, and fished out a letter from the green metal box on my bedside table.

Dearest Laura,

I received your letter today. Please, darling, don't be frightened. We'll see this through together. I don't know how, but we will. I promise you. I have to think and I need time to do that. I'm sending you this now so you know that I know and that I will not leave you to go through this alone.

Love,
Jesse

CHAPTER FIVE

Chloe's Guide for the Runaway Bride

The bride's mother sets the tone for the other mothers attending the wedding, including former stepmothers and, of course, the groom's mother. If the bride's mother has recently surgically acquired a fine new rack that she'd like to showcase, however, everyone need not wear something low-cut. In fact, the realization that your mother's boobs are higher and firmer than your own may be enough to make you start hunting for those oversize T-shirts.

The alcohol and Advil I'd taken before bed deserted my system at about five a.m., leaving my mouth feeling like it was lined with cotton. The good news was that I'd beat Etienne to the kitchen and could actually make coffee that wasn't laced with drywall dust. Jesse stumbled into the kitchen after me, looking bleary-eyed, and gave me a quizzical glance as if to ask what I was doing up so early.

I patted him on the head after I tossed back some Advil and put my head down on the table while I waited for the coffee to drip through. My new position only made it pound worse. I opened one eye and finally noticed the note left on the table. In a loping, elegant hand, it read:

Chère Chloe,
   If you would be so kind, please to empty the cupboards as
I will be from the wall removing them.

                                        Regards,
                                        Etienne

I sat up and surveyed the work that Etienne had done yesterday.

The wall was down. I couldn't believe the difference it made. The kitchen had gone from a claustrophobic shoebox to a room with a view. From the table you could look out the window at the golden hills, sprinkled with the green of scrub oak.

Unfortunately, the interior view was not quite so pretty. Along with the drywall debris, Etienne had left seven cigarette butts, two cans of Coke (one empty and smashed, the other half full) and an empty bag of potato chips scattered around on the floor. I drank my coffee and watched them as if they might get up and take themselves to the garbage. When they hadn't after an entire cup, I picked them up myself, emptied the cupboards of what few things there were, and went to take a shower.

By the time I finished showering, Etienne had arrived and had started tearing out cabinets with a glee I'd only seen matched by my nephew in the ball pit at McDonalds after his first and only Happy Meal. Jen had forbidden Rafe and me to take him there again and accused of us of trying to give him breasts with the hormone-laden beef.

There were already two cigarette butts and an empty coffee cup on the floor. No way could I stay here. I was afraid that I'd split a molar grinding my teeth or the voice in my head would tell me to slam Etienne over the head with a two-by-four.

I called Jennifer, who had just gotten back from Gymboree with Troy. If I left now I'd get to Concord just about the time he woke up from his nap and we could all have lunch.

I put Jesse and Aziza's water and food bowls outside and shooed the dogs out so they wouldn't be in Etienne's way. Jesse gave me such a sad look when I got into the truck without him that I nearly changed my mind about going. Troy loved him and the feeling was mutual, but Jen would definitely be unhappy if I showed up with Aziza in tow.

An hour and one Patsy Cline CD later (yes, I was feeling morose and there's nothing better to counteract the relentless sunshine of the Central Valley in the summer than a little Patsy, unless it's k.d. lang pretending to be Patsy), I pulled up in front of Jennifer's house. I rang the bell and she flung the door open, then flung her skinny little arms around me.

"Chloe, I'm so glad you called. I'm so glad you came." Her eyes and stomach seemed to be getting bigger while the rest of her shrank. Her arms looked like toothpicks and her face seemed drawn.

She pulled me into the house. It was easily twenty degrees cooler in there than it was outside. Goose bumps popped up on my arms.

"Bang!" Troy leaped out from the hallway that led to the bedroom. He had on a Batman cape that had a hood with Batman ears and slits for his eyes, blue galoshes with yellow duckies on the sides, and a diaper with Muppet babies dancing across the waistband. He pointed a mass of different-colored LEGOs at me and again yelled, "Bang!"

I clutched my chest and sank dramatically to the tiles. Troy cackled and fled down the hall.

"Still refusing to buy him a toy gun?" I asked from the floor. Jen rolled her eyes. "Maybe I should buy one. He turns all his other toys into firearms. Maybe if I got him one, he'd turn the gun into a baby bottle."

"Nice outfit he has on, by the way."

Jen headed back toward the family room. "He's not allowed to wear the Batman cape to Gymboree or to sleep in it. Other than that, he pretty much has it on constantly. He sneezed in it the other day and by the time I got him to let me wash it, it was nearly stuck to him permanently."

"Ick."

"You don't know the half of it."

I parked myself at Jen's kitchen counter. She pulled a pitcher of iced tea and a can of Diet Coke out of the refrigerator. "The tea is lemon-orange zinger or some herbal crap like that. Which do you want?" she asked.

"The Diet Coke," I said.

She sighed. "Can I sniff it?"

"You want to sniff my Diet Coke? It doesn't even smell like anything."

"I'm trying not to drink soda or anything caffeinated because of the baby, and I miss it so much it hurts. I miss Diet Coke more than I miss booze, and the decaffeinated stuff just doesn't taste right. Let me sniff your Coke. Please?"

She sounded like a junkie asking for just a tiny fix. "Knock yourself out."

Jennifer popped the tab on the can and then held it under her nose, inhaling deeply. "Oooh. That smells so good. Can I have one little sip?"

I nodded and she took a sip, the expression on her face nearly orgasmic. "Do you two want to get a room?" I asked.

Jennifer gave the can back to me, poured herself an iced tea, and sat down next to me. Troy crawled through the kitchen to the family room on his belly in combat mode, pulling himself along on his elbows. Jen didn't even flinch; I wasn't entirely sure she saw him.

"Gran says you're staying at Aunt Laura's."

"She has this crazy French guy remodeling it and she wants me to keep an eye on things."

"Oooh. Is he cute?" Jennifer wiggled in her chair. She has been boy crazy almost since she was born.

I thought of Etienne hocking a loogie up in the yard. "No. Kind of disgusting, actually."

"Oh." Jen was clearly as disappointed as I'd been, and she hadn't even seen the loogie. "So what are you going to do?"

Troy slipped out the sliding glass doors to the patio, then leaped onto his Big Wheel. He careened in a wild figure eight around the glass-topped table and the barbecue. Jen didn't blink an eye.

"I'm not sure," I said. "I've got two months to kill before I go back to work, too."

A piercing shriek rang from out on the patio. Jen was up and out through the sliding glass doors before I even registered where it came from. She scooped up Troy, who was holding onto his right hand and sobbing. She smothered his face in kisses, murmuring, "Poor baby. Poor sweetheart. Poor little thing," as she carried him into the house and plopped Troy onto the counter.

"Let Mommy see," she commanded. Obediently, he held out his little hand. "Chloe, could you come and make sure he doesn't fall off the counter while I go get some tweezers?"

"Sure," I said.

I took over Jen's position in front of Troy at the counter. "Can I see too?" I asked him.

Troy's sobs had slowed from howls to a kind of steady whimper. "Bee bit me." He held out the stubby index finger of his pudgy right hand. Sure enough, there was a big red welt on it and a stinger sticking out of the center.

"I see. That must have hurt."

He kept his finger in my face. "Bee bit me. Me. Troy." He sounded shocked, betrayed even.

Jennifer bustled back in with the tweezers and grabbed an ice bag from the freezer on her way past it. "Here we go," she said, shouldering me out of the way. She had the stinger out and the ice bag wrapped around Troy's finger before he could rev back up to full wail. He collapsed against her. Her arms went around him and she kissed his head over and over.

Jen whispered in Troy's ear, "Would you like to watch cartoons while I get lunch ready?"

He nodded against her shoulder and she transferred him to me. He snuffled into my neck and let his body melt into mine. I'm not sure I've ever felt anything as sweet. "Cartoon Network is on channel forty-three," Jen said.

I settled Troy on the couch with a stuffed bunny named Bobo and his yellow blankie with the ducks on it to watch Tom chase Jerry for the umpteenth decade in a row, and went back to the kitchen to see if I could help Jen.

She stood in front of the sink, her arms braced against the counter. Her body shook, her face was ashen. I rushed to her. "Jen, what's wrong? Are you okay? Are you going to be sick?"

"I don't think so. No." She ran some water and splashed it on her face. "I can't stand to see him hurt. It's like I feel the pain myself."

She'd been fine just seconds before; now she looked like she was about to collapse. "But you were so great. You took care of everything. What happened?"

"It's not like you have a choice. You have to be fine when your kid needs you. Then afterward, you can fall apart."

"Are you going to fall apart?" I tried to remember the name of the firm David worked at in Pleasanton. Maybe he should come home early?

"No more than I already have," Jen said, straightening up and trying to grin. She shoved a cutting board and a knife my way. "Help me finish up getting lunch ready?"

I chopped tomatoes and scallions while Jennifer whirred together nonfat soy yogurt, fat-free chicken broth, cilantro, and garlic in the blender. I could tell already that I was going to have to drive through In-n-Out Burger on the way home. My suspicion was confirmed when she opened a can of chickpeas and tossed them into the salad. She grabbed some plates from the cabinet and handed them to me. "Set the table, will you?"

I started laying out the plates. "Will Troy actually eat this?"

Jennifer laughed. "Heavens, no. I promised him a banana smoothie for lunch."

"Then why are we setting three places?" I asked.

She had the good grace to blush. "I invited Mom." She handed me the silverware.

"Jennifer!" All the dismay I felt sounded clearly in my voice.

"She's worried about you. She says you'll barely talk to her. Give her a chance."

"I talked to her." I set a knife and fork at each place.

"Not according to her." Jen stretched to get three glasses from the top shelf and handed them to me.

"Yeah, well, if we looked at the world according to Lily all the time, we'd be in big trouble." I smacked the glasses down on the table. Living in Lily World had already screwed up eighteen years of my life.

The doorbell rang.

"I'm not getting it," I said.

"Fine," Jen said, marching out of the kitchen.

A few seconds later, Jennifer, Mom, and Mom's new melons marched right back in. Lily was in full Suburban Splendor mode: beige slacks, light blue sleeveless silk shirt, and a tasteful string of pearls. She clasped me in a brief hug, kissed the air near my right cheek, then turned back to Jennifer. "Where's my boy?" she demanded.

"Troy," Jennifer called. "Mom-mom is here."

Lily couldn't stand the idea of being called Grandma or Granny. It had to be Mom-mom. It was faky WASPy preppy and made me cringe every time I heard it.

Troy came in, trailing the yellow blankie behind him. Bobo had apparently been abandoned to watch cartoons on his own. I considered joining him. "A bee bit my finger, Mom-mom," he announced.

Lily knelt down and looked. "You poor thing. How did that happen?"

"I was helping the bee, but it bit me."

"How awful. It stung you when you were only trying to help?" Lily looked at me. I smiled blandly back. I didn't miss her accusation. I wasn't going to let her bait me though.

"I think Troy might have run over the bee with his Big Wheel. It was pretty squished." Jennifer had started tossing the salad and was oblivious to the byplay between Lily and me. Like that was anything new. Jennifer's insistence that we were a normal family consistently won her the Cleopatra, Queen of Denial crown. "He tried to pick it up and I think he managed to jam the stinger into his own finger."

"Oh, is that what happened?" It couldn't be good that I related all too well to the squished bee. "Iced tea?"

"Thank you, Chloe." Lily took the glass from me.

Her nails were perfectly manicured, and I wondered how much time she spent on grooming these days. Manicures, pedicures, chemical peels, Botox. Then again, what else did she have to do?

"How is your grandmother?"

"Gran's fine."

Jennifer whirred up bananas, nonfat yogurt, ice, and wheat germ and presented it to Troy like a big treat. The poor kid. I could see I'd have to take him to Baskin-Robbins so he would at least know there was a reason to rebel.

Lily smoothed my hair back behind my ears and sighed. "When are you going to do something about all that hair, dear?" she asked.

My hair is long and straight and I do essentially nothing to it. Blowing it dry is as fancy as I can stand to get. Lily hates it. "Next week," I said. Who said Rafe was the only one in the family who could be passive-aggressive?

"Make sure to take at least three inches off those ends. They look dry." Lily sailed by me to the table. "And get the bangs trimmed so they're not always in your eyes. Are you sure you don't want me to make an appointment with my girl?"

I'd rather hack my hair with nail scissors than give my mother's hair minion a chance to turn me into a little clone of her. "Hey, I've got your earrings!" I'd tucked them into my bag to give to Jen to give back to Lily.

"Oh, thank you, dear. They're practically the only things of Aunt Laura's that I have."

Troy opted to enjoy his banana smoothie on the couch with cartoons, so it was just the three of us at the table. I offered to keep Troy company, but Jennifer told me not to be silly as she dished up our chickpea salads.

"Lovely," Lily said after a few bites.

"It's a Weight Watcher's recipe," Jen said eagerly. "There's not a speck of fat in that dressing."

"Really," Lily said. "You'd never know."

"You're doing Weight Watchers while you're pregnant?" I asked. Somehow, that didn't seem right to me. Knowing Jen's history made it *really* really not right.

"Being pregnant doesn't mean you can stop taking care of yourself," Lily said, stabbing her fork in the air at me like a pointer. "Quite the opposite, really."

"If you add up the baby and the placenta and all that, it only comes to about thirteen pounds," Jen said, eyes wide. "All the rest of the weight is just fat on the mother, and don't think it just comes off when you have the baby."

I took a bite of the chickpea salad. It wasn't exactly good, but it wasn't bad. "Don't you need some kind of reserve or something?"

"For what?" Lily laughed. "It's not like Jennifer will have to go out and work in the fields right after she gives birth."

No. Jennifer was not going to have to work in the fields. After getting a communications degree from San Jose State, she worked for a year as an administrative assistant at a software company where she met David. A year later they were married and Troy was on the way soon after that, but it wasn't like she sat on her hands and did nothing, either. "She has to keep up with Troy, doesn't she? And have enough energy to feed the new baby and keep her house running and all the other stuff she does." Jen's house is not exactly small. I don't envy her the job of keeping all that saltillo tile clean and shiny. It's the kind of house that Gran often refers to as a lady killer.

"Speaking of breastfeeding," Lily said. "You need to get a really good support bra, Jennifer. Otherwise you're going to wind up needing to get them lifted like I did. I suppose it was breastfeeding so many children that really did them in."

I was shocked. Not just because Lily was trying to get us to believe she'd only had her boobs lifted (she'd added at least a cup size), but also because Lily was practically a founding member of La Leche League. I'd never heard her say anything about breastfeeding that wasn't glowing.

"You only breastfed three kids, Lily," I pointed out. I realize that's plenty of human beings to have fed from your own body, but Lily was making it sound like she'd nursed legions.

"There's three of you, but I breastfed a lot of other kids, too. Kids I babysat for. Kids of friends. Things like that." Lily took another bite of chickpeas.

"Gross, Mom!" Jennifer looked a little queasy.

"It's not gross, dear. It's natural. Having a wet nurse used to be considered quite normal."

"Yeah, back when it was considered normal not to have indoor plumbing, too." Jennifer put her fork down.

"Speaking of that, when are you going to start toilet training Troy?" Lily asked. "You don't want to be dipping your hands in dirty diapers while you're breastfeeding; the danger of infecting a cracked nipple goes up exponentially."

Now I put my fork down. Dirty diapers? Cracked nipples? Was this really table talk?

"I've tried. He's not ready yet, Mom." A dark flush began to creep up Jennifer's face. "I don't want to turn it into a power struggle."

Lily laughed. "Trust me, you don't have to turn it into one. It already is one. Just don't make the same mistake I made with Rafe."

Now, that interested me. Not so much that Lily had made a mistake with Rafe, but that she would admit it. See? I never know what she's going to say or do next. My mother constantly surprises me. Too bad I hate surprises. "What mistake did you make with Rafe?"

"Listening to too much of that hippy dippy stuff about not pushing children to do anything before they were ready to do it." Lily waved her fork in the air. "If I hadn't finally gotten serious with him about toilet training, I'd still be wiping your brother's ass. You, on the other hand, were a whole different story."

"I was?"

"Oh, yes. In fact, you were toilet trained before Rafe was. Girls are always easier than boys," Lily said. "Still, you basically trained yourself. I'd be trying to get Rafe to sit on that damn potty chair and there you'd already be."

Somehow this did not come out sounding like a compliment. Of course, very little that Lily ever said about me came out sounding like a compliment.

Then, without a warning of any kind, she said, "I wish you'd told me that you had cold feet."

Okay. I knew it was coming. I mean, did I really think it *wouldn't* be a topic of conversation? Coming right on the tail of the potty training dig, though, it caught me off guard. Another Lily surprise. "I didn't have cold feet," I said.

"It's true; she didn't. Remember what the catering lady said?" Jennifer chimed in. "She said she'd never seen a bride as calm as Chloe."

The caterer had come in while we were getting dressed for the ceremony to tell me that the champagne order had gotten screwed up and they'd sent the Moët and Chandon sparkling wine instead. I figured nobody would notice as long as it bubbled, and said so. Everyone had marveled at my equanimity. I thought they were all nuts.

"Maybe too calm," Lily said, her eyes narrowing a bit. "Almost as if she didn't care."

I sat up straight in my seat. "I did too care. I just didn't care whether we toasted with sparkling wine or champagne. I cared about the important stuff."

"Like what?"

"Like Mark," I said.

Lily nodded. "And that's why you're on your honeymoon with him right now."

I hate it when Lily's right. Of course, Gran always says that even a broken clock is right twice a day.

Lily rolled her eyes. "You must have known you didn't love him. I knew you didn't love him."

That couldn't be true—could it? Had I never loved Mark in the first place? On the other hand, I was having a hard time working up a good head of righteous indignation, which is generally not a problem when I'm talking to Lily. "I didn't know I didn't love him. I wouldn't have been marrying him if I'd thought I didn't love him." I was pretty sure that was true.

Lily rolled her eyes again. If she wasn't careful, she was going to pop the stitches from her last eye tuck. "Stop posturing, Chloe. There are plenty of good reasons to marry a man like Mark that have nothing to do with love. As far as I'm concerned, marrying for love is the stupidest reason in the book." She pointed at me. "I married your father for love, and look what a complete disaster that was."

Since that marriage produced me and Rafe, I like to think it was not a complete disaster. "Thanks, Lily."

"Wait a minute," Jennifer broke in. "Are you saying that you don't love Daddy?"

"Of course not, dear." Lily patted Jennifer's hand. "Just not the kind of love that Chloe's talking about."

"So how did you know I didn't love Mark?" I asked. I hated to admit that Lily had a point, but somehow not loving Mark in the first place seemed like a better reason to have run out of my own wedding than hearing voices.

Lily waved a hand in the air. "Well, who could, besides his dried-up prune of a mother?"

"That's not true." Heat rose to my face. "Mark is an extremely successful professor at the university. He has lots of friends."

"Sycophants, more like," Lily said. "And as far as his being successful, well, he sure makes sure that anybody who's in a room with him for more than five minutes knows *all* about that."

Jennifer giggled again. "I think I can recite most of his publications from the last three years."

Lily started talking in a mock deep voice. " 'Well, when *Plant Pathology Today* decided to put my article on its cover . . .' "

"Wait! Wait!" Jennifer said, and then lowered her voice. " 'When I flew to Dallas to accept the award for my work on the citrus tristeza virus . . .' "

I held up my hands to stop them. "Fine, so Mark could be a little full of himself from time to time. Academia is very competitive. If you don't toot your own horn a little, no one will ever hear about you."

"A little? The man was puffed up so big I'm surprised there was any room for you in the same house with him, much less in the relationship." Lily rattled her ice cubes around in her now empty glass.

"There wasn't," Jennifer said. "Remember when Dr. Jensen wanted Chloe to go with him to that big conference in Germany to give that talk, because she'd done so much of the research on the paper he was giving? Remember how mad Mark got that she was leaving when his graduate seminar was giving its presentations, and he wouldn't let her go?"

The smile fell from Lily's face. "No, I don't remember that. Someone would have had to tell me about it for me to remember it."

"Jennifer, you're taking things out of context. Mark didn't say I couldn't go. I chose to be here to support him at an important moment in his career." That had been a hard choice. Jensen had been really disappointed and I had really wanted to go. But Mark had been so crestfallen when I said I wouldn't be there when he would be having a stressful time, I couldn't bring myself to abandon him. He'd needed me.

"And where was he when your career needed supporting?" she shot back.

"Right where he should be. He never got in the way of what I needed to do at work. In fact, he was always right there when I needed to work through a research problem."

"Unless you had to work late too many nights in a row. Or needed to go out of town. Or wanted to go back to school." Jen was rattling the ice cubes in her glass the same way Lily rattled hers. I wanted to slap the glass out of her hand.

"I decided not to go back to school. We talked about it and I chose not to do it. I didn't want to be in school for the rest of my life. You're confusing me with Rafe."

"At least Rafe has some ambition."

Jennifer's present job was not exactly on the Ten Most Ambitious Careers list, but pointing that out wouldn't get her off my back. All it would accomplish would be to upset her, which would mean she'd be running to the bathroom to shove her fingers down her throat to barf up what few calories we'd just consumed. There was no sense in that. "Fine. So I have no ambition. I don't need ambition. I like my job."

"Good. Because you're going to be doing the same one for the rest of your life." Lily shrugged. "So, Stuart and I have decided to remodel our master bathroom. It's about time, since we've been there for what? Ten years now? Anyway, what do you think of this tile?" She fished a tile out of her purse.

And so we were done with the topic of Chloe and her wacky behavior. For the next half hour, we discussed tile, grout, and tub enclosures. At least Jennifer and Lily discussed tile, grout, and tub enclosures; I nodded a lot. Eventually I hit the point where I felt like one of those bobblehead dolls and decided I could gracefully go.

Troy had slipped back into his Batman cape and fallen asleep watching cartoons. I guess the trauma of the bee sting had taken a lot out of him. I kissed his banana-sticky cheek good-bye. His little red mouth puckered into an *o* in response, then relaxed again. God, he was cute.

Lily gave me a perfunctory hug and then Jen walked me out to my truck.

"Thank you *so* much for coming today." Jen threw her arms around me.

"Are you always so thrilled when people invite themselves over?"

"When you do it, yes." Jen released me. "It meant a lot to me that you called today and wanted to come here to see me."

I opened the door and got in. "No problem." I just love being raked over the coals and then discussing grout color as if nothing had happened.

"It meant a lot to me that you stayed to have lunch with Mom, too." Jennifer planted herself in the open door of the truck so I couldn't shut it without slamming it into my future niece or nephew. "She's really trying, you know."

"Oh, yeah. I could see that." I tried to keep my voice flat, but the sarcasm crept in. Maybe it's habit. Maybe it's bitterness. Yeah, I'm pretty sure it's bitterness.

"It's not easy for her, you know." Jen crossed her toothpick arms across her chest. "Seriously, Chloe, give her a chance."

I laughed a little. I'm pretty sure I've given Lily more chances than a slot machine in the airport at Vegas gives. None of it was Jen's fault, though. I touched her cheek. "I'll try. Thanks for lunch."

"You're welcome. Do you think you can come for the Fourth of July? I'm thinking of having a family barbecue. I'd like you to be there."

"I don't know." A family barbecue? It sounded like torture. We could all skewer me on my poor life choices, from my ex-fiancé to my hairstyle, and then grill me. A Chloe kabob!

"Please, Chloe, please try to come," Jennifer wheedled. "I want Troy to have good memories of a happy family all together. Normal families get together on the Fourth of July and have barbecues. We'll be able to see the fireworks from the backyard."

Egads. I don't think we even knew what normal families acted like. Maybe we could pick a TV family to emulate. I'd often wanted to be a Huxtable. On the other hand, Troy was precious. A little obsessed with lining up cars by color and climbing to the top of whatever was around and jumping off it, but sweet. "When and where?"

"Here at six," Jennifer said promptly.

"How much family?"

"I want to have David's family and our family."

"That's close to fifteen people. Are you sure you want to take this on right now? Your due date is less than a month away."

"Yes. Please, Chloe, say you'll come. If you come, Rafe will come."

"If it's what you want, of course I'll come. What can I do to help?"

"Bring brownies and cookies. And give Gran a ride. Thank you, Chloe. Thank you," she squealed and finally backed up so I could shut the door. By the time I'd backed out of the driveway, she was already back in the house, probably fussing over how to get the Batman cape off of Troy without waking him from his nap.

I loved watching her with him. I liked to think that somewhere in the back of Jen's mind, she remembered the fuss I made over her as a baby and that she was passing that on to Troy. Probably not, though. Jen had been born with that maternal instinct. It had told Jen how to play with her dolls and stuffed animals by pretending to feed them and rock them to sleep, and now it had her feeling her kid's bee stings as keenly as if she'd been stung herself.

I drove back to Winters and pulled into town at a little after three. On a whim, I pulled into the Green Creek. It seemed as good a place as any to while away some time.

Til was behind the counter again. "What can I get you?"

I didn't want a drink; it was only three in the afternoon. "Diet Coke," I said.

Til tossed her rag down on the bar. "Why on earth would you come in here and order a Diet Coke? I have to charge you three bucks for it. You could go to the gas station and get one for a buck. Or to the grocery store and get a whole damn twelve-pack for three bucks."

Yeah, but I didn't have anywhere else to go. "I need a place to drink it, too."

"Oh." Til poured the Diet Coke and shoved it across the bar to me. When I pulled three dollars out of my wallet, she waved the bills away.

"Don't you have a job or something?" she asked.

"Or something." I took a sip and set my glass down, then

scooted it along the bar, making a wet streak. "I'm on a leave of absence for a couple months."

Til nodded. "And you were already shacked up with the guy you dumped at the altar, right?"

I looked up from the doodle I was making in the rings on the bar. "How'd you know that?"

She shrugged. "Your brother said."

I wondered what else Rafe had told her. I took the rag from where she'd dropped it and wiped up the mess I'd made.

"So you're looking for something to do?" Til asked.

"I guess so. I can't just sit here buying three dollar Cokes all day." Or sit at the bungalow and watch Etienne expel body fluids, or sit at Gran's and watch Rafe work, or go to the lab, or to Jennifer's or . . . I'd run out of *or*s.

"You could work here."

I looked around at the deserted bar. "More customers than you can serve, Til?"

She took the rag back from me. "Not right now, but in forty-five minutes the place'll be hopping and it'll stay that way until after seven. I could use some help getting ready for happy hour and some help winding down from it too. Even if it was only for a couple months. In fact, it might be better if it was only for a couple months."

"Why?"

"Because it'll be easier to talk my cousin into hiring you if he doesn't think it's permanent. He's a cheap bastard."

"Your cousin owns this place?"

Til nodded. "I'll talk to him tonight. Plan on being here tomorrow at four. No, make it three. Then I can pick up Hunter from preschool. He'll like that."

"Who's Hunter?"

"My kid."

That surprised me. "You have a kid? How old is he?"

"Four. He stays at my sister's after preschool until I get home. With you helping with cleanup after happy hour, I might be able to get home a little early, too."

Til had a kid to get home to. And a sister. And a life outside this stinky bar. Who knew?

"Sure," I said. "Why not?"

CHAPTER SIX

Chloe's Guide for the Runaway Bride

Your former mother-in-law-to-be is going through changes too. Now that you've run out on her son, you are clearly not the sensible girl with good taste that she thought you were. Chances are, she's drawing horns and tails on those lovely engagement photos she insisted you have taken. If you could just explain why you left the apple of her eye standing at the altar, she might be able to understand. You *do* know why, don't you?

Clearly, a cyclone had hit the yard. Cabinets, broken tiles, scraps of wood, plastic cording, and other debris were scattered everywhere. A young man wearing filthy white pants that sagged around his narrow hips, leaving a good three inches of boxer shorts sticking out, was picking up some of the debris and putting it in a garbage bag while leaving other bits that looked just as much like garbage where they were. As I watched from outside the gate, he threw out two empty cans of Mountain Dew, but left several large crinkled-up sheets of brown paper.

He turned and gave me a wave when I opened the gate. He had the same haystack hair that Etienne had, but somehow on him it worked. Of course, he was probably twenty years younger than Etienne. He also didn't have a shirt on. To be honest, this worked pretty well on him too, if you like totally buff, hairless chests with six-pack abs. Since the kid was probably all of twenty, I tried to convince myself that I didn't like totally buff hairless chests with six-pack abs, and tried to look away. My eyes seemed to have a life of their own, though.

I pulled the car through the gate and Aziza came bounding out of the garage. "Hi," I said, closing the gate behind me.

"Hey."

"I'm Chloe." I extended my hand.

He wiped his hand off on his pants and then shook mine. He had a goofy grin and a stoner's lope. It was a little like meeting a big golden retriever. "I'm Tucker. I'm working with Etienne. I'm his nephew." He ducked his head a couple of times as he spoke. Very cute.

"Oh. Great." I could probably forgive pop cans being left around much more easily if they'd been dropped by boy Adonis here, rather than Etienne. Before I could construct a sliding scale for the degree of trash annoyance and its inverse relationship to the beauty of the litterer, though, Jesse limped out to greet me. He kept his right front paw curled up, and hobbled along on his other three legs. I knelt down to hug him. "What happened, baby? What's wrong?"

"He's been like limping for a while, dude. I tried to see what was wrong, but he totally wouldn't let me anywhere near," Tucker offered.

I wasn't surprised. Jesse doesn't let just anyone handle him, especially if he's hurt. He's even snapped at me a couple times when he's had burrs in his ears that needed to be removed. He wasn't going to let me look at his paw this time either. When I tried, he drew back and growled softly.

Great. I didn't even know the name of a vet in town. I patted Jesse on the head. "Hold on, boy. I'll call Gran. She'll know where to take you."

Sure enough, she did. "Daniel Stein. He's a lovely young man. I know his mother."

"The vet's name is Daniel Stein?"

"What's wrong with that?" Gran asked.

"I just never thought about there being Jewish vets. It's kind of like finding out that there are Jewish gun nuts."

"What do you call the Israelis?"

Point taken. I called the number she gave me.

"Stein Veterinary," a voice chirped at me over the phone.

"Hi. My dog has something stuck in his paw. I need to bring him in."

"Do you have an appointment?" Chirpy asked.

Sure. I scheduled my dog's emergency weeks ago. "No."

"You know it's like four forty-five, right? Well, I dunno if Daniel, I mean Dr. Stein, can see you. He's like really busy."

"Listen, it's really an emergency. I could be there in fifteen minutes tops. Could you check and tell him that Naomi Gold recommended him? I'm her granddaughter." Gran had lived here so long that her name could occasionally open doors.

"Well, I'll check, but I can't like promise you anything."

"Thanks," I said, but she'd already put me on hold.

Tucker stuck his charmingly tousled head in. "I'm gonna, like, take off now, Chloe. I hope your dog's okay."

"Thanks," I said, waving while I wondered if anybody actually *did* anything anymore, or if they only *like* did stuff, and if I was going to start talking about the good old days when a dollar was a dollar. I sometimes feel so much older than everyone else around me.

Chirpy came back on the line. "Daniel will see you if you can come now," she said with an exasperated sigh that told me exactly what she thought about that decision.

I hung up with a promise to hustle right over there. "I've got to take you to the vet, boy," I told Jesse. I don't believe in lying to dogs or children; it just erodes their trust in you. I base this on the fact that just about every adult in my life except Gran made it a habit to lie to me. Gran was always up front about everything. When I stepped on a rusty nail in the front yard and punctured my foot, she told me the shot was going to hurt. When Bun-Bun died, she told me he had died and not that he had gone to live on a special bunny farm. She was the only one of the bunch that I trusted by the time I turned twelve.

I grabbed some towels to put down on the seat and got Jesse to hobble behind me to the truck. I opened the door and patted the seat. "Come on, boy. Hop in."

Jesse put his paws up on the running board of the truck to make his leap in and then yelped and picked up his hurt paw.

"I know it hurts, Jesse, but you have to get in the truck. Now jump in," I said, trying to sound stern and not worried.

Jesse sat down. Aziza, however, came bounding up behind us and jumped in. Jesse growled and nipped at her back leg as it went past him. She yelped and whirled around. I grabbed her collar and hauled her out.

"Jesse," I said. "Get in the truck."

He lay down and looked up at me with a "you and whose army" kind of look.

"Fine," I muttered and squatted down to try to pick him up. I felt something cold and wet in the space where my shirt pulled away from my pants. I leaped and shrieked and dropped Jesse in the process. It was Aziza, giving my exposed back a lick.

Why is it that no matter how hot it is outside, a dog nose on your lower back always feels like ice?

"Aziza," I barked, feeling rather doggy myself. Sweat trickled down the sides of my face and my back. By the time I got to the vet's office I was going to smell like a dog.

"Go. Sit." I pointed imperiously toward the garage. Aziza cringed away and I immediately felt like a jerk. She was just a dog and not a very bright one, after all. She had only wanted to give me a little kiss and a surreptitious little sniff and to be taken with us. Could I not be gracious for once?

I finally succeeded in getting Jesse's front half up into the truck and stopped for a breather. Meanwhile Aziza wiggled and cringed her way back over to us. Now she tried to wiggle into the truck next to Jesse's front half. He growled. I hauled her down again. Why hadn't I had Tucker help me get the dog into the truck? Surely, those big strong arms would have hoisted him right in.

"Okay, boy. Let's get your back side in." As the words left my mouth, Aziza snuck up and sniffed Jesse's behind. His back side went leaping into the truck and he whirled around, teeth bared so fast I barely had time to keep from getting snapped at myself.

I laughed and patted Aziza's head. "Good girl." I shut Jesse into the truck and got Aziza a treat. "Thanks for helping."

A short time later, I pulled into the side street that Daniel Stein's office was on. You could say that all the streets of Winters were side streets. Even Main Street was just a dinky little two-lane road with diagonal parking on either side. I lifted Jesse down from the truck, practically wrenching my back. "You weigh a ton," I complained.

He gave me a dirty look and a harrumph.

Chirpy was a Gothed-out teenager with spiked-up jet black hair and a powdered face, not exactly what I expected. I guess the fact that she worked in a vet's office and had that voice made me expect an apple-cheeked 4-H country girl. What did I know, though? Maybe the 4-H girls were all Gothed out these days.

"Poor handsome fellow," she said to Jesse. "Do you have a hurt paw?"

Jesse heaved a trembling sigh.

"You're being very brave," Chirpy said. "I'll let Dr. Stein know you're here."

It didn't occur to me until the door to the back area swung shut behind her that she hadn't spoken to me at all. She was back seconds later, crooking her finger at Jesse to follow her. I decided that I was invited too.

"We'll get your weight and everything after Dr. Stein takes care of that paw," Chirpy told Jesse. She handed a clipboard to me as she left the room and growled, "Fill these out."

I sat down in the orange plastic chair and started filling out our information. What kind of doctor would have a Goth teenager receptionist who spoke politely only to animals?

The answer to that was a reasonably cute vet about my age, with short dark hair, a stubbly beard, and a chest that looked like he worked out.

"So I hear you have a paw emergency," he said.

"Yes, my dog wouldn't let me look. He kept nipping at me. You should probably be careful," I said.

"You'll let me look, won't you, boy?" he asked Jesse.

Jesse snuffled.

Dr. Stein went to scratch behind his ears. I grabbed his hand. "Not the ears. He hates to have his ears touched. In fact, he's really touchy about being handled at all, especially by strangers. I have no idea what happened to him before I got him; all I know is that it wasn't pleasant and it had to do with his ears. And water. Nobody touches Jesse's ears without getting at least growled at, and nobody sprays him with a hose, either."

"So he was a stray?"

I nodded. "I guess I'm a sucker for them."

"Me, too." Dr. Stein smiled at me. Nice teeth.

He rolled Jesse on his side and scratched his belly for a minute. "So you're Naomi Gold's granddaughter."

"Mmmm." I kept waiting for Jesse to nip at him, to growl. Instead he lolled his tongue out in a big smile.

"She's a fabulous old lady."

"I don't think she'd like you saying that she's old."

He laughed. "Probably not. Don't tell her; I'd hate to be taken off her fruitcake list."

"You like Gran's fruitcake?" I didn't know *anyone* who liked Gran's fruitcakes. She made them every year and it continually amazed me that no one had ever sued her for broken teeth.

Daniel grimaced. "Not to eat. It's more the thought behind it that I appreciate."

" 'But for the honor of it all,' " I murmured under my breath.

" 'I'd rather walk,' " he finished.

I looked up at him and smiled. It had been my Granda's favorite quote. It came from an Abraham Lincoln story about a horse thief being ridden out of town on a rail.

He smiled back. Really nice teeth. And a dimple, too. "Besides, the fruitcakes make lovely doorstops until the ants get to them."

"Do ants actually eat Gran's fruitcakes?"

Daniel didn't answer; he was inspecting Jesse's paw. I waited for Jesse to snarl or snap. Nothing. Finally he emitted a low growl from his throat, but by that time Daniel was standing up with a huge sliver in his hand. "Got it!"

Jesse heaved a sigh. Stein patted his head. "Good boy," he said, fondling his ears. "Good boy."

Jesse, the traitor, licked him.

Daniel slathered some antibiotic ointment on Jesse's paw and wrapped it up. "If he'll leave this alone, he doesn't have to wear the big cone. If he starts gnawing at it, call me and we'll set you up with one. Jesse seems like a dog who would want to hang on to his dignity, though."

"You've got that right." One time Jesse tangled with some barbed wire and had to have stitches. He would only go outside at night until the hair grew back over the shaved spot.

Daniel opened the door and we all went out to the front desk. Chirpy had apparently left for the day.

"So how'd you end up being a veterinarian?" I asked as I wrote out the check at the counter.

"My mother wanted me to be a doctor. I wanted to be a cowboy." He shrugged. "It seemed like a reasonable compromise."

"What does your mother think of it? Does she think it's a reasonable compromise?"

He grinned. "I'm Jewish. My mother thinks the world rises and sets with me."

Back home, Aziza galloped out to meet us and jumped into the truck, earning herself a nip from Jesse when she crowded him on the seat. She gave him a lick and a nuzzle in return. Even bad attention was okay with her, as long as it was attention.

It was even hotter inside the bungalow than it was outside. The light on the answering machine was blinking. The first message was from Til. "Congratulations, Chloe. You got the job. Be at the Green Creek tomorrow by two-thirty. Bye." In the background, I could hear voices and banging noises and a television set. Her house sounded just like the Green Creek.

The second message was from Gran. "Chloe, I'm sure the kitchen there is all torn up. Why don't you come for dinner tonight? You can report on Etienne's progress and see what a nice job Rafe did finishing the linoleum. Be here by seven. Oh, and bring the dogs. I know you won't want to leave Jesse alone."

I love my gran.

The new floor looked great. "You really learned how to do this completely from the Internet?" I asked Rafe. I was setting the table. He was watching from the window seat, nursing a beer. Gran was out in the garden with Aziza following her around. Jesse was lying in the kitchen doorway with his hurt paw crossed over the unhurt one and his chin resting on his doggie elbow. The delta breeze was starting to pick up and the doorway was the perfect place to feel it flow through the house. He looked supremely content.

Rafe took a long swallow of his beer and nodded. "Yep. The truth shall make you free."

"It's linoleum, Rafe, not the face of God."

He got up and straightened one of the forks. "Ah, but God is in the details, little Chloe, always in the details."

"I thought it was the devil that was in the details," Gran said as she came in with some parsley she'd just cut. Aziza went over and nudged Jesse with her nose. He was so happy, he didn't even growl at her. Gran set the parsley by the sink. "Rafe, make yourself useful and rinse this parsley, please." Then she pulled the salmon out of the refrigerator. It was covered with her homemade mayonnaise, which is about as different from the stuff you buy in the jar at the grocery as homemade spaghetti sauce is from Ragu.

"It looks beautiful, Gran," I said.

She smiled. "It did come out well, didn't it? Although I'm not sure I'll be able to keep coming up with ways to serve salmon."

I knew better than to suggest that we could throw some of

the salmon out. You just don't say things like that to Depression-era babies.

She took the parsley from Rafe and scattered it around the fish as a garnish. It looked like a spread from *Bon Appetit*. As I tossed the salad, Gran pulled the bread from the oven where it had been warming and we sat down.

Nobody spoke for a few minutes, it was that good. We definitely shouldn't throw the salmon out. When I finally came up for air, I said, "So I think I got a job."

"That's nice, dear. Where will you be working?" Gran asked.

"The Green Creek," I said.

Gran put down her fork. "The bar? The one across from Billy Joe's Car Repair?"

"That's the one." I took another bite of salmon. Damn, it was good. No matter how many times I tried to do it myself, I could never get the mayonnaise to emulsify.

"What will you be doing there?" Gran asked.

I shrugged. "Tending bar. Waiting tables. Stuff like that."

"I wish I'd known you were looking for a job like that, Chloe." Gran wiped her mouth with her napkin. "I could have gotten you something at the Stag's Leap."

I hadn't thought of that. The Stag's Leap is one of Winters's finer restaurants. It's famous from Fairfield to Sacramento for its tri-tip and prime rib. It's owned by Eric and Janet Godfrey, who, like everyone else who's been around for more than a year, are friends with Gran. I'd certainly make better tips there than I would at the Green Creek. Of course, I would be making them off people who have known me since I was a baby. The clientele there is pretty much all FOG (Friends of Gran).

A huge number of whom were also guests at the Un-Wedding.

The idea of taking orders and making small talk with the people I'd left gaping at the Opera House did not appeal. Just thinking about it made the boulder in my chest ten pounds heavier. At least at the Green Creek, no one knew who I was.

"That's okay, Gran. I think I'll like working at the Green Creek."

"With Til?" Rafe asked.

"She's the one who got me the job."

Rafe ran his hand over his chin. He'd set his fork down too. "She didn't mention it."

"When would she have mentioned it?" I knew Rafe had been sniffing around Til, but I didn't think it had gotten to the point where they were sharing pillow talk.

He leaned back in his chair. "The other day. I stopped by for a drink."

"Are we speaking of Matilda Renfro?" Gran asked, her voice sharp.

"I don't know," I said. I realized I didn't even know Til's last name. "Are we, Rafe?"

He nodded, but before anyone else could speak, Jesse leaped up and hobbled over to the kitchen door. The hair on back of his neck stood up and he growled softly. Aziza bounded over after him, barking her head off. I grabbed Jesse's collar to keep him in when I let Aziza out. He gave me a look of disgust. "Sorry, boy. Not until that paw heals."

He settled down by the door, but his head stayed up and his eyes remained fixed on the door and vigilant. I hadn't even made it back to my chair when someone laid on a car horn.

I looked over at Gran, who shrugged her thin shoulders and said, "I wasn't expecting anyone."

I looked out the kitchen window. I knew that Lexus. It was Shelby, Mark's mother.

Rafe joined me at the window. "Uh oh," he said under his breath.

Gran joined us. She pursed her lips, but didn't say anything.

Shelby laid on the horn again. Aziza was really barking her head off.

"You should let her in, Chloe," Gran said.

"Do I have to?" I asked.

Gran just looked at me. I went outside. Shelby rolled down her window. "Would you please call your dog off, Chloe?"

Somehow Shelby made the words "your dog" sound like "your demonic spawn." And anyway, Aziza was Mark's dog first, not mine. I didn't feel like arguing with her, though. Actually, I didn't feel like having any kind of conversation with her at all. From the look on Shelby's face, she wasn't exactly looking forward to having a nice chat with me, either. I grabbed Aziza by the collar and told her to shush. She sat, but continued to whine and strain at my hold on her.

Shelby got out of the car. "Chloe, I didn't expect to find you here."

It seemed a lot more likely to find me here at my grandmother's than for her to be here, so why did I feel a need to explain my presence to her? "I came for dinner."

"It's just as well. I came to leave some things for you." Shelby went around and opened the trunk of her sedan. It was filled with packages. White packages with silver and golden bows. Wedding presents. She opened the back doors of the sedan. More packages jammed the backseat. "I told Mark that I'd return the gifts that had been delivered to his house. These are the ones people brought to the wedding. I thought the least you could do to help clean up this mess is to return them."

I bowed my head. "I'll get Rafe to help me carry them in."

We decided to load them directly into my truck. Shelby

stood by her car, arms folded protectively across her chest. Gran invited her in, offered her tea, and tried to make small talk about the weather, all to no avail. Shelby just stood there, tight-lipped and fuming.

Shelby had never looked at me like that before, yet I felt a shiver of déjà vu. I realized I'd seen that look on Mark's face more than once—the last time being when the glass had rolled unbroken away from his foot. I'd run then and, boy, did I want to run now.

After we loaded the last gift into the truck, Shelby got back into her Lexus. She turned it around and then glared at the gate until I went and opened it. "You know, I knew your mother in high school, Chloe."

I nodded.

"This is just the kind of stunt I'd have expected from Lily Gold. I'd hoped it had skipped a generation. I should have known better." She cruised out.

Rafe threw an arm across my shoulder and we headed back into the house. "That was fun."

"Next time maybe I'll just stick something sharp into my eye instead," I said.

"Who's ready for chocolate cake?" Gran sang out.

Rafe shook his head. "Not me. I couldn't eat another bite. I'm stuffed."

"What," I asked, "does being full have to do with chocolate cake? I don't think the two concepts are even related."

I hate it when Rafe does that. It makes him look like he has more impulse control than I do, which is totally not true. Rafe is all id. He runs on instinct and constantly seeks the fastest course to immediate gratification. Maybe it's the extra year he had in Lily's Earth Mother phase.

Of course, maybe it's being in touch with his own instincts

that allows Rafe to know when he's had enough and that eating chocolate cake will make him feel a little sick. I am completely ego. Maybe it's the fact that I'm more in touch with the external reality of the cake and its chocolatiness that makes me desire it, even though my hunger is satisfied already.

Sometimes I think that if you combined Rafe and me, we'd make a fully functional human being. Except for that icky hermaphroditic thing.

At any rate, chocolate cake was exactly what I needed. I had two pieces and washed them down with glasses of cold milk.

Rafe followed me home with Jesse and Aziza in his MG, because the truck was so stuffed with presents. Jesse started howling the second he realized that I wasn't getting in the car too. Aziza stuck her nose in Rafe's ear and gave his chin a lick, the little slut.

We got back to the bungalow and Rafe helped me unload the packages into the bungalow. I'd left all the windows open when I'd gone over to Gran's and the breeze had cooled the place off. It still smelled like sawdust, but I wouldn't choke on it anymore.

"That's quite a pile," he observed, after we'd stacked the boxes in the corner of the living room.

"It sure is." I plopped down on the couch. Just looking at them made me feel tired. The idea of facing all those people was more than daunting. I'm sure some had just bought something because they had to, but I was equally sure that some of those gifts were purchased with a lot of good wishes. Those would be the hard ones to return. "Do you think I can go around at night and leave them on people's doorsteps?"

"What?" Rafe snorted. "Like a good wedding elf? Or so you don't have to face anybody?"

"The facing thing, although I like the idea of being a wedding elf. I'd have to be better at that than I was at being a bride."

Rafe sat down next to me. "You didn't exactly give the bride thing a fair shake. Any idea why?"

I put my head down and cradled it in my arms. "If I told you that I heard a voice telling me to run, what would you think?"

"Given our family history, I'd think that you needed to see a mental health professional immediately and that psychotropic drugs were probably in order."

Pretty much what I was afraid of. "What if I told you that I finally noticed that the only people who really seem upset about this wedding are Mark and his mother?"

"I'd say you might finally be getting the hint." Rafe draped his arm over my back.

Hints were great, but they only gave you part of the puzzle. I needed to see the whole picture laid out before me, and that seemed way too difficult. "Maybe we're not genetically composed for marriage."

"Jen and David seem to be doing all right."

"She looks too thin," I said.

Rafe leaned back. "I know. I noticed at the wedding. She's only got a month or so to go, though."

"She's doing Weight Watchers." I watched for his reaction. Maybe it was just me who worried about our formerly anorexic sister doing Weight Watchers while she was pregnant. From the look on Rafe's face, apparently not. "And Lily thinks it's great."

Rafe winced. "David won't let her hurt herself, and Jen won't hurt the baby."

"Do you really believe that?" I asked.

"I don't know what else to do."

"Me neither."

Rafe hugged me good night and I put the dogs out for a last

time. I rescued the coffeemaker from the debris of the kitchen and set it up in the bathroom. Then I went back to the kitchen. Etienne had stripped it right down to its bones. And what bones they were: clean and solid. I told myself it was just idle curiosity, but even I knew I was fooling myself when I plugged my laptop into the phone jack and found a dial-up number I could use. I typed the words "arts and crafts bungalow renovation" into the search engine and waited about ten seconds (dial-up is soooooo slow) for the more than twenty thousand websites on the topic to present themselves to me.

The next two hours went by in a blur.

It wasn't until my eyelids actually stuck to my eyeballs that I realized how long I'd spent. I logged out and then fell into the bed. I was so tired I felt like there was a weight on me actually holding me down. The ceiling fan whirred gently over my head, and outside I could hear the gentle *whoosh* of the breeze through the olive trees. I closed my eyes and waited to float away to sleep.

Fifteen minutes later, I was still waiting.

I snapped on the light and sat up, and my gaze fell on Aunt Laura's green metal box.

I pulled out a letter.

My dear Laura,

I've been thinking and thinking, trying to find a way to make this work. Here is what I want you to do. Go to Sacramento to the pawn shops on J Street. I hate sending you alone there, darling. Be careful. I think you'll find many gold bands for sale cheaply there. Get one and put it on your finger, dear Laura. I'll put one there for real as soon as I can. Please believe me.

All my love,
Jesse

Holy smokes! It didn't take much to figure out what that meant. Jesse and Laura had been way more than pen pals, that was for sure. And Lily might have a cousin out there somewhere that she had never heard of. As my mind raced over the possibility of a whole other family unit, my eyes finally began to droop. I fell asleep with Jesse's letter still in my hand.

CHAPTER SEVEN

Chloe's Guide for the Runaway Bride

Returning the wedding gifts is an awkward affair. Consider returning them in the still of the night. It might be nice to leave a small note of explanation, but what could you say, really? That you heard a strange voice telling you to run? Hey, that's still good advice—dump that blender and run, honey!

I woke once again to the syncopated bangings of Etienne. I rolled over and looked at my watch. Eight a.m. It was already too hot to run. But I hadn't gotten a lot of rest anyway. I kept dreaming that I was trapped underwater and couldn't get up to the surface. I sat up, covered in sweat and gasping for air.

Once I stumbled out into the kitchen, I found both Etienne and Tucker, although Etienne was doing most of the banging. I guess that was the fun part, and he reserved it for himself since he was the boss. I let Jesse and Aziza out the front door and stumbled back to the bathroom.

I started the coffeemaker before I got in the shower so I had coffee as soon as I got out. No milk, though. I pulled on a pair of shorts and a light blue halter top (whoever started putting built-in bras in these things should be up for sainthood) and headed out with my hair still wrapped in a towel. The path from the kitchen doorway to the refrigerator was an obstacle course of construction equipment. I sighed.

My coffee made, I went into the living room, where I was welcomed by the pyramid of wedding gifts I needed to return. There were probably close to eighty packages there. Well, Gran always said to divide big tasks up into little ones and take them one at a time. If I divided them up and returned four packages a day, it would take twenty days to return them all. Even giving myself weekends off, I should have them all taken care of within a month. That wasn't too bad.

I picked four packages randomly from the pile and opened their cards. I recognized three of the four names. For all I knew, that fourth gift was from Shelby's insurance agent or her favorite uncle. There was no way to tell.

I put it back on the pile and took another one. Good, a name I knew. Except now I had two packages from Davis, one from Woodland and one from Winters. That seemed like an awful lot of driving around.

Aziza whined at the door and I let the dogs back in. Aziza barked at the packages and then flounced over to her bed. Jesse settled at my feet with a *hmmph*.

I started a Woodland package stack and a Winters package stack and continued sorting until I had four packages for people in Davis whose names I recognized. Then I grabbed the phone book and jotted down addresses. This was going to be even more work than I had realized.

Then again, at least I had something to do before I went to the Green Creek.

I braided my wet hair. When I unbraided it after it dried, I would look like Roseanne Rosannadanna, but I'd want it pulled back for serving drinks and I couldn't stand it hanging down in the heat. I finished off my coffee and ate an apple while sitting on my bed, looking at that letter from Jesse to Aunt Laura. Was he really telling her to buy a wedding ring so she could pretend she was married? The obvious answer was yes, and the reason she would need to do that seemed obvious as well. But Aunt Laura hadn't had any children. Maybe she'd miscarried. Would Gran have known about it? I loaded the four presents in the Frontier and went to say good-bye to Etienne and Tucker.

"I have to go into Davis," I told them once I got Etienne to stop swinging the sledgehammer. "Do you need anything?"

"Oh! It is so good that you asked." Etienne gave me a grin that I have to admit was charming, regardless of the tobacco stains on his teeth. "Let me make you a list. I need some things from Hubert's Hardware. Tell them to put it on my account, yes?"

I tucked the list in my purse, reminded the guys about the leftovers in the freezer and urged them to eat a lot of salmon (I felt like I was starting to grow gills) then hit the road.

The heat inside the truck was like a physical force pushing me down in my seat. I cranked the AC. The problem with doing that is I invariably forget what the air is going to feel like when I get out of the car. It slammed into me like a wall as I reached my first destination in West Davis. Luckily, all I had to do was scamper up the driveway and dump the package by the front door. I had similar luck with the next package, also on the west side.

Next, I opted to return the large, heavy package to Mark's aunt first, in the hope that Vicky would be at her apartment and invite me in for a cold drink. Unfortunately, things didn't work out that way. After driving up to where the bird streets started (most of the streets in Davis are organized by subject: there are bird streets, river streets, mountain streets, tree streets, minor president streets, etc.), I found Mark's aunt was home. In fact, she was carrying groceries in from her car. I drove right on by, hoping she wouldn't recognize my truck. Breaking into a cold sweat at the thought of talking to her, I took off for Vicky's.

Vicky, however, was not home to offer me a cold drink or warm sympathy. Judging by the number of newspapers at her door, she hadn't been home for several days. I shouldn't have been surprised. Classes were out and lots of people took vacation at this time of year. I started to set the box down anyway, but wondered what if Vicky wouldn't be back for weeks and someone stole the present from her doorway? Of course, if she was going to be gone for weeks, wouldn't she have remembered to stop her newspaper delivery? I decided not to risk it and took the box back to the truck.

Great. Of the four packages, I'd only delivered two. If things kept going like this, I'd be checking into the nursing home about the time I was done returning them.

I cruised back by Mark's aunt's house and parked across the street. The car was still in the driveway, but the trunk was closed. If Aunt Edna was home, she was safely ensconced in the air conditioning, where all sane people would be on a day like today.

I couldn't shake the idea that the second I got out of my truck and walked across the street, Aunt Edna would dart out her front door like some evil jack-in-the-box and curse me for ruining her nephew's wedding. She was one of those iron gray–haired ladies who clearly think other people consider them proper and upright, and who look like they've just bitten into a lemon and have a broomstick up their ass.

I hefted the box. I had to get myself out of the car and leave it on her doorstep.

Someone knocked on my truck window about two inches from my head. I was so startled that I jumped and honked the horn.

The curtain in Aunt Edna's front picture window twitched. There was a police officer at my truck window. I rolled it down. Hot air poured in. I smiled at the nice looking, slightly sweaty policeman. "Is there a problem, officer?"

"Do you have business here, miss?" he asked, his bushy mustache bristling with authority.

"Business? Well, not really business. I just wanted to drop something off." I felt my face flush. What is it about talking to a police officer that makes me feel instantly guilty and defensive? Hell, talking to anybody these days makes me feel instantly guilty and defensive.

The cop tilted his head to look inside the truck. "What kind of something?"

"A present." I patted the package in all its ivory and white glory on the seat next to me.

"I see." He hitched his thumbs into his belt. "Well, we've had several reports of someone casing neighborhoods in a red Nissan truck."

"I'm not casing the neighborhood. I was just . . ." Trying to avoid Aunt Edna while returning presents from my unwedding.

"Returning a present. I get it. So how about you deliver whatever you intend to deliver and move on, miss." He sauntered back to his motorcycle and got on, but didn't start the engine. He clearly intended to wait there until I'd made my delivery and left.

I looked at Aunt Edna's window. Maybe I'd imagined the curtain twitch. It could have just been a trick of the light or my eyes.

The cop was still there, pretending to look through some papers on a clipboard. I took a deep breath, picked up the package, and got out of the truck. I marched across the street as if I belonged there, dumped the package on Aunt Edna's front steps, and marched back to the truck. I was almost there when I heard a door swing open behind me.

"Chloe? Chloe Sachs? Is that you?" a voice called from behind me.

I ran. I jumped in the truck, waved, and drove off as quickly as I could, considering there was a cop watching my every move. My heart was still racing when I got to the hardware store. Aunt Edna *was* an evil jack-in-the-box and she scared me.

An older man with a giant belly that stuck out over the top of his pants gathered the items on Etienne's list, while the younger woman behind the counter quizzed me. Why was I picking things up for Etienne? What job was this for? How long would he be working on it? Would he be coming in for more supplies? Working in a hardware store must be really boring.

I stopped in the co-op and picked up some bread and fruit, since the fruit kabobs were history now. I also picked up some wine and some chocolate-covered graham crackers, clearly, my period was due any day now. I stopped in the aisle, suddenly horrified. What if the voice had been some weird hormonal thing? What if I'd run out of my own wedding because of a really bizarre case of PMS?

When I let myself through the bungalow gate, I thought Etienne was examining the exterior paint job. Then I took in his wide-legged stance and the fact that I couldn't see his hands, and put it together. He was *peeing* on my house. Great. He wasn't even housebroken.

As I got out of the truck, he did that funny shoulder-shrug, knee-bend thing men do when they're tucking themselves back in their pants, zipped up and then waved to me. "Chloe, how are you, dear? Do you need a hand?"

I quickly grabbed up all my groceries. I did *not* want those hands on my food until they'd been washed. With soap. And possibly boiling water. "I'm fine. Thanks," I said, even though the weight of the plastic grocery bags dug into my fingers like a tourniquet.

Destruction at the bungalow seemed to have spread. I picked my way to the refrigerator that now stood in the middle of the kitchen, its electrical cord stretched like a black umbilicus to the outlet. Etienne and Tucker had moved on to sanding the floors in the living room and dining room, which meant all the furniture had been moved into the second bedroom.

"Bad news," Etienne told me, leaning against the doorway. "The new cupboards, they will not arrive until next week."

I looked around the chaos that used to be the kitchen. "When next week?"

He shrugged. "Who knows? Maybe early. Maybe late. So Tucker and I, we moved on to the floor of the other rooms."

I nodded. "What kind of cupboards are they?"

The next hour slid by in a blissful discussion of cupboards and flooring.

Etienne scratched at his chin stubble. "Zees cupboards that you want, zey are actually cheaper than the ones your grandmother chose. They would have to be painted, though."

"I could paint them." How hard could painting cupboards be? Especially if they were empty.

"I like zee idea of zee cork floor, too. It would not add any time to the job. It installs just like linoleum."

I looked around at the sawdust and piles of nails and wrappers on the floor. "And it won't show dirt, either."

Etienne nodded. "I'll make some calls."

I swapped my shorts for a skirt, but left on the halter top and grabbed a sweater in case they had the air-conditioning cranked up at the Green Creek.

"Great news," Etienne said as I gave the dogs fresh water and rebandaged Jesse's paw. "Those cupboards are in stock. We can have them here in two days at the most."

If I hadn't just changed clothes or if I'd seen him wash his hands, I might have hugged him.

There were only three cars in the Green Creek lot when I pulled in past the marquee advertising karaoke night on Wednesdays. There was a dirty white Ford 150 that had definitely seen better days, a beat-up brown Dodge coupe, and a relatively clean (no car stays clean in the summer in the Central Valley—there's just too much dust in the air) new Matrix.

Inside, Til stood behind the bar watching the baseball game on the TV set. A heavyset Latino man, wearing a white straw cowboy hat that seemed a little small for his head and a plaid short-sleeved shirt that creased around his middle, sat at the far end of the bar, neck craned so he could take in the game. Two other men, one in a Hawaiian shirt and the other in a B.U.M. Equipment T-shirt, sat on the other side of the bar from Til. Hawaiian Shirt pounded the bar. "It's just wrong, Matt. Wrong, I tell you. The leagues should not meet until the Series."

"Interleague play is a fact of life, Rob, and you might as well accept it," said the guy in the B.U.M. Equipment T-shirt.

"Hi, Til," I said.

She turned. "Hey, Chloe. C'mon back." She lifted the hinged section of the bar and I slipped into new and unfamiliar territory of bottles, glasses, kegs, and levers.

"Gentlemen," she said and waited for their attention. "I'd like you to meet Chloe. She will be helping me out during Happy Hour for the next few weeks."

The two men sitting near Til both looked at me, but didn't say anything. The guy in the cowboy hat didn't turn at all. He just took a small sip of his draft beer.

"Hi," I said, giving a little wave.

Til shook her head. "Don't mind them. They'll get a lot more friendly after a few more beers."

"Speaking of which, Til . . ." The guy in the Hawaiian shirt held up an empty glass and wiggled it at her.

"You know that I don't actually know how to tend bar, right?" I asked Til.

Til grabbed hold of the Amstel Light tap and pulled it toward her. Beer ran out and into the glass she held below. She pushed the tap back. The beer stopped flowing. "Think you can handle that?"

I nodded.

"Then you can tend bar at the Green Creek." She gave Hawaiian Shirt his beer and returned to her bar stool. Her gaze went back to the TV, where the Giants led the A's three to two.

"What about mixed drinks, though? I don't know how to make any of those."

Til sighed. "Think you can figure out what goes in a gin and tonic, college girl? Or a rum and Coke? This isn't rocket science, it's just booze. Nobody orders anything fancy around here and if they do, just tell 'em you don't know how to make it and ask them what's in it. That's what I do. Nobody gets mad."

A bald man with a beard and a Harley Davidson T-shirt came in. "Hey, Til. Pull me a Bud, will you?"

Til looked at me. "Chloe?"

"Right." I grabbed one of the beer glasses and went over to the taps that were under the MY BARTENDER CAN BEAT UP YOUR THERAPIST sign. I pulled the Bud handle toward me and beer poured into the glass. I set it in front of Baldie and smiled, pleased with myself.

Til came up next to me, handed him a napkin, and asked for three-fifty. "It's important to remember to charge them," she said to me.

I blushed and nodded.

Cowboy Hat finished his beer, set a quarter next to the empty glass, and left after giving me a nod. Just then the other three men at the bar yelled out "Steerike!" in unison. I looked up at the TV and watched a dejected looking young man walk away from home plate. Hawaiian Shirt slapped a dollar down in front of B.U.M. T-Shirt.

I felt like I'd stumbled into an alien universe. Then Etienne and Tucker walked in.

"Chloe?" they said in unison.

Etienne took a handful of pretzels out of the bowl on the bar and I swore on the spot to only eat them from out of the bag from that moment on.

"It's like watching a pack of dogs," I told Clarissa when I was off duty. Now we were being served while we sat at the bar. "They really weren't behaving much like people. They're like dogs or wolves, all jostling to see who's the alpha male."

"Which one won?" Clarissa asked.

"The guy with the goatee, the untucked plaid shirt over the T-shirt, and the baseball hat on backwards."

"How do you know?"

"They all kind of defer to him. When he makes a joke, everybody laughs. If somebody else makes a joke, they all wait to see if he laughs before they laugh. If he asks for something at the same time as one of the other guys, Til gets it for him first."

Til herself came down to join us where we sat away from the baseball crowd. "Can I get you ladies anything else?"

I shook my head. "Nah. I think it's time for me to head home."

"You did a good job tonight, Chloe. I think you might be able to fly solo for an hour or two tomorrow night. If you don't mind trying, then I could have dinner with Hunter."

Clarissa's head snapped up. "Hunter?"

"My kid," Til said.

"Oh. I didn't know you had a child. I didn't even know you were married," Clarissa said.

"I'm not." Til wiped the counter in front of us. If Clarissa was waiting for more information, she clearly wasn't going to get it from Til.

"That would be great, Til. I'd be happy to fly solo for a little while tomorrow night." I stood up and pushed my chair back. "So I'll see you tomorrow then."

Til nodded. Clarissa said, "Bye" and didn't budge.

"You're staying?" I asked her.

She shrugged and studied the top of her beer glass. "For a little bit longer. I just want to finish my beer."

She'd been nursing the same beer for forty-five minutes. If she'd really wanted to drink it, the time was well past. "Do you want me to stay?"

"Oh, no." She gave me a big smile. "You go ahead. You should get some rest."

The sun was just setting as I got back to the bungalow. I love long summer nights, especially up here. The breeze comes in and the heat of the day passes. The sky turns purple and I feel like the evening could stretch on forever. I changed into a tank top and some boxer shorts, poured myself a glass of iced tea, and went out on the back deck, one of the few places you could actually sit now.

Aziza dropped her squeaky clown toy at my feet. I picked it up and hurled it into the yard. She raced for it, swooping it up as it bounced, and then careened back to me with it in her mouth. She dropped it at my feet again and I reached for it. As I reached, she snapped. I snatched my hand back. "Aziza!" I said in my most stern voice and reached for the toy again. Aziza snapped again.

Jesse growled and bared his teeth at her. She backed up. I picked up the clown and threw it. This time when she brought it back and dropped it at my feet, Jesse growled at her before I even reached for it. By the third time Aziza brought the clown back, she stepped back for me to pick it up.

This wasn't so bad, I thought as I threw the clown into the gloaming. Maybe it was a little lonely. Okay, it was more than a little lonely, but it was survivable. I'd be the weird dog lady instead of the crazy cat lady. There are worse fates.

When it started to get dark enough that Aziza was having trouble finding Clowny, we all went in. The mess was indescribable. Lumber, tools, bags of nails, balled-up newspapers, and cigarette butts seemed to be everywhere. And my bedroom was still full of the boxes I'd brought back from Mark's. I could at least do something about that.

It took an hour to unpack just two of my boxes, but it was worth it. The room looked a little bit more like mine, and I had access to a few more of my clothes. Plus, Mark had included my little television set with the built-in DVD player. There wasn't any cable to the bungalow, but now I could watch movies.

I glanced at the clock. It was barely eleven, but I was suddenly exhausted. I let the dogs out into the yard and slumped off to brush my teeth. By the time I got back to the bedroom, they were both ready to come in and go to sleep themselves.

Ah, Saturday. No Etienne banging in the kitchen in the dawn hours. I slept until Aziza poked her cold wet nose against mine. She'd just be back every two or three minutes, breathing doggy breath into my face, so I got up, let them out, and made coffee. I decided I'd drink it out on the deck. I opened up the door to go outside. The head of Aziza's squeaky clown toy sat on the mat, like a bizarre hunting trophy.

"Jesse," I said, shaking my head.

He looked at me with one of those "who, me?" expressions. Aziza trotted up with Clowny's headless body clutched in her jaw. It was pathetic, in a macabre way. I'd have to stop at the pet store for a new toy for her.

By the time I was out of the shower, it was already getting hot; I could tell it was going to top out over one hundred degrees today. I rifled through what I'd unpacked the night before and decided on a short sundress. I had it halfway over my head when Jesse charged to the door, barking, with Aziza right behind him. I wiggled the rest of the way into the dress and grabbed his collar, but let her out. "Sorry, boy. Gotta rest that paw a little longer," I told him as she streaked past him to bark at the beige pickup that had pulled up to the gate. I shaded my eyes and squinted, not sure who it was. Then Daniel Stein slid down from the front seat, long denim-covered legs first, and waved from the gate.

I walked down to let him in.

"Good morning. What are you doing out here?" I asked once we'd performed the requisite gate dance (open gate, drive through, close gate, do-si-do, swing your partner round about).

"My mom lives up the road. I promised to stop by and look at one of her horses this morning before my office hours. I was driving past and thought I'd take a peek at Jesse's paw since I was already out here." He had on sneakers and a short-sleeved cotton shirt with a henley collar. His hair was still damp from his shower and I could smell his soap. Less than a week with Etienne and Tucker, and a freshly showered man was a novelty. They should make candles in that scent.

"How many horses does your mother have?" I asked, walking toward the house.

"Six right now. The number varies with her mood and the stock market."

"Has she always had horses?"

"Since I can remember."

I opened the door to the bungalow. Jesse took one look at Daniel and rolled over on his back with his tongue lolling out. What a slut. "So the cowboy thing came to you naturally."

"I guess so." He squatted down and scratched Jesse's belly and then started examining his hurt paw. "It looks good. You're taking good care of it."

"I'm trying."

Jesse sat up and licked Daniel's face.

"He's an old soul," Daniel said.

"What do you mean?"

He shrugged, still scratching behind Jesse's ears. "Don't you get a funny feeling sometimes when you look in his eyes? Like maybe he understands a lot more than a dog should?"

"All the time."

"I see it sometimes in certain babies, too. I can't quite describe it, but I always think I'm looking at some soul that's been through all this before and has come back to try and get it right this time."

I wrinkled my nose. "You believe that reincarnation stuff?"

"Maybe."

"That's definitive."

He laughed. "It's the best I can do."

"What about Aziza? Is she an old soul too?"

We looked out at where she sat on the porch, chewing with great concentration on her headless clown.

"No." He shook his head. "Either she's a fresh one or she's been coming back as a dog over and over. And that squeak toy is totally pathetic."

I nodded. "Getting her a new one is on my list for today."

Daniel stood up. "Stop by my office. I've got tons of them. We're open until two."

I don't know how we ended up standing so close. Had I moved toward him? Had he moved toward me?

He cleared his throat. "So what else is on your list today?"

"Oh. A few errands and then work." I didn't feel like explaining that the errands consisted mostly of returning wedding presents.

"Work?" he asked.

"Yep. I'm tending bar during Happy Hour at the Green Creek."

"Good to know." He scratched Jesse behind the ears one more time. Jesse thumped his tail on the floor and Daniel headed for the door. "See you at the office, then."

I did the gate dance and watched him drive away. The day was shaping up nicely.

CHAPTER EIGHT

Chloe's Guide for the Runaway Bride

Weddings are always a great place for people to hook up. The aftermath of your un-wedding can also be a nice time for couples to meet, as they have lots in common: they can feel superior since they're not nearly as nuts as you are.

Jeff and Mary Alice Kelly live at the other end of the dirt road from Gran. Mary Alice is one of Gran's best friends and has treated me like her own granddaughter. She always remembers my birthday. She came to my graduations, lets me borrow her sewing machine whenever I want it (Gran doesn't sew), and writes poems whenever anything momentous happens in our lives. Jennifer framed the one she wrote for Troy's birth and has it hanging on his wall. I still have the one she wrote for me when I graduated from college. They are sweet, heartfelt poems.

They are also very, very bad.

They tend to have the same sing-song cadence as a limerick and they always, always rhyme.

I'd headed out to their house after picking up the trash Etienne and Tucker had left lying around and sweeping out the worst of the sawdust and dirt. I thought about leaving the pres-

ent from Mary Alice on top of her mailbox but visions of woodland animals carrying it off or at least gnawing on the package
stopped me, so I pulled up to the house.

For a minute, I thought I was going to get away with leaving
the pretty white and silver package on Mary Alice's porch and
disappearing like the good little wedding elf I wanted to be.

Fat chance. Mary Alice popped out of the house before I
made it back to my car. Were all the older women in my life
turning into evil jack-in-the-boxes?

"Chloe, is that you?"

No, my evil twin had stolen all my wedding gifts to creep
around the countryside returning them. Maybe she was the one
who'd actually run out of my wedding, after imprisoning me in
a closet. That was an answer I could live with! It wasn't me at all;
someone else did that crazy thing. "Hi, Mary Alice. How are
you? I was just dropping something off."

"Oh." Mary Alice looked down at her feet and saw the wedding present. "Oh," she said again. Then she looked up and gave
me a bright cheery smile. "So how are things going, dear?"

I didn't know quite what to say. "Fine. I guess."

"Well, that's good."

Mary Alice and I stared at each other for what felt like an
eternity or two, both studiously not looking down at the package on the porch. "Well, I guess I better be going now."

"I'll get the gate," Mary Alice said, which is basically
country-speak for "don't let the door hit you in the ass on your
way out."

I'd been dreading going into a post-mortem with each person to whom I returned a gift. It hadn't occurred to me that it
would be twenty times worse to pretend nothing out of the or-
dinary had happened. I had become the elephant in the drawing room.

Luckily, the other two packages were in town and I could leave them on porches and dash off without anyone even knowing I was there. The last package left me just two blocks from Stein Veterinary Hospital.

Gee, imagine that.

Unfortunately, Daniel was with a patient when I came in, according to Chirpy (whose name was apparently Grace). I considered waiting, but pretending I needed a veterinary consult to decide whether the squeaky hamburger would be a better choice for my dog than the squeaky bear . . . ? Even I wasn't that desperate. I bought the squeaky hamburger and left.

I grabbed a chicken taco and a Diet Coke from the Burrito Mobile and sat on one of their rickety lawn chairs in the shade. I was so grateful to eat something that wasn't salmon-based, I nearly wept. The heat and the heavy food pressed me down in the chair, and I wondered if I'd ever have the willpower to stand up again. I'd just finished licking the last spicy shreds off my fingers when my cell phone rang. I checked the caller ID. Every time it rang, I still got a little shiver of fear that it would be Mark. I didn't want to talk to him. Couldn't talk to him. Apparently he felt the same way; it was Gran who was calling.

"Hey, Gran, what's up?"

"Mary Alice says you returned her present."

I wasn't sure why this merited a phone call. "Yes. It was in that stack that Shelby gave me."

"She said you looked tired. Are you getting enough sleep?"

"I'm not tired. It's just hot out. That's all."

"Maybe you need to rest, dear. Perhaps you should rethink that job of yours."

"I'm fine, Gran, and I'm only working at the Green Creek for a few hours each day. I have plenty of time to rest."

"Well, you know best, dear," Gran said, which is what she always says when she thinks you're making a huge mistake, but knows she can't talk you out of it. I've heard her say it to Lily about everything from a boyfriend to a dress in an unfortunate shade of green. Also be warned that if Gran says, "Bless his pea-picking heart" after someone's name, it's not a good thing. She's about to say something truly devastating. I have no idea what she had against the Green Creek, but it clearly had a pea-picking heart.

"Hey, Gran, I was reading those letters again. The ones Jesse wrote to Aunt Laura?"

"You should throw those out, Chloe. None of those people are even alive anymore. If you don't want to get rid of them, give them to me."

"But there was something kind of weird in there. Aunt Laura never had a baby, did she? Or maybe a miscarriage?"

There was dead silence on the other end.

"Gran? Are you still there, Gran?"

"Yes. I'm here, Chloe. I was just thinking. What did you read that made you ask that?"

"I don't know. Something about telling Aunt Laura to get a ring and pretend that they were married."

Gran snorted. "Probably one of Jesse's schemes to get him out of trouble for something else. It would have been just like him to try to get Laura to take care of it. That man was not worth the time you're taking to read his letters. You should leave them be. Speaking of time, though, what kind of progress is Etienne making at the bungalow?"

"He's right on top of the ripping out process, but doesn't seem quite as quick on the putting back in. Listen, though, I've been meaning to talk to you about paint colors."

"I told Etienne anything in ivory would be fine."

"Yeah, well, I was looking at these websites about renovating these kinds of bungalows and, Gran, I think we could put a little more color in and it would look really great."

"What if a potential buyer doesn't like the color we've chosen?"

"Then they can repaint it."

"Chloe, ivory is fine. Just leave it be."

We hung up and I went home to check on the dogs. I looked around the living room. I could already see it with a chair rail installed around it and ivory paint above with sage green below. With the dark wood of the built-in cabinetry, the room would just sing. If I kept the color above the chair rail ivory, I wouldn't really be disobeying Gran, would I? Plus, once she saw it, she'd love it. She'd understand then why the room needed more color. Especially after she saw the green tile surround I thought we should put around the fireplace in the living room. The sage would tie the rooms together.

More cars and motorcycles crowded the lot at the Green Creek than usual. Inside, there was a group playing pool and two groups of people in motorcycle leathers at various tables, but the same three guys at the bar. The bald guy with the Harley shirt wasn't there, which made me a little sad. He had a fond spot in my heart as my first customer. There was another baseball game on the TV.

"Good-bye!" the three bar guys yelled as I walked in the door. I froze.

Til shook her head and pointed at the television, where a player trotted slowly around the bases as the crowd cheered. Two of the guys at the bar high-fived each other. The third one said something about steroid-sucking mutants, but nobody seemed to care.

Til taught me to take orders from tables and how to use the

cash register, and never ever to run a tab for anybody under any circumstances. The bar started to clear out.

"Think you can handle things?" Til asked me, glancing at the clock. It was nearly five-thirty.

I looked around the bar. Larry, Curly, and Moe (Matt, Rob, and Donald) were still at the bar and one group of leather-clad Harley guys was still at a table. Otherwise, the place was empty.

"Sure. Knock yourself out."

She threw her arms around me and gave me a quick squeeze. "Thanks so much. I'll be back by seven-thirty."

I wiped the bar down, poured a few beers, and listened to Matt and Rob discuss how much their wives spent on their hair versus how much they themselves spent on beer. The Yankees scored another run, then Matsui struck out. More people came and went.

Clarissa swung onto a barstool. It took me a second to recognize her. She had on a baseball cap and her hair was pulled back in a ponytail that slid through the back of it. She wore a short-sleeved bowling shirt, unbuttoned and open over a T-shirt. "Hiya."

"Hiya, yourself." I got her an Amstel Light and put it in front of her. "What the hell are you wearing?"

"Clothes."

"Yeah, but whose?"

"They're mine. I just don't wear them that often."

You could say that again. I'd known Clarissa for years and I'd never seen them. I shrugged.

"Is Til here tonight?" she asked.

"She won't be back until seven-thirty. She wanted to eat dinner with Hunter."

Clarissa nodded and looked up at the TV screen. "So who's playing?"

"The Yankees and the Tigers. The Tigers are totally in the cellar."

"You don't say."

"But I do."

"Do you have any idea what that means?"

"Not a single solitary clue."

Donald signaled to me from down the bar. I walked over to see what he wanted.

"I'd like a Slippery Nipple." He leaned so far over the bar, I thought he was trying to look at my shoes.

"I'm sorry," I said. "I don't know how to make one of those."

"That's okay, I do. Want me to tell you?"

"Sure."

He leered. "I usually just use my tongue."

The entire group cackled.

"And your sheep just lets you do that? Or do you have to hobble her first?" I asked.

They all laughed. Rob slapped another dollar down on the bar and they all went back to watching the game. Amazing.

I walked back to Clarissa, shaking my head.

"What was that all about?" she asked.

"Nothing." I set the glass I was drying down on the counter. "So what are you doing out here tonight?"

She shrugged. "I didn't have anything to do. I thought I'd come hang out with you."

"Uh huh." Clarissa never has nothing to do. Art openings and experimental plays and poetry slams eat up a lot of her time. She also likes to kickbox. Sure, she likes to hang out with me, but generally not in this kind of bar. Plus, there were the clothes. They sported no safety pins. Nothing was ripped and none of it was black. Something was up and I didn't like it one bit. "She's not gay."

"Who's not gay?"

"Til."

"I didn't say she was."

"You didn't have to." I poured her another Amstel Light and stared at her, ignoring the sounds of another customer coming into the bar until I heard Matt or Donald call out, "Dr. Stein! Come have a beer with us."

Daniel.

He gave me a little wave as he went to sit down with the crew near the television.

"Who's he?" Clarissa whispered.

"The local veterinarian. The one who thinks Jesse's an old soul."

"Nice butt."

Hard to argue with that.

"Don't you think you should take his order?"

Oh, yeah. I was the bartender; I had an excuse to go talk to him! I put down the glass I'd been polishing, which now shone like a diamond, and headed down the bar into pack territory. "So what can I get you?" I asked.

He paused a beat too long. There was just enough of a break for the other men to notice his silence and turn to look at us. He smiled and dropped his head, shaking it slightly from side to side. "A Michelob would be nice, Chloe."

They started mimicking him as I walked away. " 'A Michelob would be nice, Chloe.' Well, la di fucking da," Rob chortled. As I poured Daniel's beer, I watched from the corner of my eye as they punched him in the shoulder and laughed. They all went completely silent when I came back and gave Daniel his beer.

"Thank you," he said, as he handed me the money.

"You're welcome," I answered.

I walked away and they started to snicker as soon as my back was turned. What were we? Junior high students again? Still, I couldn't keep a silly grin off my face.

This was wrong. I do not react this way to dark-haired men. I always go for the big, blond guys, the WASPier the better. Then I thought about how things had gone with my last big blond guy and decided that maybe it was time for a change, and smiled some more.

Clarissa shook her head.

Til banged open the door to the bar with Rafe right behind her. "So how'd it go, Chloe?"

"Fine." I moved aside to let her in behind the bar and asked Rafe, "What are you doing here?"

"Oh," he said, swivelling onto a barstool and grinning a silly grin that was probably a mirror of the one I wore. "I was at Til's for dinner and thought I'd give her a ride over here."

Clarissa's face pinched up. "Til's for dinner?" she asked plaintively.

Rafe nodded, seemingly oblivious to Clarissa's distress, and grabbed a maraschino cherry out of the little tray on the bar. Til slapped his hand, but he just grinned at her and popped it off the stem with his teeth. She leaned one elbow on the bar and grinned back at him. There was just a little too much sugar in the air; it was like trying to breathe cotton candy.

"Yep. I got to meet Hunter and Til's sister Susan, and her kids. We had burgers. It was great." Rafe's eyes shone.

I slid out from behind the bar and sat down next to Clarissa. I sighed. My feet hurt even though I was wearing flats. "How do you stand like this every day?"

"You get used to it," Til said. "You wanna pick up some

hours tomorrow? It can get pretty busy here on Sunday after-noons." Til poured a beer and set it in front of me.

I shrugged. "Why not?" What else did I have to do anyway?

"Hey," Rafe said to Til. "Maybe you could get away and come with us, then?"

Til shook her head and said, "Nah. It really does get busy," at the same time that I said, "Who's us and where are you going?"

"Rafe is taking Hunter bowling tomorrow afternoon. He's never been and Rafe said he'd teach him." Til went down the bar to check on Larry, Moe, Curly, and Dr. Dreamboat.

"Bowling? Since when do you bowl?" Clarissa asked.

"How hard can it be to bowl better than a four-year-old?" Rafe countered.

I saw the pattern for the evening's behavior right there. The two of them were going to be battling it out and I wasn't sure whom I wanted to win. Suddenly, I was very tired. "I'm going home. Wanna come with, Clarissa?"

She shook her head. "Nah."

"We could stop by the video store and rent *Postcards from the Edge*," I said enticingly. Clarissa has a young Carrie Fisher thing, and even though she isn't actually in the movie it's enough for Clarissa to watch Meryl Streep play the part of the fictionalized Carrie that Carrie actually wrote. I myself have a much simpler Dennis Quaid thing. No, I don't need the age thing pointed out to me. I am well aware that I have daddy issues, but Dennis Quaid is cute anyway.

Clarissa turned me down flat, so I leaned over the bar and grabbed my purse. I stole a glance down the bar at Daniel. He seemed occupied and I didn't feel like I could brave the taunts of Larry, Moe, and Curly again. I willed him to look over at me, to see that I was leaving, and holy smokes, he did! He got up from his barstool and walked over to where I sat with Clarissa and Rafe.

I bent my head and fished my car keys out of my purse, hoping to hide the heat that had spread to my cheeks.

"Are you leaving, Chloe?" he asked.

I knew he was standing next to me without even looking up. "Yeah. I'm beat." I found my keys and looked up at him. He looked disappointed.

"Can I walk you to your truck?" he asked.

"Sure," I said.

I could feel Clarissa and Rafe's gazes boring into our backs as we walked out and decided I didn't care. Let 'em look.

"I'm sorry I didn't see you when you stopped by the office," he said as I unlocked my car door.

I shrugged. "It's okay. Your assistant said you were busy. I chose the squeaky hamburger, by the way."

"An excellent choice," he said, opening my car door for me. "My most discerning patients prefer it over the squeaky bear. I only keep the bear to satisfy those with more plebeian tastes."

"Exactly what I thought." I got into the car.

Daniel stood with one hand on the open door and the other on the roof of my truck. "Listen, you know this is a small town, right?"

I nodded.

"And you know how in small towns, people talk, right?"

I nodded again.

"I just thought you should know that I know about what happened at your, uh, wedding thing."

Oh. So that's what the guys at the end of the bar had been discussing with Daniel. So much for no one knowing me at the Green Creek.

"Anyway, I also thought you should know that I'm glad you did what you did."

"You are?" This was starting to seem like a theme. Were Mark and his mother truly the only ones who were unhappy about it? I was unhappy about it, wasn't I?

"Yeah. I would have been bummed if I'd met you and you were married to somebody."

For a second, I thought he was going to kiss me. I held my breath but he stepped back, shoved his hands in his jeans pockets, and gave me that fabulous smile. I shut my truck door and watched him go back into the bar. Clarissa was right. The back view was fine.

Was I shallow or what? A week ago I'd been convinced I was ready to pledge my eternal love to one man. Now I was checking out the fit of another man's Levi's without even a flash of guilt. Okay, maybe a flash, but more of the "appearance of the thing" than the thing itself. And perhaps that said more about what had gone wrong between Mark and me than anything else.

At the video store, I decided to rent *The Big Easy* instead of *Postcards from the Edge*. *Postcards* wouldn't be as much fun without Clarissa and this way I could get my dose of Dennis Quaid. I just adore it when he tells Ellen Barkin not to be afraid and calls her "chère."

I got home, fed the dogs, and let them run while I took a shower. The Green Creek's air-conditioning had the funny humid feel and smell of a swamp cooler, and I hated the mildewy smell it left in my hair and clothes. Finally, all three of us were curled up on my bed (I relented and let Aziza up too, and then almost had to shove her back down again because she got so excited I was afraid she was going to pee on me) and started watching the movie.

Next thing I knew, my head jerked up from where it had lolled when I'd fallen asleep. Either *The Big Easy* wasn't standing the test of the years, or I'd just seen it too many times. Aziza, on the other hand, seemed mesmerized.

I lifted the green metal box from my bedside table and rifled through the letters, coming up with an envelope dated August 16, 1942, from Camp Gordon in Georgia.

Dear Laura,

At last I am getting around to answering your letter. I couldn't do much writing while on maneuvers but at last I am getting caught up. I am certainly glad that the maneuvers were called off. Three weeks of that was plenty—in fact, too much. I don't know how I would or could have taken the full two months. I was getting as ugly as a full grown Grissley Bear. Of course I wasn't alone on that score—everyone else was the same way. Getting cut short on your sleep, food, and water doesn't help your disposition any.

The only thing I think that could make my mood better now, though, is to see your shining face.

Love,
Jesse

The next one was on a tiny piece of paper in a brown envelope from the War and Navy Departments. It was dated July 9, 1944.

Hello, Darling,

This is just a short note to let you know that I am safe and sound in a nice quiet hospital and enjoying myself very much. All that I can tell you is that I was wounded in ac-

tion but it isn't anything serious. It is giving me that vacation that I always dreamed about—you know—do nothing but eat and sleep. There is no telling when I will get a chance like this again.

How is everything on the home front? Are you still working at your office job?

Well, it's time to be signing off again, but as soon as I can get my hands on some paper I will write you a nice long letter.

Love,
Jesse

I wondered how badly he'd really been wounded. I picked a few more letters out, hoping to find one that had been written later, but only came up with ones from 1942 and 1943.

"What I need to do," I told canine Jesse, "is take all the letters and put them in chronological order. Then I'm sure the whole thing will make sense."

He wagged his tail and barked twice. I looked hard into his eyes. What was it that Daniel had seen in there? Some glimmer of an old soul? There were moments that I knew just what he meant. I put away the letters and turned off the light.

The next morning, I took the bandage off Jesse's paw. It looked great so I decided to take the dogs for a walk. It was already close to eighty degrees out and by noon it would be unbearable. We made it two miles or so and I was soaked with sweat. I showered, picked out some presents to return to Davis, and headed off to get a binder and some plastic sleeves to put Jesse's letters in, and maybe a couple of magazines on interior design. Aunt Laura's bungalow had so many possibilities, I got excited just thinking about it.

The excitement sped me along as I crossed Road 99, where the countryside's Road 102 turns into Davis's Covell Boulevard. The windows of the truck were open and the wind was in my hair and I was singing along with the radio . . .

. . . and there was a cop on a motorcycle behind me with his siren blaring.

Oops.

I pulled over to the side, but not before I got a glimpse of my speedometer. I'd blown through the section where the speed limit drops without ever touching my brakes.

I rolled down my window and rested my head against the steering wheel.

"License and registration, please," the cop said.

I looked up and we both did double takes. It was the same cop who had watched me return Aunt Edna's present.

"You again?" he asked.

"Hi." I gave a little wave.

He peered in through my open window at the stack of white boxes in the passenger seat. "Are you returning more presents? What'd you do? Run out of your own wedding?" He smirked.

"Actually, yes."

To his credit, the smirk died. I can't say I was disappointed. I hate smirks and the smirkers who smirk them.

He cleared his throat. "I still need to see your license and registration. Do you have any idea what speed you were going?"

"No," I said as I rifled through my glove compartment for my registration. I figured I might be able to get away with lying if I wasn't looking at him. Gran has told me hundreds of times that I have a "glass face" and am incapable of lying with any success. Rafe, on the other hand, could shit on your head and tell you it was a winter cap and you'd end up believing him. I handed the officer my registration.

"Are you aware of what the speed limit is along this stretch of road?" he asked.

"I think it's thirty-five." I handed over my license.

He took a minute to look over the license and the registration before he handed them back to me. "When was your wedding supposed to be?"

I had to think about it, and the answer was like being hit with a ton of bricks. "A week ago today."

"Oh!" he said. "You're *that* runaway bride."

I put my head down on the steering wheel. Were there more of us? Maybe we should all start a support group.

He started writing. "I'm going to let you off with a warning, Ms. Sachs. Just so you know, though, I had you clocked going fifty-five in a thirty-five-mile-an-hour zone. Fifty-five would have been just fine a hundred yards back, before you crossed Road Ninety-Nine. But you're supposed to slow down when you hit the city limits, okay? It's a safety thing." He handed me the ticket.

"Thanks," I said.

He leaned into my window. "And Chloe, it wasn't a coincidence that I was right there where the speed limit changes. Do you understand?" He took off his sunglasses and looked me right in the eye.

"I think so," I said. "You mean it was a speed trap and you guys are there a lot?"

He straightened up. "I can't comment on that. But don't sing along with the radio unless you can watch the speed limit at the same time. It's important. It's a safety issue, Chloe."

"Okay, Officer."

"Musciano," he said.

"Excuse me?"

"Officer Musciano. It's written on your ticket, too."

I swung by the bungalow again before I went to the Green Creek. Jesse lay on the porch, licking his paw. Aziza kept wiggling closer and closer to him. I wasn't sure if she wanted to lick his paw too, or wanted Jesse to lick her. Whatever she wanted, he was intent on ignoring her. Poor thing.

I dropped off the plastic sleeves I'd bought at the office supply store and then took a minute to leaf through a couple of the magazines I'd picked up. Maybe field stone would be a better choice for the living room fireplace. No, I preferred the tile surround. Etienne hadn't started tiling the kitchen counters yet, so maybe there was still time to use the same tile in the living room and the kitchen. That would really tie it all together. I almost picked up the phone to call him, but I didn't have his home number and it was Sunday, after all. I'd catch him first thing in the morning.

Cars and trucks jammed the Green Creek's little parking lot. I angled into a small spot between a beat-up Honda Civic and a white pickup and had just barely enough room to squeeze out my door.

I wasn't even all the way through the door when Til started barking orders at me. "Go over and see if those guys by the pool tables need another pitcher and then check the three tables by the bathroom to see if they need refills."

I grabbed an order pad and skedaddled. It took about half an hour, but things did settle down with me circling the room and delivering drinks and Til pouring a nearly endless variety of beers with the occasional shot to accompany them.

"Whew! I'm glad you got here when you did," Til said, handing me a Diet Coke. "I was starting to worry I wouldn't make it until Karen got here."

"Karen?" I sat down.

"That's right. You haven't met Little Miss Hardbody yet. Well, you'll have the pleasure this afternoon. She should be here about four."

"Little Miss What?"

Til waved her hand. "Never mind. You'll see."

Things stayed busy, but I felt like I was getting into the groove: take a few orders, pull a few beers, watch a little baseball, turn around and do it all again. I was filling a pitcher for the two couples who were playing pool when I heard the door open behind me and sensed someone sit down at the bar. I turned around and nearly dropped the pitcher. Daniel. With the nice smile, the dimple, and the great teeth.

"Hey," I said.

"Hey, yourself."

"Chloe, you're dripping," Til said.

Something cold hit my foot. Oh, yeah, the pitcher. I righted it. "I better just . . . uh . . . go . . . you know."

He nodded. I grabbed four fresh glasses and delivered the pitcher to the pool table and came right back. "So what can I get you?"

"A Michelob." He was still smiling.

I poured it and set it in front of him. "What brings you here?"

He shrugged. "My Sunday clinic hours are over and I didn't feel like heading home just yet."

"That's nice." Doh! What was nice about not going home? I sounded like an idiot. "I mean, it's nice to see you."

"Nice to see you, too."

We just kind of smiled at each other for a while. Cotton candy was starting to fill my lungs.

"How's Aziza like her new chew toy?" he asked.

"Not as well as I'd hoped. She really liked that clown and she's still carrying its body around. I tried to throw it out, but she knocked the garbage can over to get it back."

"Maybe I should stop by sometime and see if I can help her make the transition," he offered, propping his elbows up on the bar. Wow. He had really nice shoulders.

"Maybe you should," I said, feeling a blush rise up to my cheeks.

He smiled again and headed down the bar to watch the game with the guys.

"Dr. Stein is too nice to be your rebound guy," Til said behind me.

I whirled around. I had forgotten she was there. I'd forgotten anybody but Daniel and I were there. "Who says he's my rebound guy? Right now, he's just my vet."

"Yeah, right. A vet who makes house calls to see if your dog likes her squeak toy." She set down the glass she was filling and started filling another.

"Okay. Maybe he's not just my vet." I couldn't help the hint of a smile that went along with that thought.

"So then he's your rebound guy, and I'm telling you that Dr. Stein is too nice for that. Leave him alone." Til stomped off to give the beers to the table by the jukebox.

I had to leave Daniel alone for the next hour, because a group of ten bikers came in and all wanted separate checks. Damn lawyers. I barely got to wave good-bye to him when he left. At about three-thirty, Rafe came charging in.

Til didn't even say hello. "Where's Hunter?"

"Outside in my car." Rafe's lips were tight.

"Why? What happened?"

Rafe gestured for Til to come closer and spoke to her in a low voice. She threw the rag she was holding down on the bar. "Can you hold the fort for a while, Chloe?"

I looked around. "Sure. No problem."

"I'll be back as soon as I can." Til lifted the hinged section of the bar and started out.

"I'll come with you," Rafe said.

But Til held up her hand to stop him. "Thanks, but you've done enough." She slammed out the door.

Rafe put his head down on the bar. "Geez, Chloe, I really blew it."

"What happened?"

"I took Hunter bowling. I thought it would be fun. I'd get to know him a little. He'd get to know me."

I hated what I was hearing. Hadn't the two of us been through enough "uncles" and "special friends" to know that we should leave the poor kids alone? I could never decide which was worse: the boyfriends or girlfriends of our parents that were assholes, or the ones we actually liked and got attached to that didn't last? The Charm was the exception. "Oh, Rafe."

"Don't start with me, Chloe. It seemed like a good idea. We went over to the MU on campus. It's air-conditioned. There's food there. They have these bumper things in the gutters so you can't throw a gutter ball."

"Sounds like a nightmare so far." I'd like to bowl with bumpers. I might actually have a double digit score if I had bumpers.

Rafe lifted his head to give me a dirty look and then put it back down.

I poured him a Coke. "So what went wrong?"

"I don't know." Rafe pushed himself up and took a sip of the Coke. "It wasn't like I'd planned. I was going to be all patient and cool and fun, and he was going to be all cute and sweet and fun. Instead, Hunter was all over the place. Jumping on the chairs, not standing still, not tying his shoelaces. Racing over to the arcade when it wasn't his turn. Not listening to me when I tried to show him what to do."

"Acting like a four-year-old, then," I said.

"A hyper four-year-old."

"Oh, like you were Kid Calm and Controlled? Weren't you four when you spray-painted the inside of Lily's washing machine?"

Rafe glared at me. "It was worse than that, Chloe."

I was surprised. I expected Rafe to be good with kids, maybe partly because he wasn't all the way grown up himself. "You didn't just run around the arcade with him?"

His brow creased. "I was trying to be the grown-up, you know? The adult?"

"That's a first."

He ignored me. "He was getting ready to take his turn and he started swinging the ball around and around. I was afraid he was going to let it slip and hit someone, so I yelled at him." He stopped.

"And . . . ," I prompted.

"I must have yelled louder than I thought or sounded scarier than I meant to, because he wet his pants."

"Oh."

"Chloe, it was the weirdest thing. It was like all of a sudden I heard Stuart's voice coming out of my mouth. Remember when we first moved in with him? How all of a sudden he'd just bark at us?"

Yeah. I remembered. It hadn't taken much to push Stuart to the end of his rope.

"We wouldn't even know we were doing anything wrong and then he'd be there, shouting. Do you remember how big he seemed?"

I remembered that, too. Of course, most grown men seem big to little kids, but when Stuart got mad, he loomed.

"Actually, I was looking at him at your wedding and feeling surprised that he really isn't that big a man. I'm taller than he is. I remember him as being huge."

"And scary," I said.

"I don't want to be him, Chloe. I don't want to be like that." Rafe took my hand.

"I don't think you have to be, Rafe."

"I don't know about that. I didn't feel like I had a choice today. It just happened. That was my first reflex, my first reaction—to shout at Hunter and literally scare the piss out of him."

"It could be worse," I said.

"How? Til's furious with me. The kid's scared of me. How could it be worse?"

"You could have scared the shit out of him."

Before Rafe could comment on that, a young blond woman walked into the Green Creek and flipped up the hinged area to come behind the bar.

I stepped back. "Who are you?"

"I'm Karen. The evening shift. Who the hell are you?"

Ah, Little Miss Hardbody? I could definitely see how she'd earned the nickname. "Buff" didn't do this girl justice. "I'm Chloe."

"Where's Til?"

I looked over at Rafe, who ducked his head. "She had a family thing that came up. She'll be back in a little bit."

Karen rolled her eyes. "There's a shocker. She's lucky this whole damn bar is a family thing, or she wouldn't have a job at all."

I didn't know quite what to say. I looked over at Rafe, who was still studying the bubbles in his Coke. "Yeah. Well. I guess it's time for me to go." I slid out from behind the bar.

"So, you're the chick who ran out of her own wedding, huh?"

Didn't anybody have anything else to talk about? "So you heard about that," I said.

Karen laughed. "Everybody's heard about that. It's been the major topic of conversation for most of the week. I'm just surprised that Deborah Lo Guercio hasn't written a column about it yet in *The Winters Express*."

I cringed.

"Of course, now everybody's rooting for you and Dr. Daniel." Did her mouth never stop moving?

Rafe looked at me, head cocked to one side. "Dr. Daniel?"

"The vet," Karen said, and poured the old pot of coffee down the sink. "He can come keep my inner animal purring any time; he's a hottie. And you must be Til's new man," Karen said to Rafe, who was still apparently counting bubbles in his Coke.

He shrugged.

"So is your grandmother fit to be tied about you two right now?"

I looked at Rafe. Gran was bothered by my working here, but I wasn't sure why and definitely didn't feel like discussing it with Karen. I mumbled something about it being a long day and gathered my stuff up to go home. As I was about to walk out, a very nice looking guy with fashionably messy hair strolled in.

"Goddammit, Malcolm," Karen said, "you're late. You were supposed to be here fifteen minutes ago and you were supposed to bring me dinner."

"I'm sorry, babe."

"Yeah, that's what you said this morning, too," she snapped. Ooh. Burn.

Etienne and Tucker had installed the new cabinets and they looked wonderful—even better than I'd thought they'd be. I could just imagine them with dishes stacked inside. Maybe a few bowls in different colors. Fiestaware! That's what they needed. Actually, what they really needed was to be painted. Etienne and Tucker had taped them off and left a can of primer and a couple of paintbrushes out, so I put a kerchief on my head and got to work.

Clarissa came by about an hour later. She popped some baby quiches and some artichoke pesto torta into the oven to warm up, then changed into a pair of my shorts and picked up a brush. "So isn't your grandmother paying someone to do this?"

"Yeah, well, I kind of changed what she ordered, so I'm picking up a little bit of the slack." Even with the tape, it was tricky to paint the edges of wood that separated the panes of glass. I dabbed at a drip of paint on the glass with a wet paper towel.

"Aziza, cut it out." Clarissa had sat down on the floor to paint the lower cabinets and Aziza was licking her ankle.

"She's moved up from your toes." I moved over to the next cabinet and got on the step stool to reach the top.

"If I let her, she'd lick me from my toes right up to my head," Clarissa grumbled.

I looked down at her. "All in all, we've both probably had worse dates."

"I hear that."

We painted for a little longer in silence, then Clarissa started clearing her throat repeatedly.

"Just ask. What's the problem?" I said.

"I was just wondering how Rafe did with Til's kid."

I filled her in. "Happy?" I asked, seeing the smug expression on her face.

Clarissa feigned surprise. "Me? Happy at another person's misfortune? Chloe, how could you think such a thing?"

I kicked her.

Later on, curled up with the dogs, I dumped the contents of the green metal box out on the bed. On the bottom there was a tattered piece of red fabric with a little bit of white along one edge, and three smaller boxes of deep blue. I flipped one open. It was a medal in the shape of a star and was accompanied by a creased piece of onionskin paper. I carefully unfolded it.

HEADQUARTERS
4th INFANTRY DIVISION
APO 4, US ARMY

AG 201-Hernandez, Jesse (O)

Subject: Unexpurgated Citation to Award of Silver Star

To: Second Lieutenant Jesse Hernandez, 02011717, Infantry, 8th Infantry

Citation:
"JESSE HERNANDEZ, 02011717, Second Lieutenant (then Staff Sergeant), Infantry, 8th Infantry, for gallantry

in action in the vicinity of Bettendorf, Luxembourg, 21 January 1945. The rifle company with which Lieutenant HERNANDEZ served as a squad leader attacked a pocket of enemy resistance in the vicinity of Bettendorf. Another company of his battalion had been repulsed by this same enemy force the previous day, after sustaining heavy casualties. One of these casualties was a lieutenant, believed to have been killed. Lieutenant HERNANDEZ, acting as platoon guide, assisted in leading the platoon through heavy enemy automatic and rifle fire to a point from which the lieutenant was discovered to be helplessly wounded but still alive. In spite of the hostile fire which covered the area, Lieutenant HERNANDEZ moved forward about twenty-five yards to the side of the wounded officer. He then dragged him across terrain which was under direct enemy observation and fire, a distance of at least 100 yards, to a point from which his evacuation could be completed. Lieutenant HERNANDEZ's courageous and forthright actions undoubtedly saved the wounded officer's life and reflect credit upon himself and the military service."

H.W. BLAKELEY,
Major General, U.S. Army,
Commanding.

Wow. He was a hero. A real one.

He'd also gotten the Bronze Star for defending a "vital hill" from enemies who threatened to "encircle and overrun his position." I figured the Purple Heart had to be for whatever had landed him in the hospital. I slid the fragile paper into the page protectors and snapped them into the binder.

I tried to put the letters into the sleeves and got them in date order without reading them, but after three or four, temptation got the better of me.

Sunday Night
November 19, 1944
Hello, Laura,

The mailman brought me a letter from you today so I wanted to get on the ball right now with an answer.

A baby girl! Corazon is a perfect name. You know you always have my heart. The footprints are so tiny. No bigger than my thumb. It's hard to believe a person could be so small. I know this is all so hard, darling, but I will make it right as soon as I get home. I promise.

Which brings me to my news. For a while I thought that I was going to be 3ld but don't have to worry about that anymore. They decided against it because I will be ready for duty in about a month and it will take longer than that to get me home. They explained that I would be better off here than get sent back and have my rating taken away from me plus a very good chance of ending up in the South Pacific.

You know there isn't anything wrong with me to keep me out of combat once my stomach clears up. Then as long as I am over here and Germany falls, my chances of getting discharged in a hurry are much better.

I don't think the war is going to last very much longer. Don't ask me why I think so because I can't tell you—it's just a feeling I have. I hope I am right. Ha ha.

Well, it's time to be signing off again.

Love,
Jesse

A baby girl? Aunt Laura had had a baby nobody talked about. What had happened to her?

I closed the box of letters and crawled under the covers. Why hadn't Gran ever said anything? Did she not know? How could she not know? And if she did know, how could she have lied?

CHAPTER NINE

Chloe's Guide for the Runaway Bride

Ah, the honeymoon. That magical few days after the wedding for you and your groom to relax and enjoy each other. Or, it can be that magical time when your ex-groom can try to get laid by someone else. Remember when those nonrefundable tickets seemed like a good idea?

Jesse now gets to go with me to the mailbox without a leash. Judging by the way he waltzes out the gate with his head high, this is apparently the Nobel Prize of doggie treats. He's earned it by being good. He's good on walks, and generally behaves like a reasonable creature.

Aziza doesn't get to go to the mailbox at all. She can't control herself well enough to keep from tripping me when I walk across the room. She is wildly jealous and Jesse clearly knows it. He smiles and lolls his tongue while shooting many backward glances at unhappy Aziza who races up and down the fence yipping.

I peeked into the mailbox. My mail had finally caught up with me. All those people offering me credit cards and discount mortgages could finally reach me. I could probably throw out half the mail.

We were almost back when Jesse stopped in his tracks. His entire body stiffened. His tail stuck straight up and he quivered. He stared at a bush. The hair on the back of his neck bristled and he let out a low, menacing growl.

"What is it, Jesse?" I asked, afraid to get closer to the bush. What if it was a snake?

He took two stiff-legged steps forward, hair still high on his neck. I grabbed a stick and poked it in the bush, ready to jump back if something rattled, hissed, or slithered. Instead I heard a whimper, a tiny little cry.

I dropped to my hands and knees and peered into the brambles. I could see a little bit of fluffy fur. I lifted a branch. A kitten! It was a wee tiny white kitten with little gray spots.

Jesse took another step forward, his tail still straight up, his nose still quivering. He nudged the kitten with his nose and then gave it an experimental lick. It cried. Jesse moaned.

I scooped the kitten up into my hands, and Jesse and I ran back to the house to call Daniel.

"I don't know, Chloe," Daniel said, cradling the kitten in the palm of his hand while it suckled at his pinky finger in my kitchen. "Don't get too attached."

"Is there something wrong with it?" I peered at the little white and gray ball of spotted fur, trying to see any obvious damage.

"She's just so small. It's hard to know."

"Are there tests you can do?"

"Sure, but half of them won't mean anything. She shouldn't be away from her mother yet." He looked up at me with those melting chocolate eyes. He was worse than Rafe. "I want to make sure you know what you might be in for. This kitten might not make it."

"Why do you keep saying that, if you don't see anything wrong with her?"

"Sometimes a mother sees something in her baby that we can't see. If she has limited resources, she'll abandon the ones she thinks she can't successfully raise, the ones that are too damaged to make it."

Tears sprang to my eyes. She wasn't damaged. She was perfect. I took the little fuzz ball from his hands. After a mew of protest, she snuggled into my hand and started to purr. Dan went to the sink and started washing his hands.

"She *might* make it," I said.

"So what are you going to name her?" he asked.

"Spot," I said.

He frowned. "That's a dog's name."

"Says who?"

"Says me and I'm a professional."

"You're a professional veterinarian, not a professional namer, and the kitten's name is Spot."

"Fine, then. Be that way." He smiled at me and gave Spot a scratch under the chin with his pinky finger. She purred back. "Bring Spot in later this week and we'll check her for worms and take some blood. Meanwhile, keep her warm and see if you can get her to eat. If she can't handle kitten food, you could try baby food or I could bring by Kitten Milk Replacement."

I leaned against the now-clear kitchen counter. There was still a fair amount of debris lying around, but I'd gotten most of the kitchen stuff back in the cabinets. A little order was emerging in the chaos. "Thanks, Daniel. I appreciate you coming out here."

"You're welcome," he said, but his eyebrows pulled together. "I just hope you're not setting yourself up for heartbreak here. Are you sure you want to do this?"

I held Spot up next to my chin, rubbed her soft fur against my skin, and listened to her tiny, determined purr. "I'm sure."

He looked at his watch. "Okay then. I need to get in. My office hours started about fifteen minutes ago. See you later."

After I did the gate dance with Daniel, I grabbed the stack of envelopes I'd brought in from the mailbox and settled myself on my bed with a cup of coffee and Spot in my lap. Two credit card offers, one book of coupons for local businesses, my Visa bill, and an air mail envelope. I opened the air mail envelope first. In it was one of those photos they take of people at tourist trap restaurants that you can buy for a few bucks.

It was a nice picture, sharp and clear with good color. In it, Vicky was giggling and playfully pushing Mark away while he tried to stick his tongue in her ear. I turned it over and tried to catch my breath. There was an inscription: *Having a great time. Glad you're not here.*

I looked at the postmark: Tahiti. Mark was on our honeymoon with Vicky. No wonder she wasn't picking up the newspapers at her apartment. She was too busy boinking my boyfriend.

Jesse leaned against my legs and looked up at me with his big soulful eyes. I looked down at Vicky's laughing ones, then called Clarissa.

"McMurphy, Slater and Ramirez," she said.

"Runaway Brides, Incorporated," I answered.

"How may I be of service to you today, O Flakey One? Are the voices telling you to stay home and clean the guns?"

"I need to know the proper reaction to finding out the man you left at the altar is on your honeymoon with another woman."

"Ooh. Burn," she said, then there was a pause. "Who? Who went with him?"

"Vicky Montoya."

"The brunette with the boobs from the University?"

"The very one." I squinted at Vicky's chest in the photo. Her boobs weren't that fantastic. They couldn't hold a candle to my mother's.

"Oooh. Double-D cup burn."

"Clarissa!"

"Hey, it's not my fault that she's got a nice rack. What was the question?"

"What's the proper reaction?"

"I don't know. How do you feel?"

"Stunned, I think. Maybe a little jealous." But not really any more jealous than you would be about any ex-boyfriend getting it on with someone. My epiphanies might come slowly, but maybe there *was* a reason I left Mark at the altar. I filed that away for future thought.

"Under the circumstances, I think a dignified silence might be your best choice. We can send him dog poo in the mail when he comes home."

"Nah. He'd know it was us."

"Doesn't make it any less fun to think about."

"I guess so." I didn't really feel it, though. We hung up.

Jesse and I were still sitting at the table, staring at the photo when Etienne showed up.

"A nice looking couple," he rasped, tapping ash from his cigarette into the palm of his hand. I must have looked really upset since he didn't tap it onto the floor. "Ees that your sister? Or a cousin?"

"Nope." We both had long, dark straight hair and brown eyes. Vicky was a few inches shorter than me, but now that I was looking, I realized we looked more like sisters than Jen and I did. Jen had Gran's lighter coloring; I was dark, like Lily. "Just a friend. At least, she was a friend before she went on my honeymoon."

Etienne snorted, which then necessitated a trip outside to spit. I picked up the photo, ripped it up into tiny pieces, and then dropped them on the floor. "Etienne, let's talk tile," I said when he walked back in.

Tucker showed up bleary-eyed about ten minutes after Etienne, although Jesse almost didn't let him out of his car. He sat by the driver's side door and every time Tucker would open it, Jesse would bark his head off. I finally dragged him back to the bedroom where I'd left Spot. After making sure that Tucker was safely inside, I put the dogs outside with food and water, then drove to Davis to return my wedding present quota for the day.

I pulled up in front of my major professor's house in North Davis Farms and parked. There was a tap at the window. I jumped about a foot. I couldn't believe my eyes. I rolled down my window. "Officer Musciano?"

"Hi, Chloe. How's it going?"

"Fine," I said, drawing the word out a little like a question.

Officer Musciano seemed oblivious. He was looking at the houses. "Wow. You had people from this neighborhood at your wedding?"

I nodded.

"Must have been quite a do, to have people this fancy."

"It was supposed to be." I blurted, "My ex-husband-to-be is on my honeymoon with one of my girlfriends. Ex-girlfriends."

Officer Musciano's eyebrows went up so high, they arched over his sunglasses. "Ouch."

Double-D cup ouch. "Officer Musciano?"

"Yes, Chloe?"

"Did I do anything wrong?"

"I dunno." He shrugged. "The guys at the station were wondering if maybe he hit you or something. I said I didn't think so. I figured maybe he was a jerk and deserved to be left at the altar. Anyway, if you were that unsure, it's probably better you didn't get officially hitched."

Great. I was a topic of conversation for the local police, too. "I meant, did I do anything wrong while I was driving?"

"Oh, no," he said. "I saw you driving into town and thought I'd say hi. Good job slowing down at the speed limit change. You may want to check your rearview more often, though. I was following you for a lot of blocks and you never noticed me." He kick-started his motorcycle and drove off. I watched him go and wondered what you're supposed to do if a police officer starts stalking you.

I grabbed the heavy box with its white shiny paper and silver bow and walked up the driveway to Mike's house. If I ever went to another wedding, I would wrap the gift in red paper. Or black. Or purple with pink polka-dots. Just the sight of white wrapping paper was beginning to make me itch. Is it possible to be allergic to a color?

Mike flung the door open as I set down the package. "Chloe, what are you doing here? And why did you need a police escort to do it?"

Mike is a gentle bear of a man with a surprisingly soft voice. Just seeing him made me smile. I picked the package up and held it out to him. "Returning packages."

He took the big box and balanced it on one hand as if it weighed nothing. "Return to sender, eh? Well, come in and have a beer."

"It's a little early."

He waved his hand. "Sun's over the yardarm somewhere. So what have you been up to since your wedding, besides returning presents?"

"Eating a lot of leftovers and working at a bar outside of Winters until my leave of absence from Chromonology is over."

"Well, you certainly gave us all something to talk about over at the ag school."

I winced.

Mike clapped me on the back. "You did us a favor. If we don't have something juicy to gossip about, we pick at each other like a bunch of psychotic chickens and you know how nasty that can be."

I've seen psychotic chickens, and they don't hold a candle to academics on a roll. "Always happy to help."

"You could help more." Mike pulled a beer out of the refrigerator and waggled it at me. I shook my head. "Have you ever thought about coming back?"

"To the university? As what?"

Mike shook his head. "As a doctoral student."

I shrugged. "What would be the point?"

"I dunno," he said, throwing his long arms wide as he sat down at the kitchen counter. "Better jobs. More money. More recognition. More prestige. More options. Pretty much more of everything."

"Yeah, but I'd have to pay out big time for the more."

He shrugged. "Nothing's free, Chloe, but I don't think you'd have to pay as much as you think."

I shook my head. "Mark and I went over this a hundred times."

Mike's eyebrows went up. "And?"

"It never made sense."

Mike leaned back in his chair, but I could see his body tensing. "It made sense for him to have his Ph.D. and more money and more mobility, but not for you to have it?"

"You're making it sound different than it was, Mike."

"How different could it be, when he clearly talked you out of pursuing the next step in your career?"

I started to protest, but Mike cut me off. "Come in and talk to me at the university. Give me a chance to tell you my perspective on it."

I sighed. "I'll come by," I said, "but that's all I can promise."

"It's all I'm asking for."

"I'm bored." Karen crossed her arms over her chest. It wasn't terribly exciting at the Green Creek today. Even the baseball watchers weren't excited; something about the All-Star break. I leafed through an issue of *California Bungalow* and wondered who had enough money to furnish a place like the ones they showed in the magazine, and where all their crap was. Where was the junk mail that had just arrived or the pile of newspapers to be recycled or the books they were reading at night? And what was with the green apples? Were people in bungalows only allowed to eat Granny Smiths? I'm a Braeburn girl myself, except for that brief snappy tart period when the Gravensteins are in season. Mark liked Fujis and as a result, I don't think I'd had an apple in over a year. Maybe I'd stop by the store and buy myself a bunch of Braeburns on the way home.

Karen pushed a ten-dollar bill across the bar to Malcolm. "Go make yourself useful for once and entertain me. I dare you to go hit on that girl." She gestured at a table with her chin.

There were three women at the table. "Which one?" he asked.

"The one in the stripes," Karen said.

Why do the manufacturers of women's clothing still make

items with horizontal stripes? It's just cruel. No one looks good in them. Even skinny girls look dorky in horizontal stripes. Remember Gwyneth Paltrow in *The Royal Tenenbaums*?

This young lady never needed to worry about being mistaken for Gwyneth Paltrow. Maybe two or three Gwyneths roped together. Truth was, Malcolm was not in her league. Malcolm was not even in her universe. I'm not saying she wasn't a good person or a smart person or a worthy person, but everyone has a league and we all know it, and she and Malcolm weren't in the same one.

Malcolm looked horrified. "It'd take more than ten bucks to get me to hit on her. Do I have to?"

Karen tapped the ten with her fingernail. "Ten bucks and I pay for the drinks you buy her. Come on, Malcolm. It'll be fun. I'm bored." She leaned over the bar toward him, plumping her cleavage up on her folded arms.

Malcolm's eyes almost rolled back in his head. Poor guy.

"Ten and you buy both her drinks and mine," he said.

Karen shoved the ten at him and poured two beers. "Have at it, then." She sat back down and crossed her legs.

I watched Malcolm saunter over to the table. From behind the bar we couldn't hear what he said, but the three women looked up, smiled in delight, and then made room for Malcolm to sit with them. Striped Shirt's face lit up when he placed the beer in front of her. My gut twisted.

Karen poked me with the toe of her boot. "Stop staring. They'll figure out something's up."

"You don't think they're already wondering why someone who looks like Malcolm is hitting on them?" I countered, but I did stop staring.

Karen shook her head and took a sip of her coffee. "That's why it's so funny. The three of them have gotten all dolled up and talked themselves into thinking they're beautiful. They're going to buy it hook, line, and sinker. You'll see."

I didn't want to see, but it was a little like driving past a car accident. You can't stop yourself from looking. All three women's faces were lit up and turned toward Malcolm. I felt my heart sink. Then Daniel walked in and my heart leaped up and did a little happy dance instead.

"Hey," he said.

"Hey, yourself," I replied. "What can I get you?"

He grabbed the basket of stale Chex mix on the bar and took a handful. "How about a Diet Coke?"

Til let herself behind the bar. "Dr. Stein, what are you doing here?"

"I have an hour or so before my evening clinic hours. I thought I'd stop by." He took a sip of the drink I'd handed him.

Til's eyes narrowed. "Don't you usually go to the café?"

"I thought I'd shake things up a little." He smiled at me. He was doing such a good job of shaking things up, my knees felt a little wobbly.

Til's eyes narrowed more. "You shouldn't be drinking before clinic hours."

"It's just a Diet Coke, Til. It won't affect my judgment." Daniel looked earnestly at Til with just a hint of a smile quirking at the corner of his mouth.

"If you're buying three-dollar Cokes in a bar, your judgment's already off." Til stomped away.

"What's with her?" Daniel asked after she'd gone over to the pool tables.

"She thinks you're too nice to be my rebound guy," I said.

His eyebrows shot up. "Am I?"

"Which? Too nice, or my rebound guy?" I leaned over the counter. I kind of wanted to know myself.

He leaned forward too. Our noses were nearly touching. "Either. Both."

He smelled nice. "She might be right, you know. I might not be completely stable."

"What makes you think I am?" He was close enough now that if I put my head down it would rest on his shoulder.

Malcolm slapped the bar next to us and we both jumped.

Karen came gliding down to Malcolm. "Well?"

He held out his hand. "Lay it on me, babe. I got me a date for Friday night."

Daniel's brows drew together. I shook my head. "You don't want to know. I wish I didn't know."

"It took you long enough," Karen said, arms crossed over her chest. "What were you doing over there for so long?"

"I didn't want them to be suspicious!" Malcolm grabbed the bowl of Chex mix. "Melanie found me very interesting. She wanted to know all about me."

Karen shook her head. "That should have taken about five seconds."

Daniel looked down at his watch. "Listen, I've got to go. My clinic hours start pretty soon. What are you doing tomorrow?"

"I'm going to my sister's to pretend to be a normal family having a normal family barbecue."

"Which part is pretend: the family or the barbecue?"

"The normal part. How about you?"

"Pretty much the same. We're pretty good at pretending to be a normal family, though." He smiled and my heart did the happy dance again. "I'll call you."

I jotted my cell phone number down for him on a bar napkin, then watched him go, perfectly well aware of the sappy grin on my face but unable to wipe it off.

Til came up beside me. "You shouldn't toy with him. He's a nice guy."

"Who says I'm toying?" I demanded.

"I do," she said, and started pouring beer. "What else could you be doing? You left a guy at the altar about two seconds ago."

The girls had stood up to leave, swinging their hair and giggling as they grabbed their purses. Striped Shirt gave Malcolm a little wave as they walked by.

"What will you say to her on Friday?" I asked, curious despite myself.

Malcolm popped a pretzel in his mouth. "Nothing. I won't be here."

"But I will." Karen grinned.

I looked back and forth between the two of them. "You've done this before, haven't you?"

Karen shrugged. "A few times. It keeps things interesting when the bar gets slow."

"Don't do this, Karen," I said.

"Oh, c'mon," she said. "It's a hoot!"

"It isn't a hoot. It's cruel and childish and nasty." My face burned. I felt dirty standing by and watching it happen.

"Well, it's not my fault that you don't have a sense of humor or that those girls are as stupid as they are ugly."

I took off my apron and stowed it under the bar. "I'm going home."

I ran into Etienne in the parking lot, and learned that they'd installed the chair rail in the dining room and that the tile for the fireplace surround had come in. I couldn't wait to see it! It was going to tie the living room in with the kitchen just perfectly.

*   *   *

I spent the next morning at Gran's baking brownies and cookies to take to Jennifer's that evening. Gran had been assigned potato salad and was making enough to feed several large army battalions. The pile of peeled potatoes nearly blocked my view of her.

"I don't know why I'm bothering to make these," I said. "Jennifer won't touch them and neither will Lily."

"Everyone else will appreciate them, dear," Gran said, picking up another potato to peel. "Troy will like them."

That was pretty much enough reason to get me to do anything and I decided to add M&Ms to the cookies along with the chocolate chips. I sipped my coffee happily. Gran's microwave worked, so I had gotten to steam my milk the way I liked it. Everything was always better at Gran's.

Thinking about Troy made me think about babies, which made me think about those letters from Jesse to Aunt Laura. "I've been reading more of those letters," I told Gran.

"Mmmm." She carefully whittled an eye out of one of the potatoes.

"Gran, are you sure that Aunt Laura never had a baby?"

She not only looked up from her potatoes, she even set her potato down. "I already answered that question, Chloe. I've told you to get rid of those. I don't want to talk about them anymore."

"But Gran, you should read them. It really sounds like maybe she had a baby. Could she have given a baby up for adoption and not told you about it? She worked in one of the factories in Santa Barbara for a while, didn't she? Maybe she had a baby then."

"I don't need to read them. I lived them." Gran pressed her lips tight together, the same way she used to every time Lily would drop Rafe and me off here so Lily could go on a trip with a new uncle.

"There was a letter where he talked about a baby girl named Corazon. I'm trying to put it together. I didn't remember anybody ever saying anything about Aunt Laura having a baby."

Gran grabbed the pot where the eggs were hard-boiling off the stove top, using her apron as a hot pad. "That's because she didn't. I don't know what that man was referring to, but he was always unreliable. You can't believe anything he said."

"But Gran, why would he make something like that up?"

"Chloe, I'm telling you." Gran whirled around, potato peeler back in hand. "Let sleeping dogs lie. Whatever he wrote to Laura is in the past and there's nothing to be done about it now."

"But, Gran . . ."

"Chloe, I told you. That's enough. Now drop it."

Gran almost never spoke to me in tones that sharp. Once when I was about eight and threw a tantrum because I didn't want to take a bath, she had rolled her eyes, said I was becoming just like my mother, and informed me in no uncertain terms that I could get my skinny little rear end into the bathtub or it would be put there forcibly. She had that same look now, too, so I dropped it. I absolutely never wanted to be told I was just like my mother.

CHAPTER TEN

Chloe's Guide for the Runaway Bride

Wedding announcements in newspapers are de rigueur. Un-announcing is trickier. Going the newspaper route seems unnecessary. Besides, everyone's talking about it anyway.

Gran and I decided to drive together to Jennifer's for the Fourth of July Normal Family Barbecue, since she doesn't like to drive at night anymore.

As I pulled up the steep incline of her driveway, Gran came out with a big box in her hands. She had on pale blue slacks with a white shirt whose pocket and collar had details in the same material as the slacks. The handle of her red pocketbook was cinched in the crook of her arm.

"Is that everything?" I took the box from her. "Is there more inside?"

"No. This is it."

She grimaced a little getting into my high front seat, then adjusted her seat belt so it wouldn't crinkle her blouse where it crossed her chest.

I wracked my brains for something to talk about that

would dispel the strain that was still there from this morning. By the time I thought of something, however, her head had already lolled over to the side and she was snoring gently. I changed the radio from the classical station back to the local alternative rock station, but kept the volume low. She woke with a start as I pulled into Jen's driveway behind Stuart's BMW. Rafe's MG wasn't there yet, nor was David's parents' Buick.

"We're here already?" Gran asked.

I nodded and smiled.

"I slept the whole way?"

I nodded again.

"I'm sorry, Chloe. I meant to be better company than that."

"It's fine, Gran. You're great company even if you're asleep." And I didn't have to field prickly questions about what I was doing at the Green Creek, and she didn't have to field ones about Jesse and Aunt Laura.

David answered the door when we rang the bell. "Come on in. Jen's in the kitchen."

Gran walked in first with me behind her. David grabbed my elbow as I walked past. "Here, let me take that box from you," he said in a funny overloud voice. After Gran had gone ahead, he whispered to me, "She's out of control."

"Jen?" I asked unnecessarily. I mean, who else could he be talking about? Maybe Courtney Love had stopped by?

He nodded. "You'll see in a second, but I thought I'd give you a heads-up."

I stepped cautiously into the kitchen. Jen's kitchen and family room looked like the Fourth of July aisle at Party City had exploded all over it. She'd strung red, white, and blue bunting everywhere and those honeycombed folding paper bells, and a lot of flags, too. Jen herself was decked out in a short white skirt with a flag motif maternity top. Her little white Keds had red stars and blue stripes.

"Chloe, you're here!" She clapped her hands. "Where's Rafe?"

"He's coming on his own. I'm sure he'll be here any minute. There wasn't any traffic."

Her brow creased in a frown. "On his own? But that means he'll be late. What if he isn't here when it's time to sit down? What will we do?" She wasn't even stopping to breathe between sentences.

"He'll be here. And if he's not, we'll start without him like we always do." I started taking things out of the box that David had set on the counter for me.

"But I don't want it to be like we always do. I want it to be like we're a real family." Jennifer's lower lip quivered.

It would be nice to blame all this on pregnancy hormones, but the "real family" and "normal family" stuff has been a mantra lately for Jen, whether she's pregnant or not. I think it's to impress David's parents, which I found even harder to fathom than pregnancy hormones.

David's father was one of those men who wore his pants cinched up under a protruding belly and talked about nothing but his golf game. David's mother was one of those women who walked around with her mouth pursed up as if she'd just bitten into a lemon while she said things like, "Isn't that nice" and "How lovely." Kind of a Northern California version of Dana Carvey's Church Lady.

"We are a real family," I said. "We're just a real family with one member who's habitually late." And others who are habitually drunk and others who are habitually mean-spirited and others who run out of their own weddings.

Lily sauntered in, a tall glass of clear liquid in her hand. I hoped it was water. "I take it Rafe's not here yet."

"He'll be here." I shifted some things around in the refrigerator to fit in Gran's tubs of potato salad. There were individual parfait glasses layered with strawberries, blueberries, and whipped cream in a red, white, and blue motif and a sheet cake that was decorated like a flag. I stood up, turned around, and practically bounced off Lily's new boobs.

She grabbed me by the shoulders and took a long look. "You know, dear, you really need to start putting sunscreen on your neck and chest. Otherwise you're going to look like a chicken by the time you're forty."

"Good to see you, too, Lily," I said.

"Stop it," Jen said. "Stop it right now."

I took a deep breath and asked where Troy was. Smart cookie that he was, he was in his room playing. I went to say hello and see if I could hide out with him.

There's nothing like a good game of Candyland to help you forget your troubles. I was pursuing Troy through the Bubblegum Forest when I heard the doorbell ring. It was either Rafe or David's parents and I wasn't particularly anxious to see any one of them, so we kept playing.

I had been dumped by the Jelly Bean Monster back to near the beginning when the doorbell rang again. I made a slight modification to the rules so Troy could win (it is not my job to teach him to be a good sport; it is my job to spoil him), and told him I thought we should join the party. He agreed and strapped on several belts, bandolier style. The fact that one of the belts had a Barney motif added a lot to the ensemble. He shoved a LEGO gun in the waistband of his Pull-Ups and indicated he was ready to go.

As my heavily-armed escort and I headed down the hall, I heard my name mentioned.

"Chloe?" said David's father, Howard. "Isn't she the one who ran out of her own wedding a few weeks back?"

"Yes, dear, but I don't think you should mention it."

"Why'd she do it anyway?" he grumbled. "Did she catch him dipping his wick in somebody else's candle?"

"Not that I'm aware of. She apparently just ran out and won't tell anyone why." I could hear how pursed up Margaret's mouth was by the way she was speaking.

"Bunch of damn squirrels, the lot of them," Howard grumbled. "Jennifer's the only one of 'em worth a bean."

"Hush," Margaret said. "Just try to be nice for the evening. Do it for Jennifer. It's important to her that her family's here tonight. Lord knows why."

I looked down at Troy. He looked back up at me and then pulled his LEGO gun. "Bang!" he said. "You're dead."

"If only," I replied.

We went into the kitchen. Rafe was sitting at the corner, drinking a beer and munching on tortilla strips and salsa. I kissed the top of his head and he gave my hand a squeeze. Lily and Margaret were there, too. I took a tortilla strip and dipped it in salsa.

It was halfway to my mouth when Lily said, "Do you really need that, Chloe?"

I shoved the whole thing in my mouth and chewed as noisily as I could.

"There you are," Jennifer said, in a too-bright tone that made me nervous. "We were just heading out to the patio to have appetizers. Would you grab that plate, Chloe? The one with the pesto torta on it?"

There were four plates covered with appetizers, one with green stuff that could be pesto, so I grabbed it. "Where's Gran?"

"She's lying down for a few minutes. She said she's tired." Jen started to slide the door open with her elbow. Margaret raced over to get it for her, even though her hands were also full already. Lily kept sucking on one of the ice cubes in her drink as if she could lick off the last traces of vodka.

"But she slept in the truck on the way here." I followed everyone out and set the plate I was carrying down on the red, white, and blue festooned patio table, then went back to shut the door.

"Well, she's sleeping again, Chloe," Lily snapped. "I guess she didn't realize that she needed your permission."

Howard and Stuart were over helping David with the grill, which seemed to consist of watching while David did everything.

"So what's new with you, Chloe?" Margaret asked.

My mother rolled her eyes.

"Oh, not much." I took a big gulp of lemonade. "I walked out of my own wedding not too long ago. That's pretty much my big news."

Jennifer choked on an ice cube and Rafe snorted.

"Now I have no place to live since I was shacking up with my fiancé and I'm on leave from my job," I continued. "Other than that, well, I found a sick kitten and adopted it."

"Oh, Chloe," Lily said. "Another pet?"

"That's right, Lily. A little tiny kitten whose mother abandoned it," I said breezily.

Lily took another long drink from her glass. That *so* wasn't water. "You should use the money you waste on those animals to get yourself a decent haircut and a manicure. Your nails look like you've been living in a barn."

Boy, was Margaret ever going to be sorry she'd asked me her nasty little dig of a question. At least I'd gotten her to unpurse her mouth; it was hanging open like she was trying to catch flies. Sadly, she excused herself to go check on David over by the grill. But it did satisfy me to have hoisted her by her own passive-aggressive petard.

Stuart chose this moment to come over and join us. "Princess," he said to Jennifer. "Everything is just exquisite. You've done a beautiful job."

Jen beamed. "Thanks, Daddy."

"Another drink, Lily?" Stuart held his hand out for Lily's empty glass. She nodded and the two of them went off to find the liquor.

Jen waited until the door was shut to hiss at me. "Why do you always have to do that?"

"I'm sorry about smarting off to your mother-in-law, Jen. She was asking for it, though."

"Believe me, Margaret can take care of herself. That's not what I'm talking about. Can't you get along with Mom for just one night?"

"She started it."

Jen shook her head. "I'm going to check on Troy." She left.

I considered walking some of the appetizers over to the group by the grill, but as Howard turned sideways, giving me a full view of his gut hanging over his belt, I decided to eat the pesto torta myself.

At least acting like a normal family was filling.

In the end, the food was so good, I was glad I stayed. Jen had been marinating beef tenderloin in port and cranberry juice all day, and David did an excellent job at the grill. I was trying to score thirds on the tenderloin when Lily rattled the ice cubes of her empty glass at Stuart in the international sign of "Baby, get me another vodka tonic." Stuart obediently took the glass and started to leave the table when Gran said, "Do you really need that, Lily?"

Ooh. Burn! And using the very words Lily had burned me with earlier. Maybe this normal family thing wasn't all bad.

Stuart paused. Lily's eyes narrowed, but she sighed and motioned for Stuart to sit down.

Lily truly didn't need another vodka tonic. She'd already had two or three and there was wine on the table, too. Once she started slurring her words, I knew we were going to be treated to a show.

She leaned conspiratorially over to David's mother. "Sho, Margaret, whaddaya think about your boy knocking up my daughter again?"

"Excuse me," Margaret squeaked, her eyes wide.

"Must be packin' some high quality shperm." Lily smiled around the table. "They hadn't done it but once or twice without the rubbers before the deed was done."

"Mama," Jennifer broke in. "This isn't a dinner table conversation."

"Oh?" Lily looked around the table, still beaming. "Anybody here not know where babies come from?"

No one raised their hands.

"Shee, Jen, everybody knows. Shouldn't be ashamed about shex, should she, Margaret?" Lily leaned over to give Margaret a big wink.

I'm pretty sure all Margaret's sphincters snapped shut at that moment.

"Lily," Gran said. "I think that's enough."

Lily waved Gran away like an annoying fly. "Maybe that's your problem, Mom. You always thought it was enough. Maybe you should have had more."

"Lily!" Gran stood. "I will not tolerate this kind of talk."

"So go, you old bat." Lily stood too, but had trouble steadying herself. She tried to brace herself against the table, but her arm slipped and she went down hard on her elbow. Stuart grabbed one arm and I grabbed the other, and we helped her back into her chair. She swallowed hard and her face turned a little green. She looked up at Stuart and said, "Baby, I don't feel sho good."

Stuart and I didn't miss a beat. We raced her to the closest bathroom. We just made it.

Practice does indeed make perfect.

"Shweet Chloe," Lily slurred as she patted my face. The storm had passed and I was tucking her into the bed in Jennifer's guest room to sleep it off a little before Stuart took her home.

"Go to sleep, Mom," I said, pulling the blanket up over her shoulders.

"You always hang in there with me, don't you, darling? Through everything."

"I do my best, Mom. Now go to sleep." I didn't want her to sit up and get the spins. Jennifer would have an even bigger hissy fit than the one she was having now if Lily barfed on the carpet.

"No matter what, Chloe hangs in. Even before you were born. Tried my best to shake you loose, but I couldn't do it." Lily closed her eyes.

I went still. "Mom? What does that mean? What do you mean, you tried to shake me loose?"

She opened one eye and patted my hand. "Not to worry. Years ago. All fine now."

I stayed until she started to snore and then stumbled into the bright lights of the hallway.

"How is she?" Jennifer asked from the sink, where she vigorously scrubbed at a frying pan. Gran waited next to her with a dishcloth in her hands. Margaret and Howard had left without even waiting for the fireworks—or perhaps our family pyrotechnics were enough.

"Asleep," I said.

Rafe raised one eyebrow at me as he meekly dried the wineglasses on the draining board. "Think she'll puke again?"

Jennifer growled. "She better not."

"I don't know why you're so upset." I picked at the edge of the cake. "She was very tidy about it. No mess at all."

"I'm upset because that beef tenderloin cost about nineteen dollars a pound." It looked like Jennifer might scrub the nonstick coating off the pan, and she wasn't even using the scrubby side of the sponge. "Could she have gotten bombed at Thanksgiving and barfed up the dollar twenty-nine per pound turkey? Nooooo. She had to puke up the really expensive stuff. And, of course, she had to do it in front of David's family."

"I'm sure your mother didn't do that intentionally." We all whirled around. Stuart stood in the doorway to the kitchen. I hadn't heard him come in. By the looks on Rafe's and Jennifer's faces, they hadn't, either. Gran didn't say a word, but her lips tightened.

Jennifer went crimson to the roots of her beautifully highlighted blond hair. "I'm sorry, Daddy."

"Me, too, princess. I should have been watching." Stuart

came into the kitchen, looked at me, and shrugged. "I didn't notice that someone had set the wine bottle right by her plate."

I shut my eyes. I didn't know how this had worked its way around to being my fault, but it had. "That was me," I said. "I didn't realize she'd be sitting there. I just put it on the table."

"Mmm," Stuart murmured noncommittally.

I wanted to punch him in his Pillsbury Doughboy face.

Jennifer kept scrubbing at the same damn pan as if she could scrub the blight of this dinner off it if she worked hard enough.

Rafe, however, set his towel down and turned, leaning against the kitchen counter. He crossed his arms over his chest. "So, it's either Chloe's fault for leaving the wine near her, or your fault, Stuart, for not watching her closely enough. Or maybe it's Jen's fault? Hey, Jen, if you hadn't invited your family to your big normal family barbecue, it wouldn't have happened. It's your fault."

He snapped his fingers. "No! I've got it! If those damn forefathers hadn't signed the Declaration of Independence this day, Jen wouldn't have made a big dinner and Chloe wouldn't have set the wine bottle out. It's Thomas Jefferson's fault that Mom got so drunk that she puked. Let's blame Thomas Jefferson and George Washington. It certainly makes more sense than blaming Mom." He turned back to the stack of dishes.

"You're a fine one to be talking about taking responsibility for your actions, Raphael," Stuart said in his bland beige voice. He is always at his most dangerous when his voice is at its most bland and beige. It's the calm before the storm.

Instinctively, I took a step away from him. I swear I saw even perfect princess Jennifer flinch, although to my knowledge, she'd never felt the sharp sting of Stuart's backhand across her face.

Rafe whirled around, a spatula clenched in one hand, a towel in the other. "At least I'm making an effort," he hissed, waving the spatula at Stuart.

"Put that down," Stuart said. "Get it out of my face."

Rafe looked down at his hand and threw the spatula down as if it had suddenly grown white-hot. The dish towel followed and he stomped out of the kitchen to Jennifer's backyard.

I took the pan out of Jennifer's hands, gave it to Gran to dry, and gave Jen another dirty one.

She barely looked up. "You couldn't just act normal for one night. Not even for me."

"Jen, you can't seriously blame me for Lily getting so blotto that she threw up. She's a grown-up. We shouldn't have to worry about how close she is to the wine bottle." My face felt hot.

"You just don't get it, Chloe, do you? I don't blame you because you put her too close to the wine bottle. I blame you because you can't get along with her for even one night. Then she gets upset and she drinks too much and throws up my beef tenderloin."

I didn't want to argue with Jen. I didn't want to argue with anyone, including Lily. That, however, never seemed to be an option.

"I don't know why it's so important that we look like a normal family in front of David's parents anyway, Jen. They think the world of you; you don't need to impress them. They think the rest of us are nuts, but they like you."

Jen stared at me, eyes wide. "You think this is about David's parents? You think this is about impressing them?"

"Isn't it?"

Jen put her head in her soapy hands. "Maybe it was at first, but not anymore. The stakes are much bigger now, Chloe." Jen's hands fell to the rounded mound of her stomach.

"You could have thought about someone besides yourself for once, Chloe," Stuart said, the sanctimonious bastard.

I followed Rafe outside. It seemed a better response than spitting in my stepfather's face. Rafe had done that once when he was twelve and the results had not been pretty.

Rafe stood by Troy's swingset, his face pressed against the big metal bar. I wrapped my arms around myself. I felt chilly, even though it was easily in the seventies.

"So what were you going to do with the spatula, Rafe? Flip him to death?" I asked.

"Did I look as ridiculous as I felt?"

"Pretty much. The dish towel with the geese was an unfortunate accessory choice. The pink ribbons are not manly."

"Do you know, I'm still afraid of him on some level?" Rafe's voice cracked as he spoke and I regretted the accessory joke.

"It's a hard habit to break. More addictive than heroin, they say." I was a little afraid of Stuart myself.

Rafe snorted. He extended one arm out to me and I let him pull me to him. "Jesus, Chloe, why do we do this to ourselves? Why do we keep coming to shit like this?"

"Different reasons, different times. We came tonight for Jennifer."

"Yeah, I bet she's in there just thanking her lucky stars that we came."

"At least we gave David's family something to talk about."

"And to feel superior to," Rafe observed.

"We did them quite a service. I bet David's in there right now thanking Jennifer for inviting us."

We turned to look in the kitchen window. David was holding Jen. He didn't look like he was thanking her. He looked like he was trying to keep her from flying apart.

"Yeah," Rafe said softly. "I'll bet that's just what he's saying to her."

In the east, a giant anemone of sparkling light burst into the sky. A few seconds later we heard the boom. The fireworks had started.

CHAPTER ELEVEN

Chloe's Guide for the Runaway Bride

Running out of your own wedding may have made you
a little bit notorious. Even if you have handled things politely and in a way that did not cause nationwide news
coverage, people will still remember. Try to stay away
from situations like bar fights that may give others an
even worse opinion of you.

"Well, your mother certainly made an impression again,"
Gran said drily as we pulled out of Jennifer's driveway.

"I think we all did." I rolled down the driver's window and
let the cool night air wash away the stuffiness. I wished it could
blow away the headache that throbbed in my temple as well. I
couldn't stop thinking about Jennifer with her hands on her
tummy bump.

Gran yawned. "Lily never has brought out the best in people."

We turned out of the subdivision and began the winding
drive through the foothills to the interstate. "Why is that,
Gran?" I'd never questioned why Lily was the way she was. I'd
always felt like it was trying to understand why hurricanes happen. They just do and you have to clean up after them, no matter why they do what they do.

"I don't know, Chloe." She yawned again. "It does seem like blood will tell."

I zoomed up the entrance to the interstate and spent a few moments merging in and getting over a few lanes in the post-celebration traffic. "What do you mean by that, Gran? What blood?"

There was no answer.

I looked over. Gran was asleep. I sighed and clicked the radio back on.

She slept all the way back to Winters, waking when I pulled up to her gate. "I'm so sorry, Chloe. I slept all the way again, didn't I?"

"It's okay, Gran. I'm just a little worried about how tired you are. Are you feeling all right?"

She patted my arm. "I'm not such a spring chicken anymore. In fact, I'm just about ready for the soup pot."

"Don't say that." I helped her down from the truck and then pulled her box of empty Tupperware containers out of the back-seat. Jen must have scoured each one until she took off a layer of plastic.

"Not saying it doesn't make it less true." She walked slowly up her steps and unlocked the front door.

I followed her inside and set the box on her kitchen table. "Do you want me to make you a cup of tea?"

She waved her hand. "No, dear, I just want to crawl into my own little bed. You head on home now. Oh, by the way, I may have found someone who would take Aziza off your hands."

"You did?" My heart sank a little. I'd gotten used to her being around.

"The Ridders up the road might be able to take another dog. We can talk about it tomorrow. I'm just too tired right now."

Her lights were out before I even got to the gate. I didn't remember Gran ever being this tired. Maybe I could convince her to go for a checkup tomorrow.

Aziza and Jesse were waiting by the gate for me when I got back to the bungalow. Inside, Spot was still asleep in Jesse's bed. I guess kittens must be like human babies and sleep a lot. I gave her a little head pat and she opened one eye to look at me. The other eye didn't open quite as much. I knelt down to take a better look. Spot's left eye was crusted shut. I wiped the crust away with my thumb and she pulled her head back, clearly affronted. Then she sneezed at me.

I laughed and, with Spot in one hand, I went and poured myself a glass of wine.

I'd left the windows open in the bungalow, so it wasn't as stuffy or as smelly with Etienne's chemicals as it might have. There was nothing much to steal, and I doubted anyone would come out this way to steal it. Besides, anyone could probably reach in through the doggie door and let themselves in if they wanted to. The living room was still a mess. The pyramid of wedding gifts was dwindling, but now there was a pile of tile for the fireplace surround and wood for the chair rail. There were dropcloths on the sofa and a nail gun on the recliner.

I went into the bedroom, and the phone rang. It was Daniel. Even hearing him smile over the telephone made my heart do that little pirouette.

"So how was acting normal?" he asked.

"We failed miserably. How 'bout you?"

He chuckled. It was a nice sound. "I think we might be too good at it. There might be something to letting all the not-normal stuff out. My sister's dating a total asshole and everyone's too polite to point it out."

"I think it might be okay if it's just a trickle of not-normal instead of a flood. Let's face it, the family's got to be in sad shape when I'm the sane one."

"You seem pretty okay to me."

"Daniel, I ran out of my own wedding a little over a week ago."

"Yeah, but I didn't see it. It doesn't have the same impact when you just hear about it."

"Next time I have an un-wedding I'll make sure to invite you."

"Well, gee, I'm flattered. Listen, I should go. I just wanted to say hi and to remind you to bring Spot in sometime this week. I'd like to check her out more thoroughly."

"Okay. Good night, then."

"Good night."

I didn't hang up, though. I waited to hear his click first. I didn't hear it. I could still hear him breathing though.

"Daniel?"

"Yes, Chloe?"

"You're supposed to hang up after you say good night."

"You didn't hang up either. Why do I have to be the hanger-upper?"

"Because you're the one who has to get up for work tomorrow?"

"Oh. Yeah. Okay, then. Good night."

This time the phone did click, but it still made me smile.

Jesse's letters to Aunt Laura lay on my bedside table. I snuggled Spot into my lap and plucked one out of the pile.

Sunday Night
April 28, 1945
Dear Laura,

   How is my new family getting along? Jacob's deferment is about up now, isn't it? I have been sweating this war out hoping that it will be over before the draft board catches up with him. If it ends before they do, I don't believe they will ever call him.

The situation does look good now but these Krauts insist upon fighting to the last man. If we get that last man now we won't have to fight them twenty years from now. Germany will remember this war for a long time anyway. When we get through these villages riding tanks, the tankers leave them burning like the devil. It's not a pretty sight to see the people fleeing from burning villages and trying to salvage little items, but if it wasn't for them backing the army there wouldn't be a war now. From now on they will have to take what they have been giving out for the past four years.

I dream every night about coming home to you and Corazon. I don't think it will be long now, and we will be able to put an end to this masquerade we've been living.

Love,
Jesse

A yellow envelope in the pile caught my eye. I fished it out. It wasn't a letter. It was a Western Union telegram. I could hardly believe what I was reading.

Miss Laura Gold,
We regret to inform you . . .

It took a second for all the words to register. I dropped the telegram—the dreaded telegram. That's how they always refer to it. Jesse had died. He'd been killed in action. That's why he hadn't come home to Laura. Tucked into the telegram envelope was another letter from the government detailing how it happened. Only snippets of phrases registered in my brain.

Second Lieutenant Jesse Hernandez, 02011717,
sustained mortal wounds while out on patrol
near Wiesbaden, Germany . . . service to his
country . . .

I looked over at my Jesse, lying on the floor, his big brown
eyes trained on me expectantly. "That other Jesse wanted to
come back to Laura. He didn't disappear at all."

The mention of his name made his ears prick up. "Aroooo
roooo," he said.

My hair was stuck to my neck when I woke up. Either it was already unbearably hot or it was matted to me with cat spit. Or
possibly both. Spot had curled up on my pillow right behind the
nape of my neck as I'd fallen asleep. I'd thought it was really cute
until about two a.m., when she'd started kneading my neck and
nibbling on the hair right along my hairline. I'd shifted her to a
different place on the bed, but she kept coming back.

It was so sticky that when I got out of the shower, I couldn't
get dry. I'd been thinking about staying to help Etienne and
Tucker paint the living room, but decided Clarissa was right.
My grandmother was paying them to do it, and I could return
wedding presents and stay inside my air-conditioned truck.

There was one stop I needed to make first. I tucked the letter from Jesse into my purse and hit the road to Gran's.

"Chloe, what a nice surprise." Gran had on a big straw hat,
an enormous pair of gloves, and plastic gardening clogs. Today's
blouse and slacks outfit were in a khaki and rose color scheme.
She could have been a catalog model for gracious gardening
supplies.

I sat down next to her in the grass. "I wanted to see how you
were doing. You were so tired when we got back last night."

Gran waved my concern away. "You know us old people. We just can't party like you young things."

"Speaking of knowing people, Gran. Would you take a look at this?" I handed her the letter from Jesse that I'd read the night before.

"Chloe, what is this?"

"It's one of Jesse's letters to Laura. Remember? The ones I told you about. Gran, I don't know how she managed it without you knowing, but I'm sure Aunt Laura had a baby, a baby girl. Her name was Corazon."

Gran's lips pursed. "I told you, Chloe, digging into the past like this will do no one any good."

"Gran, listen, I found out something important about Jesse. He didn't desert Laura, like you thought. He was killed, Gran. That's why he didn't get back." I grabbed the yellow sheet from my purse and handed it to her.

"I know, Chloe." Gran's mouth stayed tight.

"Then why did you tell me he disappeared? You made it sound like he ran off."

"What difference does it matter why he didn't come back?" Gran stood now and brushed imaginary dirt from her slacks. "We were better off with him not coming home anyway. He'd made more than enough trouble before he left."

"Gran, how can you say that? I can tell from these letters that he really loved Aunt Laura, and I think she must have really loved him, too. Maybe that's why she never married. She still pined after him."

Gran headed for the door. "That is not why your aunt Laura never married. She wasn't pining for anyone." She turned in the doorway. "People make mistakes, Chloe. They do their best to fix them afterward, but no one wants them dug up. Especially if they've been buried for a while. You need to learn to let things be." Gran's voice started to rise and her thin frame began to shake. "Don't meddle in this, Chloe. None of it can be changed. It's all water under the bridge."

"Gran . . ." I reached my hand out to her.

She straightened her shoulders and glared at me. "Do you know who you're acting like, Chloe? You're acting just like your mother. This is the kind of thoughtless, selfish thing I've come to expect from her, but I thought you were different."

I drove to town in a daze. I couldn't understand Gran's reactions. I could see Aunt Laura trying to keep the baby a secret back in the forties, but who would judge her now? I was relieved when my cell phone rang.

"Hello, Chloe. Can you hear me?"

I recognized The Charm's voice immediately. "I can hear you just fine. How are you? How are Cara and Jackson?"

"We're all fine, honey. They're out of school, underfoot and making me crazy. How are you doing?"

"Okay. Keeping busy."

"Well, I guess that's a good thing. Listen, the reason I'm calling is that your dad's birthday is tomorrow and I was hoping you'd come for a little visit."

Dad's birthday. I would have to get him a present. There was no one worse to buy a gift for than Dad. He had tons of money to buy what he wanted himself, was incredibly picky, and really didn't care if he hurt your feelings by telling you your present sucked. After all, he was just being honest, wasn't he? He wouldn't want you to waste money in the future on something he didn't want. You wouldn't want that either, would you?

"You could sit by the pool and I'd pamper you for a day," she wheedled.

"I've got the dogs, and now I've got a kitten, too. I couldn't impose." No one wants two big dogs in their house, especially if one of them is Aziza. I don't even want two big dogs in my house when one of them is Aziza, and I had become attached to her.

"Bring 'em with you. I'll make Jackson pick up the dog poo and maybe he'll stop pestering me to get him a dog. You'd be doing me a favor."

I didn't say anything.

"You don't have to make up your mind right now. Think about it. We'd love to see you."

"I'll think about it," I promised. I wouldn't mind seeing Cara and Jackson or spending some time with The Charm. Dad, on the other hand, was another story.

"One more thing and I'll let you go. I know you're busy."

"Okay," I said, bracing myself.

"Don't forget that if you need to talk, I'm just a phone call away."

We said good-bye, and I asked myself for the hundredth time what a nice woman like that saw in my father.

I cruised around Davis, but there was no good place to park at the university. There never was. I kept a close lookout for Officer Musciano in my rearview mirror and was disappointed when he didn't show up. What kind of useless stalker was he, anyway?

I ended up parking at Rafe's rented house and walking over to Mike's office in the blast-furnace heat. I stopped off at the Memorial Union to grab a bottle of water so dehydration wouldn't set in before I made it to Briggs Hall. As I turned from the cashier's counter, I spotted Vicky at one of the tables.

It would be ridiculous to pretend I hadn't seen her. Besides, what would I do the next time I saw her? Because there would be a next time. Davis is a small town, and the world of plant pathology is even smaller. I'd be running into Vicky at conferences and symposia with the regularity of a monarch's migration from Canada to Mexico until the day I retired, and probably beyond that.

"Hi, Vicky," I said, stopping by her table.

She looked up and, to her credit, a guilty flush suffused her face. "Chloe."

I said, "Look . . ." at the same moment she said, "I'm so . . ."

We both laughed, but it was a nervous, tittery laugh. "You go first," Vicky said.

Oh, sure. It sounds gracious, but it totally put me on the spot. What was I supposed to say? *Heard you had fun on my honeymoon?* Or *Hope you're enjoying banging my boyfriend?*

But Mark wasn't my boyfriend. He was fair game and that had been my doing, not Vicky's. She may have been opportunistic, but she wasn't to blame.

"I just wanted to say that there are no hard feelings. At least, not on my part," I said, feeling very mature. "I hope you and Mark are very happy."

Vicky rolled her eyes. "There is no me and Mark."

I sat down next to her. "He sent me a picture of you and him in Tahiti. It sure looked like there was a you and Mark."

Vicky shrugged. "The tickets were nonrefundable; it seemed a shame to let them go to waste. It also seemed a shame to let Mark go to waste, until I spent a few days alone with him and found what he's like. Jeez, Chloe, I can't believe you almost married that jerk. I'd heard he could be kind of difficult, but he looked like such a catch. You really can't judge a book by its cover, can you?"

My mouth opened and closed a few times, but nothing came out. This woman had gone on my honeymoon with my ex-fiancé, and now had the nerve to complain that he wasn't good enough for her?

"At first I couldn't believe you'd left him like that, but some people don't know how good they've got it." Vicky looked at me and flushed a little.

I felt my own face grow pink. Say what you will about Dad, he always made sure that we weren't dropping out of school for lack of money. I knew Vicky struggled to make ends meet.

"I thought, hey, an all-expense paid trip with a cute guy. What's not to like? But after three days I was trying to figure out how to exchange those tickets. He's cute and he's got a great job and everything, but the way he was suddenly bonkers about me? That was the first creepy thing. I thought it was part of the whole rebound deal, but then he didn't want to let me out of his sight for a second. He even came to my apartment and watched me pack." She shuddered and took a long sip of her soda. "Although now I think he just wanted to see what I was bringing, so he could plan which outfit I was wearing when. He's such a control freak. I don't know how you put up with it."

"Control freak?" I fiddled with the label on my water bottle.

"Oh, please. Don't tell me he didn't try to control you. It's way too ingrained a habit for him to have only done it to me. The never-ending 'are you going to wear thats' and 'why did you put that theres.' I thought I'd go out of my tree by the third day!"

Mark likes things just so—Vicky was right about that. I never thought of it as controlling before, though. "I don't think Mark really means to control. He's just trying to help." The words sounded lame even to me.

Vicky's eyes narrowed. "How is acting as if everything that you do is wrong helping? How is constantly rearranging your hair, straightening your top, or cleaning almost invisible specks of dirt off your shoes being helpful?"

"He just has this need to fix things that he sees are wrong. Do you really want your hair to be mussed or your top to be crooked or your shoes to be dirty?"

Vicky gave me a look that said I was crazy. "Of course not. But I also know that someone who's constantly trying to fix you is implying that you're broken."

I left Vicky at the MU and headed off to Mike's lab. I found him reading e-mail with a half-eaten sandwich on his desk. "Chloe," he said, rising from his desk.

"Mike." I returned his hug, and then we both sat back down.

"So what can I say to get you to come back and do your doctorate?" He crossed his arms over his belly.

"Tell me why I should," I threw back at him. This was why I loved working with Mike; he was always challenging without being confrontational.

"We covered that at my house: Money. Prestige. More opportunities. More chances to travel. More interesting work. More control over what you do. How's that for a start?" He'd ticked each item off on his fingers and grinned at me over the thumb he had sticking up. " 'Dr. Chloe Sachs' has a very nice ring to it."

"Don't talk to me about rings," I grumbled, and he roared. It felt good to joke about it. "Besides, Chromonology pays me just fine. Prestige doesn't interest me much. I have plenty of opportunities. Who would take care of my dogs while I traveled? My work is plenty interesting because Dennis gives me a huge amount of control over what I do." I grinned back with my thumb pointing downward.

Mike steepled his fingers and stopped grinning. "Seriously, Chloe. I don't understand why you don't want to come back for the Ph.D. I could really use a student of your caliber right now. I've got two new students, but they're green as grasshoppers."

I outlined the basic argument about how much I made at Chromonology and how much I would have to give up to be in school and how I wouldn't make that much more.

Mike's fist came down so hard on his desk that his sandwich jumped. "Who the hell told you that?"

"Mark and I worked it out for ourselves."

"Figures," Mike muttered. "Listen, Chloe, I hope you don't mind, but I took the liberty of talking to Dennis after you left my house. You wouldn't have to give up your job at Chromonology. In fact, you could use the research you're doing there as part of your thesis topic. You'd probably have to cut back to three-quarters time, maybe half time toward the end, but you wouldn't have to quit altogether."

I leaned forward. "You'd do that for me?"

"Chloe, we do it for people all the time. You know that."

"Yeah, but I thought that was for special students, people you really really wanted here."

"What makes you think that you're not one of those people, Chloe?"

I sat back. What *did* make me think that? The only person who had ever made me feel not quite up to snuff with my research capabilities was . . . Mark. I may be dense, but even I was starting to see a pattern here.

"Please don't say Mark made you think that, Chloe," Mike said quietly. "I'd have to beat the shit out of him."

In all those conversations with Mark about whether or not I should go for my Ph.D., I don't ever remember him saying that they wouldn't do this for me, but had it been implied? I knew it had. The real question, though, was why I had believed it so readily.

"Tell me you'll at least consider it, Chloe."

"Of course I will." There was one more thing bothering me. "But it would be pretty awkward to be back here, running into Mark all the time."

Mike smiled. "You may not have to worry about that."

"Mike, it's too small a place to think we won't cross paths."

"You won't cross paths if he's not here."

I stared at him. Mark, not get tenure? It didn't seem possible. "Are you serious, Mike? Is Mark's tenure package in trouble?"

Mike shook his head. "You know Mark's a damn fine scientist. Hell, Mark makes sure everyone in a ten mile radius knows that. I heard he's had an offer from somewhere else. A very attractive offer."

We said our good-byes, and I left the over-air-conditioned building for the heat outside.

Me, with a Ph.D. I mused about it as I walked. It would certainly please Dad to no end. That was one strike against it. It would be a huge time commitment, but the thing I hated most about my present situation was the empty hours that stretched in front of me each day. Dennis apparently already thought it was a good idea. *Dr. Chloe.* Mike was right; it had a nice ring to it.

And I had to admit: whether I took Mike up on his offer or not, it was nice to be wanted.

"So where's your brother been?" Til asked.

"I figured you'd have a better handle on that than I would." I popped a maraschino cherry in my mouth and chewed.

Til's jaw tightened. "Well, I don't."

"We had a family barbecue yesterday at my sister's. I don't know what he did after that."

"I should have known," Till said, under her breath.

"Known what? That my sister was having a barbecue?"

Til slapped the rag down on the bar. "No. I should have known that I wouldn't hear from him after I slept with him."

My eyes got big.

"What?" Til said, sarcasm dripping from her words. "You thought we were playing patty-cake?"

I shook my head. "No. I try not to think too much about my brother's sex life." It would take a lot of thinking if I did. Rafe was girl Velcro. He walked through a room and they just stuck to him.

"Well, apparently, he tries not to think too much about it either." Her words were angry, but I could see the tears gathering in her eyes.

Karen came back with a tray of empty glasses. "Who tries not to think about what?"

"Nothing. Forget it, Karen. It's none of your business," Til said quickly.

Too quickly, really. I could see Karen's interest pique.

"Seriously, who are you talking about? Chloe's brother? The hunky professor wannabe?"

I wasn't sure who I felt more mortified for, Rafe or Til. I seriously doubt he'd want to be referred to as a professor wannabe, even a hunky one.

Til kept wiping down the counters.

"Aw, c'mon. You can tell your aunt Karen all about it," Karen cooed.

Til's shoulders stiffened.

"You slept with him, didn't you?"

Til set down her rag. "Drop it, Karen."

"You did, didn't you? Now he hasn't called, has he?" Karen shook her head. "Don't say I didn't tell you so. He got his little piece of hot trailer trash lovin' and he's moved on."

"I am not trailer trash," Til hissed between clenched teeth.

Karen shook her head again. "You can take the girl out of the double-wide, but that don't mean you can take all the double-wide out of you."

For a second I thought Til was going to slug her. Instead, she grabbed her purse from under the bar and said, "My shift's up. I'm going home."

Karen watched the door bang shut with a little smile on her face. "You notice she didn't deny sleeping with him."

I grabbed an order pad and went out to see if anybody needed fresh drinks.

By the time my shift was nearly over, Clarissa still hadn't shown up. I let myself behind the bar, grabbed my cell phone out of my purse and dialed her number. It rang about five times and went to her voice mail. "Hey. Where are you? I thought we were meeting at the Green Creek. My shift's up so I'm heading home. Call me when you get this."

"Did you see who else is here?" Karen asked after I hung up.

"Who?"

She nodded over at one of the tables. Striped Shirt was back with her girlfriends.

"So? They came in for a drink. So did a lot of other people." I gestured around the bar.

"Yeah, but those three came in to see Malcolm." Karen giggled. "She's so hot for him, she can't even wait until Friday. She's hoping she catches him now."

I slung my purse over my shoulder and headed out the door. The blast-furance heat felt good; maybe it would burn off the oily residue that I felt on my skin after talking to Karen.

Striped Shirt and her friends came out of the bar practically on my heels and started to load into a little white Honda Civic, giggling to each other. I hesitated for a second, then walked over to the Honda Civic and knocked on the window. Striped Shirt was driving. She rolled the window down.

"Listen," I said. "I just wanted to warn you. That guy in there the other night—Malcolm—he's not going to show up for your date on Friday."

Striped Shirt opened her car door and got out. "What are you talking about?"

She really wasn't that unattractive. She was carrying a few extra pounds and could use more forgiving jeans, but she wasn't a bad looking girl. She was no Karen, however, with her gym-toned muscles and made-for-Levi's physique. "He won't show up. He only made the date with you on a bet with the bartender. She's his girlfriend."

The other two girls were getting out of the car. The one in denim capris said, "What is she saying, Melanie?"

"She says Malcolm won't show up for our date on Friday, that he only came over and talked to us on a dare."

"She's just jealous," the one in khaki shorts said.

"Is that it, bitch?" Melanie said, taking another step toward me. "Are you jealous?"

"Look. I was just trying to help." I turned to go back to my truck.

"Sure you were," one of them called after me. Something sharp hit me in the back. "Stupid wetback."

I whirled around. "What did you say? What did you call me?"

Denim capris cocked one hip in a classic tough girl stance. "I called you a stupid wetback. Whatcha gonna do about it?"

What *was* I going to do about it? Correct the racial epithet, insisting she take back the wetback and call me a yid or a kike instead? Or throw a rock back at her and start a brawl? Then I could be known as the chick who ran out of her own wedding *and* started fights in bar parking lots.

I turned back around and walked to my truck, hoping they wouldn't throw any more rocks.

"That's right, bitch. Keep walking," Melanie yelled after me.

I got in my truck and reversed out of the lot.

On my way up to the gate, I stopped at the mailbox. I'd gotten another credit card offer, an announcement about an upcoming sale, and a delayed postcard from Tahiti with a picture of a waterfall on the front. On the back, Mark had written: *We made love here. Thank God I'm here with someone who's actually halfway decent in bed.*

After talking to Vicky today, it didn't burn that much.

CHAPTER TWELVE

Chloe's Guide for the Runaway Bride

Weddings are a great time for families to get together and share memories of special times. Your un-wedding can also stir up family memories—like the story of how you almost weren't born.

As if this wasn't enough to make my day complete, my mother decided to call.

"Chloe, it's Mom. I just wanted to make sure you knew I was all right. I think it was just a case of too much rich food, combined with a touch of a virus." She laughed a little. "My stomach just can't take that anymore."

I tapped Mark's postcard against the table. Too much rich food and a virus? How about too much vodka and red wine?

"What rich food? I thought all Jen's recipes came from Weight Watchers."

"Those M&Ms brownies definitely weren't Weight Watchers, and you know how I love chocolate."

So now Lily was blaming me for bringing a dessert that was too yummy? Did I bring the imaginary virus, too?

"Anyhoo, I knew you'd be concerned so I just wanted to set your mind at rest."

Whether my mother was okay after drinking so much that she'd vomited hadn't crossed my mind. What had crossed my mind was another matter entirely.

"I did have one question," I said.

"Shoot, darling. Ask anything."

I rolled my eyes. Lily was always extra nice after she'd done something embarrassing, but shouldn't she be darlinging Jennifer and not me?

"What did you mean when you said you'd tried to shake me loose?" I asked.

Silence.

"Are you still there?"

"I am."

"So what'd you mean by that? How did you try to shake me loose?"

"When did I say anything about shaking you loose?"

"When I was tucking you into Jen's guest bed after you got sick." Because you drank too much. Not because I made brownies.

"I honestly don't remember, darling." Nervous laughter. "Darling, Stuart's calling. I'll get back to you. Okay?"

Oooh. Tittery laughter *and* darlinging me? This was big. But I'd never get anything out of Lily while she was sober and wanted to get off the phone with me fast. I would have to remember this for the future when I didn't want to talk to her.

"Sure. No problem. See you later."

I tore up Mark's postcard and threw the pieces into a pile of sawdust and scraps in the corner. Spot came into the kitchen and mewed desperately at me, then hunched over. Jesse nosed her a little, and she sat down and wrapped her tail neatly around her little front feet.

I knew the one person who would tell me anything that Lily

didn't want me to know, and I had an invitation to go to his birthday tomorrow. I called Til and told her I wouldn't be in to work and then called The Charm and told her I'd be there for Dad's birthday celebration.

"Wonderful! If you leave first thing in the morning, you can be here by one o'clock if the traffic's not bad. We'll have lunch and then sit by the pool."

Santa Cruz is beautiful. I'm a sucker for the ocean, and just knowing I'm near it makes me happy. It's not that I don't appreciate the Central Valley, it's just the flattest place on the planet. Flat. Flat. Flat. Flatter than even Kansas, which has been scientifically proven to be flatter than a pancake. Anyway, Dad's house is gorgeous. It's a creamy white stucco with a red tile roof. Inside, it's all dark tile and warm leather furniture.

As I headed there, I plugged the earpiece in on my cell phone and called Jen. "So Mom called. My brownies made her sick."

"She only called you once? Lucky you. She's been phoning me every ten minutes." Jen sighed. "It took a lot of nerve to put those M&Ms in the brownies. You want the flower to be green?"

I needed a new earpiece. That made no sense at all. "What?"

"Oh, sorry. I'm coloring with Troy. He doesn't like to do the actual crayon work himself, so he tells me what colors he wants where."

"Why?"

"How should I know why he wants the flower to be green? I would have made it pink or red, but it doesn't seem worth fighting over."

"I meant, why doesn't he want to color it himself, Jen?"

"Oh. He gets frustrated. He doesn't have the coordination to stay inside the lines."

I thought about Jen's thematically decorated house and the precisely layered strawberries and blueberries in the matching parfait glasses and her coordinated outfits, and figured that Troy's obsessive apple didn't fall far from the compulsive tree. "So you're all recovered from the barbecue?"

"Who, me? What would I need to recover from? Would that be you making my mother-in-law gasp like a fish on a dock? Or perhaps my mother drinking herself into a stupor? Or having my brother threaten my father with a dirty spatula?"

"Old Lemon Mouth deserved the gasping. Rafe didn't really threaten Stuart with the spatula, he just waved it at him. And technically, Lily didn't drink herself into a stupor. A stupor would imply that she would have kept her mouth shut rather than discuss your sex life with your mother-in-law."

"A stupor would have been preferable, then."

I heard Troy asking for something that sounded like purpur on the grass. "Seriously, Jen, are you okay?"

"Seriously? No. I'm heartsick that you couldn't all behave for one night, and my blood pressure spiked up high enough that my doctor is threatening me with bed rest if I don't get it down in the next week."

"But you're eating, right?"

I was treated to a long pause. "I'm taking in plenty of calories."

"Plenty for whom? A supermodel with a runway gig the next week or enough for you and the baby? It's not just about you right now."

"The baby will take what it needs from me." I could almost hear the way Jen's jaw was clenching.

I started to argue, but she cut me off. "Look, Chloe, I have to go. And I don't want to discuss this anymore, anyway. Let's face it: It's not like your life is in such great order that you can go around telling the rest of us what to do."

That shut me up fast. She had a point.

At Dad's, my little brother and sister both had friends over. Jackson and his buddy, Philip, were delighted with Aziza's soccer playing abilities and devised a complicated game of dog/boy ball. Cara and her friend, Tiffany, were sitting poolside, drawing pictures, taking turns holding Spot and making plans for The Charm to give them both hair wraps later. It was all so idyllic and calm and happy. It amazed me that I was related to these people.

"I hope you don't mind having lunch here," The Charm said as she handed me a plate mounded with fruit salad and quiche. "I don't like to leave the kids alone by the pool."

Since The Charm and Dad's backyard was a miniresort, I couldn't see why anyone would mind. "It's fine."

"That's nice of you. I was sort of hoping for a girlie lunch, but maybe we can do that tomorrow. What are you doing to keep yourself busy?"

I told her about the Green Creek. She nodded while rubbing sunscreen on her bare legs and arms. She had on khaki shorts and a tank top, a nearly identical outfit to mine. She handed the bottle over to me. "It's important to keep your skin healthy. Put some on."

It always cracks me up when The Charm tries to "mom" me, since she's only five years older than I am. Still, her heart was in the right place. I set down my fork and put on the sunscreen.

"When do you go back to Chromonology?"

"End of the summer."

"Are you sure you want to go back? I was talking to that old professor of yours at the . . . Well, anyway, he seemed to think you should go back for your Ph.D." Charm took a bite of her quiche.

"You know, you *can* be successful even if nobody calls you doctor." I didn't want to get Dad's hopes up about me going back for my Ph.D. before I'd made a decision, and I knew The Charm would pass anything I told her on to him.

She held her hands up. "I know. It's just that your dad seems to think you're wasting yourself, and now your professor is sort of saying the same thing. Maybe this is a good time to make a change, since you're making so many other ones."

The only change I'd made was not to marry Mark, and in some ways that wasn't a change, either. After all, I was staying single.

The Charm kept her word about pampering me for the day. I lay by the pool with Spot in my lap. She brought out popsicles that she'd made with real fruit juice and let me read her copies of *Entertainment Weekly* and *InStyle*, and Jackson had to pick up all the dog poo. After having to deal with Aziza's special fairy circles, he was changing his tune about wanting a dog and considering the advantages of a nice gecko.

When Dad got home at four-thirty, the popsicles were replaced by margaritas. Since The Charm makes the kind with crushed ice, the only real difference is the buzz. The extra kids were shooed home and Cara and Jackson were sent in to bathe.

"Chloe, good to see you." Dad sat down next to me.

"Happy birthday, Dad." I kissed his cheek. "How are things?"

"Fine."

This is typical of conversations with my father that I originate. He doesn't quite know what to say to me or do with me. Rafe and I possess a certain charm for Dad as reminders of his hippie past, but beyond our roles as mementos, we're kind of annoying for him.

"How's your brother?"

"Fine also. Busy."

"So busy that he can't make it to his old dad's birthday?"

"Apparently." I braced myself for one of the two lectures that was most likely to follow. These situations generally brought forth either an elegy on the Ingratitude of Children or an oratory on How His Children Were Stolen by His Mean-Spirited Ex-Wife.

"Not like he's got classes to teach this time of year," Dad grumbled.

Ah, it was to be the elegy. I settled into my chaise longue, focused on my margarita and tried to let Dad's words wash over me without sticking.

Then Dad changed into his Speedo to swim some laps, which I took as a cue to get away from the pool. Seriously, has the man never heard of trunks? I really don't want to have any information at all about my father's package and the Speedo provided way too much information. I took a shower, put on a sundress that I hoped wasn't too wrinkled, and went to help The Charm in the kitchen.

"Let me retie the bow in the back," The Charm said after telling me that my dress looked nice on me. It was too bad Dad hadn't married her until I was already in my twenties. Of course, if he hadn't waited that long, he might have been arrested for statutory rape.

"Can I do anything?"

"Absolutely. Clean the asparagus."

I did, and I helped make the salad. The other guests—two couples from the neighborhood—arrived and hors d'oeuvres and drinks were served while The Charm lit the grill. At a signal from her, Dad went out and grandly put everything The Charm had prepared on the grill.

Both the couples had bought Dad booze. Now, why hadn't I thought of that? Of course, I couldn't exactly afford the hundred-dollar bottles of scotch and port that they'd brought. No. I was definitely safer with the book I'd chosen. I tensed as Dad opened it anyway.

"Mr. Know-It-All?" He turned it around to show everyone the title. I breathed a sigh of relief. It was always a good sign when he showed it around.

"You hardly need that, do you, Bob?" One of the men—it was a little hard to distinguish them in their gray-haired, khaki-slacked sameness—guffawed and clapped him on the back.

Another person would probably not have noticed the flicker that crossed my father's face. Of course, another person wouldn't have spent a good deal of their life tuned in to those little signs that you'd done something wrong, because that other person wasn't going to be punished for it. I wanted to kick the guy right in the teeth.

"Chloe apparently thinks I need it," Dad said, his eyes just a little bit aglitter.

"I just thought you'd find it interesting," I protested. "I'd read a review . . ."

"Well, it's the thought the counts," Dad said, setting it face-down next to him.

The company finally departed and Cara and Jackson were sent to bed. Dad went off to his study and The Charm went to do the dishes. I told her I'd be there in a few minutes to help, then went off to find Dad.

He was behind the big desk in his study with a glass of something amber in his hand, probably a sample of one of his birthday presents.

I took a deep breath and summoned my courage. I generally try very hard not to bring up the subject of Lily with Dad or vice versa. Their divorce has not been a friendly one. Neither of them have much nice to say about the other and both subscribe to an "if you can't say something nice, say it extra loud" policy. Still, I didn't know anyone else to ask about this. "Hey, Dad, can I talk to you for a minute?"

He swiveled around to face me. "What's on your mind, Chloe?"

I cut right to the chase. "Dad, why would Mom say something about not being able to shake me loose?"

He swiveled back and forth in his chair, but his gaze stayed on my face. "What brings that up?"

"Something she said the other night, when she was . . . not feeling well."

"You mean when she was drunk."

I shrugged. I didn't feel like asking if he was the pot or the kettle, as he knocked back his scotch after his third or fourth glass of wine. I didn't think it would help get my question answered and with Dad, I always try to keep my eye on the prize.

"I'm surprised she said anything like that, even if she was plowed," he mused. "I've always wondered, though. . . ."

"Wondered what?"

"Hold on a second." Dad went over to the bookshelf and after a minute or two of searching came back with a battered album. He flicked through the pages and then handed the book over to me. "Here."

The page he showed me had a picture of toddler Rafe brushing his teeth in the nude, another of him playing in the mud while nude, and one of my mother in cut-off shorts, a gigantic T-shirt that didn't hide her pregnant belly, and a leg cast.

"What's with the cast?" I asked.

"She fell down the stairs." Dad took another sip of scotch without taking his eyes off me. "At least, she said she fell."

"Dad, I don't feel like playing games. What are you trying to tell me?"

"Your mother's never been a clumsy person. Not even when she was pregnant. Not even when she's drunk." He set the glass down and leaned back in his chair, hands steepled in front of him.

"You're saying that Mom threw herself down a set of stairs to try and miscarry? That's what she meant when she said she tried to shake me loose?"

He didn't say anything.

"I don't buy it, Dad. That was Mom's Earth Mother phase. She was running around northern California breastfeeding complete strangers and spouting peace and love."

"True enough. On the other hand, talking the talk is a lot easier than walking the walk."

"Why wouldn't she just have had an abortion?"

"Roe v. Wade was in 1973, Chloe. You were born in 1972. Plus, an accidental stumble and a deliberate abortion are two different animals, aren't they? Which one would jibe better with being an Earth Mother?"

Tears pricked at the back of my eyes. "Did she tell you she didn't want me?"

Dad grimaced. "I don't think it was that she didn't want you. Things between your mother and me were tense by then. We already had Rafe. We knew a baby was a lot of work. Rafe certainly was. He was never an easy child."

Ah, yes. The saga of Rafe. The difficult child. The child who needed all the special treatment. Always ahead of me, forging pathways to places I never wanted to go. I stared at my father as he turned gently back and forth in his big leather chair.

"I'm surprised this hasn't occurred to you before, Chloe," Dad said, taking off his glasses and rubbing the bridge of his nose. "You're a perceptive young woman. You must have picked up on some of this."

Had I? Maybe Dad was right. Maybe I had known, deep in my heart, that I hadn't been wanted. Not even by my own mother. Not even before I was born. She had been willing to risk breaking her neck in a fall down the stairs just to shake me loose, and I had tenaciously clung onto her. I'd fought hard to stay.

I felt like I'd been socked in the stomach, and at the same time, a whole bunch of things suddenly became clear.

"Did you want me, Dad?" I asked.

He sat back as if shocked that I would ask. "Chloe, of course I did. I love you. I love all my children."

Yeah. Right. That's why he was always so thrilled when I called. I mumbled an excuse about helping The Charm and left.

I left early the next morning. The Charm was sad that I cut my visit short. She'd been hoping we could do a little shopping together or that maybe I'd go to her spinning class with her. She really was sweet, but I couldn't stand another minute of my father's watchful gaze on me.

I maybe could have stayed if I'd thought he was watching so he could be there to help, but that's not my father's way. He'd never been there to catch me, any more than he'd been there to catch my mother when she'd fallen.

I took my time driving up the coast and stopped several times to let the dogs run, so it was late afternoon and hot as Hades by the time I got home. Etienne and Tucker must have left already because the driveway was empty. All I wanted was to grab a beer and sit on the porch, anyway. I didn't need company for that.

But I kind of wanted it. I kind of wanted to be wanted at all.

When I got out of the car, Jesse and Aziza bolted out instantly. Spot stood at the edge and mewed pitifully. She didn't look quite right. I don't think she'd liked the car ride much. She'd spent most of it curled up between Jesse's front paws, looking a little carsick. I scooped her up and she nuzzled under my chin and purred. She couldn't be too sick if she was purring like that, could she?

The kitchen looked great. Etienne had tiled the counters and they had actually swept the floor. I was tempted to go out and cut some roses to put on the table but I wasn't sure which ones Etienne had peed on, so I decided to buy some from the store.

I set Spot down and she wobbled a bit and abruptly lay down. There was definitely something wrong. I pulled my cell phone out of my purse to call Daniel but before I could flip it open, it rang.

It was Daniel.

"You have great timing. I was just about to call you."

"I'm flattered."

"Don't be. There's something wrong with Spot, so I want you to come and look at my cat."

"You know, Chloe, as pickup lines go, that's pretty pathetic. You could at least use a synonym for cat so it sounds dirty."

I couldn't help but smile. "Seriously, she's not okay. Can you come over?"

"Absolutely. Have you eaten?"

"No."

"Give me half an hour and I'll be there."

Half an hour. Time enough to shave my legs and have a quick shower, in case he wanted to check more than my cat.

As I got out of the shower I heard a car pulling through the gate. Damn, he was early! It had only been fifteen minutes. I wrapped a towel around myself and darted through the construction obstacle course in the hallway to look out the kitchen window.

Jesse and Aziza bolted through their doggie door. Jesse ran over and head-butted Clarissa. Aziza squatted and peed next to her tire. I opened the kitchen door.

"Tell me again why you took that dog?" Clarissa called to me, glaring at Aziza while patting Jesse on the head. She reached into the open back of her Rav4 and pulled out two bags of groceries.

"Because no one else wanted her."

"I can relate to that."

Spot stumbled into the kitchen and mewed desperately at me before lying back down. Jesse nosed her a little and she flopped her tail once in response.

"What's that?" Clarissa asked.

"That's Spot," I said.

"Who no one else wanted?"

"You got it." I picked Spot up and got a reassuring purr in response.

"Maybe we should form a club." Clarissa started pulling out six-packs of beer and bags of chips. She saw my raised eyebrow and said, "I was worried you wouldn't have enough alcohol to meet my inebriation needs tonight."

"You've certainly taken care of that. Come talk to me while I get dressed." I squinted at her. "What did you do to your lip?"

She touched the swollen spot on her lower lip. "It's a long story."

"Save it, then. We don't have much time." In my room, I set Spot down on the bed and started rummaging through my closet.

"This place looks amazing, Chloe. I can't believe how much it's changed. Did your grandmother design it?"

"No. I guess I did."

Clarissa eyes widened in their raccoon eyeliner. "You? Where'd you learn how to put this all together?"

"Internet."

"I'm guessing you're expecting company, since you seem to be looking for something other than boxer shorts and a tank top." Clarissa lay down on the bed next to Spot and took a long pull of her beer.

I took a long denim skirt out of the closet and pulled it on. "Daniel is coming to look at my cat."

Clarissa grinned. "So that's what you kids are calling it these days?"

"It's not a euphemism, Clarissa. The cat's not okay." I yanked a halter top over my head and grabbed a brush to yank through my hair. Spot sneezed, as if to illustrate my point, and I heard a car coming up the road. "That's him now."

I ran out to open the gate for him with Clarissa calling after me, "How come you never run out to open the gate for me?"

I closed the gate behind Daniel's truck and walked up to him as he got out of his truck. He had on jeans and an untucked light blue dress shirt with the sleeves rolled up. "Whose car?" he asked, nodding toward Clarissa's Rav4.

"My friend Clarissa's."

"She inside?"

I nodded and braced for the disapproval that I wasn't alone. Mark would have been furious.

"Guess I better do this now, then." He took my face in his hands and cradled it to him and kissed me.

It was a really good kiss. A really, really good kiss. So good I felt like I was swimming in it. It didn't feel anything like disapproval or irritation.

Daniel broke off the kiss but left his hand on my cheek. "I guess I should check on Spot now."

"You should probably check Jesse's paw, too."

"You're absolutely right. Anything else I should check?" He grinned.

"I'll make a list for you, doctor," I said primly, and headed into the bungalow.

Inside, Clarissa whispered in my ear, "Are you sure it wasn't a euphemism?"

Daniel went to check Spot and I started unloading the bags he'd brought with him: burgers, fries, and salads from the Putah Creek Café and, surprisingly, Gerber Lamb and Lamb Gravy from the Town and Country Market.

Clarissa helped herself to some fries. She poked at one of the salads. "Do you think these have meat in them?"

"Probably."

She sighed. "I was thinking of becoming vegetarian, but it's trickier than it looks."

Daniel came back in with Spot cradled in a towel. "How long has she been like this?"

"Only since this afternoon, but when I think about it, I guess it's been coming on for a while."

He nodded. "Is she eating?"

"A little, but she's so tiny. I think she fills up fast."

"Drinking?"

I thought. "Not much of that, either."

Daniel handed her back to me. I sat down in one of the kitchen chairs and he leaned against the counter. Clarissa handed him a beer.

"Chloe, there are a lot of reasons for a kitten to fail to thrive."

I nodded, trying to be the good student, as always.

"Some of them we can treat. Some we can't."

"Which is this one?" I crossed my fingers. *Be one you can treat. Be one you can treat. Be one you can treat.*

Daniel took a deep breath and let it out. "I don't know. I don't like the way this is going though. She needs to build some strength. I brought some baby food. We should try and feed her every hour. I'll show you how."

He opened up the baby food containers and got a syringe out of his bag. He took Spot from me and held her on her back, carefully coaxing in the food one cc at a time. She turned her head away, but he just kept coaxing her. When he decided she'd had enough, he cleaned off her little face and set her down. Jesse was right there to nose her.

I poured Clarissa's chips and salsa into bowls and took out some of the scones and raviolis and mini-pizzas and baby quiches. Everyone grabbed plates and we headed out to the porch, followed closely by Jesse and Aziza. The second we were outside, Aziza dashed off to retrieve her headless clown doll, which she then dropped in Clarissa's lap.

""Ewww!" Clarissa held it up between her thumb and fore-fingers. "It's covered with dog spit and it doesn't have a head!"

Daniel took it from her and threw it. Aziza flew off the porch to retrieve it. "I guess the squeaky hamburger didn't make the cut."

I shrugged. "I think she likes to chew on something with legs."

Clarissa snorted and choked on a chip. Aziza dropped Clowny at Daniel's feet and backed off two steps without even a growl from Jesse, just as Rafe's MG turned onto the dirt lane.

And to think that I'd been lonely for company just an hour ago. Now I felt all warm and fuzzy inside.

I let Rafe in the gate.

"Who's here besides Clarissa?" he asked, eyeing Daniel's truck.

"Daniel." I started back to the bungalow.

Rafe followed. "The vet?"

"The very one. He's here to check on my cat."

Rafe snorted and I shook my head. "It's not a euphemism."

"Whatever you say." Rafe grabbed two beers on his way through the kitchen to the porch. "This place looks fantastic. Has Gran seen it?"

I blushed. "No. I'm not sure she's even talking to me right now."

That stopped him. "What on earth could you do to make Gran stop talking to you?"

"It's those letters, Rafe. The ones from Jesse to Laura. I think Laura had an illegitimate baby and every time I try to talk to Gran about it, she gets upset."

"Have you considered not talking about it?"

"No. I want to know what happened."

"Why? What difference could that make?" he asked curiously.

By then we were on the porch and Rafe plopped down in one of the Adirondack chairs with his two beers, one of which was half gone already. I noticed Clarissa had a few empties by her already as well. "So what are you two drinking off?"

"Til," Clarissa and Rafe said in unison.

Rafe raised his bottle and Clarissa clicked hers against it. "To Til." They both drank deeply.

"What is it about her that's got the two of you in such a dither?"

Rafe and Clarissa exchanged glances. Finally, Rafe said, "The woman is sex on legs, Chloe."

"Always has been," chimed in Daniel. We all turned to look at him. "I went to high school with her. It's been like that since she was twelve. She walks through a room and every man knows it."

"Damn straight," Clarissa said, draining her beer bottle. She stood and swayed a second. "I'm going to get another beer. Anybody want anything?"

"I'll come with you. I want to check on Spot," Daniel said.

Rafe and I sipped our beers and I leaned back in my chair. The sky was so phenomenally beautiful, with the stars clustered thick above the silhouettes of the oak and eucalyptus trees that dotted the hills. The Seven Sisters twinkled down at me as if they had a message they needed me to understand. I pulled my sweatshirt around me. "So if Til's so damn hot, why'd you ditch her?"

"I haven't ditched her."

I waited for him to say more. He didn't. "So where have you been?" I asked.

"At work."

"Chickenshit." This is how Rafe breaks up with women. He disappears. He will change his routine, his grocery store, his favored post office, even his apartment to avoid seeing a woman and telling her face to face that he doesn't want to see her anymore.

Normally, this doesn't bother me so much. This time it did, and I knew why.

"You know, it's bad enough that you broke Til's heart, but you, of all people, should have been a little better about breaking Hunter's heart."

"Hunter is why I left, Chloe. I would think you, of all people," he said in a very pointed inflection, "would understand that."

"Enlighten me, because I don't see it."

"Then you're not paying attention. I made that kid wet his pants just by yelling at him, and I wasn't even that mad. Then the other morning at breakfast, he spilled his milk. When I reached for the napkins to clean it up, he cowered, Chloe. He cowered away from me." Rafe sounded as incredulous as Troy had about being bitten by the bee. "Maybe you're right, we're like poison," he said. "Any relationship we're in turns toxic and unpleasant. I don't think I'm willing to inflict that on another generation."

"I didn't say we were poison. I said we might be genetically incapable of having a decent relationship. Besides, you were right: Jen's not doing it. She's not inflicting it on Troy."

"Yet," Rafe said. "And look how hard she's fighting it. One more family dinner like July fourth and she might kill herself. Let's just face it, Chloe: Maybe we're not made to be in relationships. Speaking of which, I went down to see Dad for his birthday." He gazed up at the stars.

"Excuse me? I was there for Dad's birthday and you, sir, were not there."

"I just missed you. I was a little late."

Try twenty-four hours late. Rafe would get away with it, though; he always did. Yet I'd get the lecture on how inconsiderate he was the next time I was there.

Rafe took another long pull of the beer that dangled between his fingers. The man was born to hold a longneck. "He gave me a present."

"You went to see Dad for his birthday and he gave you a present. You know it's supposed to be the other way around, right?"

Rafe shrugged. "It would have been rude to refuse his offer. Besides, I've been wanting to read that book."

My heart sank. I already knew the answer, but I asked anyway. "What book?"

"Mr. Know-It-All."

I put my head down on my knees.

"He gave me a sweater, too." Rafe pulled a light blue cashmere sweater from out of his backpack.

I glanced up and put my head back down on my knees. "That's the sweater I gave him for Hanukkah. I gave him that book the day before yesterday." Dad must have really been pissed about that pencil-necked jerk's know-it-all comment. He knew perfectly well that Rafe would show me the book and the sweater.

"Dammit. I knew it was too good to be true." He dropped the sweater back into his backpack. "It wasn't my color anyway."

"Do you know how much that sweater cost?"

"Not a clue."

"One hundred and eighty dollars."

"What was one hundred and eighty dollars?" Daniel came back out and sat down next to me. He reached out and took my hand.

I stared at his hand on mine for a moment, surprised at how natural and good it felt.

"The sweater Chloe gave my father for Hanukkah that he has now regifted to me. You must have really teed him off while you were there, Chloe."

I explained about the dickhead's comment and Rafe cringed. "Ouch. No way you could have stopped that one."

"And for that, your father is taking all the gifts you've given him and giving them to Rafe?" Daniel asked.

Clarissa came out with a tray full of pizzas and quiches. "You know, you just don't get sick of these things, do you?"

Personally, I could go a long time without ever eating another mini-quiche. Do not even talk to me about salmon. "Knock yourself out."

"And the sweater cost almost two hundred dollars?" Daniel asked.

I nodded.

"You know, you could return that and go out for a damn nice dinner," Daniel observed.

"I like the way this man thinks!" Rafe pulled the sweater back out of his backpack. "It even still has the tags on it."

CHAPTER THIRTEEN

Chloe's Guide for the Runaway Bride

A runaway bride may be pursued by the police even if she didn't pretend to be abducted. This can, on occasion, work in her favor.

The second I walked in the Green Creek's door that afternoon, Til was there waiting. "Why didn't you tell me Clarissa was a lesbian?" Til demanded, hands on hips. The place was empty, deserted. And very, very silent. Til didn't even have the TV on.

"Excuse me?" I said, even though I was pretty sure I knew what she was talking about. It all started to click together now. Til had stormed out of here the other night at about the same time that Clarissa was supposed to meet me. They must have run into each other in the parking lot. Til was what had "come up" for Clarissa the other night. All those comments about not being wanted the night before started to make sense, too.

"Don't play stupid. Your buddy Clarissa. She's a dyke. She decided to tell me she was gay by kissing me, and I was so damn surprised I nearly bit her lip off."

I couldn't help it. I snorted. That explained Clarissa's swollen lower lip.

"It's not funny, Chloe," Til said. "What is it with you people? What did I ever do to you? Is this some kind of game you play? Is it to show how much smarter and better you are than everyone else? You're no better than Karen and Malcolm and that stupid game they play. Did your grandmother put you up to it? Is that it? Did your snobby grandmother tell you to come down here and torture all the poor stupid people who don't quite meet her standards?"

"My grandmother?"

"Yeah. Everyone knows what she's like. I thought maybe you were different. I don't know why."

Donald and Matt came in, cutting off our conversation. I flicked on the TV to ESPN and took their orders.

Til left and Karen arrived, not that she did much work. She got on her cell phone almost the second she came in. "Malcolm, pick up your damn phone, you dolt."

By seven-thirty, I was exhausted. I'd been up half the night with Spot and was anxious to get back to her. I took off my apron and told Karen I was clocking out. She nodded and grabbed her phone.

As I headed out to my car I heard the door open and shut again behind me, but didn't think much of it until someone yelled behind me. "Hey, you!"

I turned around. Great, it was Striped Shirt. She had on a pink top over a denim mini and high-heeled sandals, all of which were quite cute, but which were why she was having a hard time catching up with me in the parking lot. High heels and gravel do not mix.

"Can I help you?" I asked.

She stomped unsteadily over to me. "I think you've helped enough. Don't you, Wetback?"

Good God, would she never insult me correctly? Then I

realized that it was Friday night. She was here for her big date with Malcolm. That's why Karen had frantically been calling him.

I sighed. "Let me guess. Malcolm didn't show up."

"No, he didn't." She had caught up with me now. "You had something to do with that, didn't you?"

She was standing way too close. I hate people who don't respect my personal space. I took a step backward. "No, I didn't. I told you. He was never planning on showing up. He won the bet when you agreed to meet him." I turned away and walked to my truck.

"That's not what she says. That bartender chick, the one you said made the bet, she said she doesn't know what you're talking about."

I glanced over at the window, wondering if Karen was looking through it and cackling over the mess she'd created. "Do you really think she'd admit to it? That she'd just come clean and tell you she'd made a bet like that?"

That slowed her down for a second, but only for a second. "I think you had something to do with it. I think you wanted Malcolm for yourself and told him not to come."

"Let me guess. Karen told you that, too." I unlocked my car door. "You can think whatever you want. It doesn't matter to me."

She grabbed my shoulder and whirled me around. "How 'bout I make sure it matters to you?"

I suppose I was lucky that she wasn't used to fighting in heels. When she whirled me around, her balance wobbled so her punch went wide and hit me in the shoulder.

I have never ever been in a fist fight. Girls in Walnut Creek High School simply do not do that kind of thing. Abigail Dunlop and Missy Sample had gotten into a hair-pulling/slapping kind of thing junior year, but it was only that once and was the talk of the school until we graduated.

I grabbed my shoulder and yelled, "Ow! That hurt!"

"It was supposed to hurt!" Striped Shirt yelled as she used my truck to right herself. "What are you? A dimwit?"

I squinched my eyes shut and prepared for her fist to hit me. That was my entire idea of self-defense: to not look as someone creamed me. Sometimes it amazes me that I've survived this long.

I heard Striped Shirt grunt and then a male voice saying, "That's enough."

I opened my eyes. Officer Musciano? He had Striped Shirt's arm twisted up behind her back while he pressed her against my truck.

"Officer Musciano! What are you doing here?" I gasped.

"I was riding by and it looked like you needed help." He rubbed at his mustache. "You look like that a lot, Chloe."

He was wearing bike shorts and a road bike was lying on its side in the gravel. No wonder we hadn't heard him drive up. And wow. He looked great in the bike shorts. Love that lycra!

"Thank you! I don't know what would have happened if you hadn't come by."

"I would have pounded your face in. That's what would have happened." Striped Shirt tried to wiggle free and he wrenched her arm up a little higher. She grunted and stopped fighting.

And that was when Malcolm drove into the parking lot. We all stopped and watched him get out of his car and saunter over. "Hey, Melanie, I'm sorry I'm late."

She blushed to the very roots of her hair and my mouth dropped open.

"You ready to go?" Malcolm said. "I thought we could go over to the Stag's Leap. I could use a change of pace. It's quieter there. We can talk."

Melanie jerked her arm away from Officer Musciano and straightened her shirt. "That's okay, Malcolm. I'm just happy to see you." She linked her arm with his and sashayed across the parking lot with one last scowl in my direction.

Officer Musciano retrieved his bicycle. "What was that about?"

I shook my head. "I'm not sure anymore myself."

"So you live out here?" He swung his leg over the bike.

"Yeah. Right before you get to Lake Solano." It seemed too complicated to explain about Aunt Laura's bungalow, but it also felt strangely right to say I lived here. Really, where else did I live? "How 'bout you? Do you live out here?"

"Nah, I live in Davis. I just like to ride my bike out here. It's a good workout."

"We're fifteen miles from Davis."

"Like I said—good workout. You okay getting home?"

"I think so. Thanks again."

He waved, pushed off and rode off into the summer night. That was one handy stalker to have around.

Back home I coaxed a few cc's of pureed chicken into Spot, stroking her throat to help her swallow, and followed it up with a few drops of water. She shivered in my hands. I turned on the heating pad that I'd set on my bed and made her a nest with an old wind-up clock and a soft strip of blanket.

She seemed to get limper every time I picked her up to feed her. She gave a little chirp of distress as I set her down, and tears sprang to my eyes. "Sorry," I whispered.

Jesse stuck his nose over the edge of the bed and snuffled

Spot, who craned her head around to look and mewed. Jesse licked her and then settled on the floor next to the bed.

I set my alarm for midnight and shut off the light.

We repeated the exercise at one, two, and three. Each time, Jesse stood by the bed, watching me feed Spot and snuffling her when I was done. Each time, Spot's little body felt smaller and lighter in my hands.

At four a.m., when my alarm went off again, Spot's body was limp in my hands when I picked her up off the heating pad.

I turned her on her back and rubbed her tummy with my finger. "Spot," I whispered, my voice sounding loud and harsh in the quiet bedroom. "Spot, wake up."

I heard Jesse get up and felt the cold wet of his nose against my hands. I started to shake. Jesse licked my hands until I lowered them enough for him to sniff Spot. It only took him one sniff to confirm what my heart wouldn't believe yet, and he sat down by my bed and began to howl. That's when I began to sob.

"Stop apologizing. I'm glad you called."

Daniel had wrapped me in a quilt and held a glass of brandy to my lips. The first sip had made me cough and splutter, but then had sent warmth flooding through my bloodstream. I still shook, but not with the bone rattling intensity that had made it difficult to dial the phone. "Didn't know what else to do," I whispered through my chattering teeth.

"I told you. It's all right." He held the glass to my lips.

I took another sip. "She's so little, Daniel." I looked over at where Spot lay in the shoebox that Daniel had brought with him.

"Too little, Chloe."

"I know. You told me."

"I'm sorry. It seems like some little creatures weren't meant to make it. I'm afraid Spot was one of those. It doesn't make any sense, but you have to be ready to let them go."

"How do you know?" I whispered. "How do you know which ones will make it and which ones won't?"

He shook his head. "You don't. Not really."

"But you knew about Spot. You could tell when you first saw her." I took the brandy from his hand and took a sip; I'd stopped shaking enough to hold it without spilling.

"Sometimes I just have a feeling. You still have to fight, though, whether or not you think they're going to make it. Whether or not they're fighting, too." He stroked a finger down Spot's soft fur. "Especially the little ones. For them, you have to fight extra hard."

"Why didn't she fight harder?"

He shook his head and put his arm around my shoulder. "Some of us are fighters and some of us aren't. Some beings have a will to survive and thrive that's simply born into them. Some don't. Some are just too damaged to fight anymore." He shut the lid on the shoebox. "If it makes you feel any better, I can't keep myself from fighting for the little lost ones, either—no matter how many times they break my heart."

We buried Spot by some climbing America roses near the fence as the sun started to come up over the yellow hills. Jesse stood beside us as solemn as a minister. I started to say something about Spot being a good kitten, but my voice shook and broke. Daniel hugged me and told me to go get some sleep and left, but I wasn't quite ready to leave Spot just yet.

I sat under the climbing roses with Jesse and Aziza pressed up against either side of me. Aziza got bored and ran off to chase a squirrel, but Jesse pressed closer against me. I blew my nose for the fifteenth time, then stood up to go inside.

When I did, a thorn jabbed my head. Ouch! I tried to duck out from under the rosebush, but my hair had gotten caught on the thorns. I turned, managing to snarl my hair further.

I froze, my deer-in-the-headlight reflexes coming to the rescue for once. I reached up and gently started untangling my hair, and Aziza chose that moment to come up behind me and sniff me. There is nothing like a cold dog nose up your butt to get you out of a rosebush fast. Unfortunately, I left quite a bit of hair behind.

I was emotionally worn, and exhausted, but I knew I wouldn't be able to sleep now. Spot was gone and even though I'd only had her a short time, she was going to leave a much bigger hole than the one I'd just left in my scalp. To distract myself, I grabbed the box of Aunt Laura's letters. A heavy envelope had sifted to the bottom, and I decided to check it out.

I slid a butter knife under the flap so I didn't rip the envelope, then pulled a yellowed, brittle piece of paper out and carefully unfolded it. It was a hospital birth certificate from Community Hospital in Santa Barbara, the old-fashioned kind with the baby's little footprints on the bottom. It was for a baby girl named Corazon Hernandez, and her birthday was January 27, 1944.

The exact same birth date as my mother's.

"Rafe, I've got to show you what I found in that box." I set the birth certificate down in front of him.

After I'd realized what I was reading, I'd shot out of bed like a bullet and drove into town and shook Rafe out of bed.

He glanced it over and then set it back down again. "So?" He put his head down on the kitchen table.

I nudged the Starbucks coffee that I'd gotten him against his arm. "What do you mean, 'so?' Don't you see?"

"Apparently not."

"Look at the birth date, Rafe. It's *Lily's*. I don't think Gran is Lily's real mother. I think Aunt Laura was!"

Rafe cocked his head to the side and his eyebrows went up. He thought about it for a second. Then he shook his head.

"What difference would that make? Lily was barely a mother to us. How would it matter who her mother was?"

I blinked, totally stunned. "What do you *mean*, what difference would it make? This is huge! Our family has been living a lie for more than sixty years." I shoved the birth certificate back at him. "Doesn't that make any difference to you?"

So much had whirled into place for me when I'd seen the date on that birth certificate. Everything from Melanie calling me a wetback, to Etienne thinking I could be Vicky Montoya's sister, to a million other times that people assumed I could speak Spanish or knew what to order at a Mexican restaurant. I couldn't believe that Rafe couldn't see it.

Rafe shoved the paper right back at me. "If I got excited about every lie our family lived, I'd have a heart attack. I admit, this is vaguely interesting. We have a whole different set of genes than we thought we did, but beyond any relevance to our medical histories, I don't see how it really has any impact on us."

"Well, I'm going to ask Gran about it." I folded the paper back up and put it back in its envelope.

"Why would you do that?"

"To find out the truth. To find out who our grandparents really were."

Rafe leaned both elbows on the table. "Chloe, don't you think that if Gran wanted us to know this, she would have told us about it a long time ago? Leave it alone."

"Maybe she was just waiting for the right time."

"I'm pretty sure that there is no right time for that kind of conversation. So if that's the case, we may be waiting for a really long time. Plus, has it occurred to you that Gran probably has some pretty strong feelings about this?"

I slumped back in my chair. "Yeah. It has."

"How exactly do you plan to approach with her this?" He imitated my voice: "So, Gran, I hear that Lily isn't your daughter after all, and you've been lying to the world for sixty years?"

"I had planned to be a little more delicate than that."

"That's a relief. What did you plan on saying?"

"I don't know. I need to think about it."

"Maybe you should think about whether you need to say anything at all."

But I had thought about it, and I did need to say something. Maybe Rafe was right, and the only difference this would make was that we wouldn't have the family history of diabetes that came to us from my grandfather. But I still needed to know what had really happened—and if I didn't ask Gran now, I might never ask at all.

In the twenty minutes it took to drive from Rafe's house to Gran's, I rejected half a dozen ways to start the conversation. Gran always appreciated a straight shooter, so I didn't want to beat around the bush. She also appreciated a certain amount of tact, so I didn't want to blurt out that she'd been lying to all of us for sixty years. In the end, I decided that I'd tell her that I found the birth certificate and knew that Lily was Corazon. I'd play it by ear after that.

When I pulled up to the house I expected her to already be out on the porch. I knew she could hear a car arriving, but she wasn't there. I walked up the stairs and knocked on the door. "Gran? It's me, Chloe. Gran, let me in!"

Nobody answered.

"Gran?" I called again.

Still no answer.

The screen door was latched, but the inner door was open. She should be able to hear me anywhere in the house. My heart started to beat faster. Why wasn't she answering?

"Gran?" She could be in the bathroom, I reminded myself. Or she could be hurt.

I gave the screen door a good hard tug and the hook and eye latch pulled right out of the old dry wood.

Gran wasn't in the kitchen or the living room. She had to be inside somewhere; she couldn't latch the door from the outside. I came around the corner into her bedroom and I found her lying on the floor, her eyes staring ahead. I ran back to the kitchen and dialed 911.

"I'm afraid Mrs. Sachs has heart problems," the doctor told us, as if it were a news flash. Lily, Stuart, Rafe, and I were clustered in the small waiting room off the cardiac care unit as the nurses got Gran settled in a room. I'd called everyone on my cell as I'd followed the ambulance to the hospital.

"We know that. That's why she had the pacemaker put in five years ago. That fixed it," I said, impatient to get the pre-liminaries out of the way.

Dr. Engel ran a hand over his pale, tired face. The man looked like he never saw the outside of the hospital. "I'm afraid her condition had gotten too serious for the pacemaker to fix."

"So what do we do? How do we fix it?" I asked. Everyone else still looked shell-shocked, even Stuart.

"We don't," Dr. Engel said in a soft voice.

I leaned back in my chair, suddenly dizzy and sick-feeling. "We don't?"

"Chloe," Lily said, reaching for my hand.

I snatched my hand away from her grasp and glared at her. "We let her die? We just sit here and watch while she suffers and dies?" I couldn't believe what I was hearing.

Dr. Engel shook his head. "We'll do everything we can to assure that your grandmother experiences as little pain as possible. I've already ordered a morphine drip. It will help ease her breathing, as well."

"Thank you, doctor," Stuart said, all solemn and serious.

Thank you? Thanks for what? Drugging her to death? Why was Stuart even here in the first place? I felt a snarl starting deep in my throat. Rafe grabbed my shoulder, his fingers digging in hard enough that it hurt. I sat back in the chair and he released his grip.

"Can you tell us why there's nothing else to be done?" Rafe asked in a reasonable tone of voice. I shot him a look that I hoped was filled with gratitude.

"It's what your grandmother wanted," Dr. Engel said. "She's known for some time that her heart was enlarged and that her congestive heart failure would continue getting worse. She made her wishes quite clear to me. I urged her to inform her family, but if she didn't, that was her choice to make."

The nurse came in to let us know that they had finished settling Gran in her room. We all trooped in. Her eyes stayed closed, even after I took her hand.

After a couple of minutes, a little dark-haired nurse came in. "You should probably all go home and get some rest. She'll be fine tonight. Come back in the morning."

Lily and Stuart whispered to each other and then agreed to leave. Lily gave Gran a kiss on the forehead. Rafe left a few minutes later, but I wanted to stay.

I had to stay.

The last thing my grandmother had said to me was that I

was selfish and thoughtless and just like my mother. I needed to show her it wasn't true.

Gran still hadn't woken when morning came around and Lily came back to the hospital. Once Nurse Jackie had figured out that I wasn't going anywhere no matter how often she suggested it, she'd brought in a roll-away bed for me. I had dozed a little, but not much. My mouth felt dry and my tongue felt like it was coated with cotton.

"You've been here all night?" Lily asked.

I nodded. "I wanted someone to be here in case she woke up."

"I'm here now. Go home and get cleaned up. You look like hell." Gotta love that maternal instinct in Lily. It runs true every time.

I stood up and stretched. "I should have seen it coming—she's been so tired lately. You know how she hates to ask for help. I should have seen it and been there for her. She's always been there for me." *Like you've never been.* The words hung in the air between us.

Lily's eyes narrowed. "This is so typical, Chloe. It has to be all about you, doesn't it?"

"What?"

"This isn't about what you did or didn't do, Chloe. It's about your grandmother getting old. And possibly dying." She held up her hand to cut off my protest before it even left my mouth. "That's what happens to people. They get old and die. Accept it." She stood and brushed herself off. "I'm going to get some coffee."

I sat there in the dim light for a few minutes after she left, listening to the steady beep of the machines hooked up to my grandmother. Then I stood and looked at myself in the mirror. My mother was right; I did need a haircut. My bangs hung into my eyes, there were chunks missing from the incident in the rosebush, and the ends were dry and brittle looking.

I grabbed the nail scissors from my grandmother's toiletry kit and started to cut.

I walked into the Green Creek to let Til know I wouldn't be able to work today. She was clearing off one of the tables near the pool tables.

"Hey, Til."

She turned and almost dropped the beer glasses she was carrying.

"What . . . did . . . you . . . do . . . to . . . your . . . hair?" she gasped.

Just in case you're considering it, trimming your hair in a poorly lit mirror is not one of your better beauty choices. "I trimmed my hair," I said.

"No, you didn't." Til shook her head vehemently. "You hacked it off. That's like amputating a leg and saying you got your toenails trimmed. That's like cutting down a tree and saying you trimmed the branches. That's like—"

I held up my hand to stop her. "I get the point, Til. Don't hurt yourself making up metaphors."

She looked uncertain for a moment, which Til never does unless someone uses a big word, then set down her tray and flung her arms around me. "When will you stop this, Chloe? When will you stop punishing yourself?"

I struggled out of her arms. What on earth was she talking about? So I'd given myself a bad haircut. "I'm not punishing myself. I got sick of my bangs being in my eyes and I tried to cut them myself."

"I'm calling Susan."

"Who?"

"My sister. She'll fix it."

"I don't have time to mess with my hair, Til. I only came in to let you know that I can't work today or probably tomorrow either. My grandmother is in the hospital." I would've just called except I needed to feed the dogs and it was on my way.

"She'll be fast. I promise." Til was already dialing.

"No one's that fast. I'm going to go take a shower and feed my dogs and go back to the hospital."

Til's eyes narrowed. "We'll come to your place, then. You're not going anywhere else with your hair like that."

I shook my head and left. I'd be long gone before they got there.

CHAPTER FOURTEEN

Chloe's Guide for the Runaway Bride

Running out of your own wedding seems monumental at first. But at some point, you realize that your own personal little drama doesn't mean squat.

Twenty-five minutes later I was in the truck and driving away. When I got back to the hospital, Nurse Jackie was gone. Nurse Lucy was presently on duty.

"Oh, you must be the granddaughter," she said. "Your mother just left to get some lunch. I thought she was the granddaughter. She looks so young."

"Yes, she does." It was true; everyone said so.

"And she's so pretty!" She walked with me into the room.

A covered tray sat on the bedside table, untouched. Gran lay still in the bed, each breath heaving her chest up and down.

"Yes, she is." Also another one of those things that everyone says about Lily.

"You have great genes," Nurse Lucy said.

Well, appearances can certainly be deceiving. I pulled a chair next to Gran's bed and sat down. "Has she woken up at all?"

Lucy shook her head. "No. I'm afraid not." She adjusted the

sheet across Gran's chest and pressed some buttons on the IV tree.

"Do you think she will?"

"I wish I could tell you. Everybody's different. It's hard to predict." She squeaked out of the room on her crepe-soled shoes.

I'd grabbed a paperback from the gift store as I came up, and now took it out of its bag. It was a mystery novel by a British author that I knew Gran enjoyed. I opened the first page and started to read it to her.

I didn't make it far. Two nights in a row with next to no sleep caught up with me, and I dozed off.

In my dream, a truck backed toward me. The steady *beep-beep-beep* of its warning grew louder and louder as it got closer and closer. My feet were stuck in concrete and I couldn't move. I kept signaling to the driver, but since I couldn't see his mirrors, I knew he couldn't see me. There was no one there to save me, no one to tell the driver to stop. I had to get his attention. I filled my lungs to scream as loud as I could and . . .

. . . sat up straight in my chair, choking a little on my own drool as I did. The box that controlled Gran's IV kept beeping.

Lily glanced up from the magazine she was leafing through. "Nice hair," she said.

"Water?" Gran croaked. She'd finally woken.

"Mom?" Lily said at the same moment I said, "Gran?"

"Water?" she asked again.

The water in the pitcher at Gran's bedside was warm so Lily grabbed it and went to get some more.

We were alone. "Gran, what happened to Corazon?"

"Corazon?" Gran's watery eyes slowly focused in on me. "Who do you mean?"

"The baby. The baby that Aunt Laura had. I saw her birth certificate. Is Corazon my mother?"

Each breath cost her so much. I could see the artery in her neck leaping with each tortured rise of her chest. She waved the question away. "I've asked you not to call her that, Laura. It will only confuse the child. Her name is Lily now. That's what Jacob wanted. Lily, after his mother. It's the least we can do for him. He is raising another man's child, after all."

Gran's eyes seemed trained over my left shoulder. I wanted so much to know the truth. Pretending to be Laura felt terribly wrong. Still, this might well be my only chance to find out who my mother was and who my grandmother was. I don't know why, but I knew in my heart of hearts that Rafe was wrong. This was bigger than whether or not we had a family history of diabetes.

"Naomi, can you remind me why we did this?" I asked. "Why did we pretend that Lily was your daughter instead of mine?"

Gran's head turned back and forth on the thin pillow. "Don't be ridiculous, Laura. An out of wedlock baby was bad enough. But one of mixed blood? What else were we to do? Who would even want to adopt a child like that?"

"Mixed blood?"

Gran nodded. "Mustn't tell. Mustn't let anyone know. Too humiliating."

"And I never tried to marry anyone else?"

Gran's hand waved distractedly in the air and then eventually settled back onto the bed like a wounded bird finally coming to rest on the ground. "Jesse Hernandez ruined you. Damaged goods." Her eyes closed again. "Lily, too. Damaged goods from the start. But Jacob and I tried and tried. Never could make a baby. Never could make a good one for ourselves. Had to make do."

Lily hustled back in just then, her heels clacking on the hard tile floors. Who wears strapless sandals to a hospital? I guess the same woman who would wear linen trousers and a silk top (which would be my mother). "I've got fresh water and another pillow, Mom," she chirped.

She poured the fresh water into a glass and held the straw to Gran's lips. Gran took a sip and then waved it away. Lily set the glass down and started adjusting the bed, her movements jerky and uncoordinated. Gran groaned and Lily jumped back. "Where does it hurt, Mom?"

"Everywhere," Gran croaked. She pointed at the water and Lily held the straw to her lips again.

"That's because you're all squished up." Lily set the water down. "Let me get you more comfortable."

She shifted Gran in the bed and propped her pillow. Her movements were awkward, but tender in their own way. A silver flash of memory dazzled my mind for an instant. Lily sluicing cool water down my back as I burned with fever. What had it been? Chicken pox? Strep throat? Something with a rash. Something hot and itchy that my mother soothed as she hummed. Why hadn't I ever remembered that before?

I squinted my eyes as if maybe I could see past the shiny smoothness of Lily's surgically tucked face and plumped lips to that other mother who seemed like a dream.

"There. That's better, isn't it?" Lily said.

Gran shut her eyes and said, "It won't last."

She fell asleep a few minutes later, her fingers fluttering spasmodically every few minutes until she'd dropped off.

I said I needed a walk, and practically streaked for the exit doors. The whoosh of air as they opened propelled me through into the sunlight. I stood for a second, grateful for the hot air on my frozen face.

My grandmother was not my grandmother. She had raised my mother out of a sense of duty mixed with shame and resentment, but she had not been her mother. Not biologically. Maybe not emotionally.

Gran had always been my ally in the wars I waged against Lily. I always knew she'd back me up, give me a place to stay, help me stand up to my mother and dismiss her. At least, that's how I'd always thought of Gran, as my ally. Maybe I'd been more her pawn.

How do you survive having a mother that never loved you? That couldn't be right, though. Gran must have loved Lily at some level. She'd fed her, educated her, kept her clean and safe and warm.

And at some point, Lily had tried to soothe my feverish itchy back in a bath while she hummed. A flood of other memories seemed ready to pour like rivers through my brain. Lily cutting my peanut butter sandwich into the shape of a heart. Lily reading me a story about a mother bunny who wanted to be the Easter Bunny. Lily wrapping me in a warm towel as I got out of a bath.

They were all there, buried deep under the memories of Lily drunk at a piano recital, Lily flirting with my fifth grade teacher, Lily telling me to lighten up or change my hair or how I dressed, sat, ate, spoke, breathed. Because that's the only way she knew to mother.

I'd at least had Gran as my ally. Who had Lily had? Gran was wrong. I wasn't the one who was like Lily. She was.

When I went back into the hospital, Rafe was there sitting by the bed as Gran breathed laboriously.

"Hey," I said.

"Hey, yourself." He squinted at me. "You look pale. Are you okay?"

I shook my head. "I don't know."

"What's with the hair?"

I sank into the chair that Lily had been in earlier. "Long story."

There didn't seem to be anything more to say, so we just sat there.

Around six o'clock, Til walked in with two grocery bags full of sandwiches and fruit and chips and cookies. Hunter clung to her leg as she hesitated in the doorway. "I thought you might be hungry," she said.

"Oh, Til," I said, tears welling up in my eyes.

Hunter peered around her leg at Rafe, his eyes wide.

"Hey, buddy." Rafe waved at him.

Hunter let loose of Til's leg, scampered across the room and into Rafe's lap. As the little boy snuggled in, making himself at home, Rafe looked over at me in astonishment and then back at Til. She shrugged and started pulling out food.

I had had no idea that I was hungry, but once I started eating I couldn't stop. I ate two sandwiches, most of a bag of chips, an orange, and three cookies. I don't think I even looked up the whole time. Honestly, I'm not sure I chewed. I couldn't stuff it in fast enough.

"Hey, Rafe, will you take Hunter to the men's room?" Til asked.

I looked up. Hunter was doing a little wiggle dance and grabbing his crotch.

"Sure. C'mon, buddy," Rafe said, taking Hunter's hand.

"He freaked himself out when he made Hunter wet his pants," I told her after they left the room. "He's worried he'll hurt him."

Til chewed her sandwich in silence for a moment. "He won't."

"How do you know?" I didn't know if Lily had meant to hurt me or that Gran had meant to punish Lily for all those years, but I suspected not. There are so many things we do that happen out of the grasp of our reason, that happen on an instinctive level, that seem to control us more than we control them. How could she know that Rafe would never hurt Hunter, whatever his intentions might be?

"Because I won't let it happen."

"Til . . ."

"Look, he's not going to be perfect. Nobody is. You just have to do the best you can and hope the kid forgives you for the rest of it. Kids forgive an amazing amount of stuff."

I couldn't help thinking that there's also some stuff that kids won't forgive. Ever.

The three of them—Hunter, Til, and Rafe—left together a little while later. I heard Hunter giggle as Rafe swept him up onto his shoulders in the hallway. I shut my eyes and whispered a little prayer for them.

I'd decided to spend the night again. Til had called Daniel and he'd offered to take care of Jesse and Aziza for me, so there was no reason not to. The night slid into the next day in the weird seamlessness of days and nights in the hospital. Jen, Rafe, Clarissa, and Lily all came and went as the day went by.

Gran's fingers plucked at the sheet that covered her. "Do you think she's too warm?" I asked Nurse Lucy on one of her frequent trips to check on us.

"She might be experiencing some distress. Should I give her more morphine?"

Shouldn't someone more qualified than me be deciding that? Nurse Lucy looked at me expectantly while I thought. I leaned over to Gran. "Gran? Do you want more morphine?"

She didn't answer, but her fingers kept picking at the sheet.

"Will it hurt anything to give her more?" I asked Lucy.

Lucy shook her head, a sad smile on her face. "No. Not at this point."

Her message was clear. Nothing really made a difference at this point. Tears welled up in my eyes. I looked away. "Go ahead then."

Lucy punched some buttons on the box on the IV tree and then left. Gran's fingers stilled. I sat and watched the pattern of the sunlight shift across the room. About twenty minutes after Nurse Lucy left, Gran's eyes suddenly flew open. She stared so intently at the spot where the wall met the ceiling, just to the left of the ceiling-mounted TV, that I turned to look too. There was nothing there. Not even a cobweb.

"What is it, Gran? What are you seeing?"

Gran didn't even glance in my direction. Her lips moved soundlessly and she raised her hands as if to take hold of something being offered down to her.

The hair on the back of my neck stood up. I touched her cheek. "Gran?"

Her eyes swiveled toward me with no sign of recognition or response. She looked back toward the ceiling. The pause between her breaths grew longer. An alarm started going off and Nurse Lucy hurried back in. She pushed more buttons and the beeping stopped.

"More?" Lucy asked me.

Gran's chest heaved with the effort of getting in each breath. She grimaced.

I nodded to Lucy. "Yes. More."

I took hold of my grandmother's hand and held it to my cheek. "It's okay, Gran," I whispered to her. "You can go if you want."

Ten very long minutes later, she did.

*   *   *

I went to the waiting room to make all the phone calls. I called Lily and Stuart's house first. Stuart answered and I left him to tell Lily. Rafe answered on the second ring. "Hello?"

"It's me, Chloe." Then I couldn't say anything more.

"Chloe? Are you there?"

"Yes," I whispered into the phone. "But, Rafe . . ."

"Chloe, is it Gran?"

I couldn't answer, but I figured the sound of me sobbing pretty much answered the question. He asked if he should come and I was able to choke out a no. What would have been the point? I told him to call Jen.

I went back into Gran's room. She was still there, physically at least. I took her hand. The warmth had already left it. Her skin felt waxy and damp, but I held her hand anyway.

Nurse Lucy came in. She put her hand on my shoulder. "You don't have to stay, Chloe. We can take care of the rest."

I shook my head. "I'll stay and wait with her until the funeral home comes."

"If that's what you want, okay. But why don't you go out now? I have to wash her body and prepare it to be picked up."

"No," I said. "I'll stay and help."

Lucy removed the IV tubing from Gran's arm. She rolled Gran's body toward me and I held her as Lucy rolled the sheets up beneath her. Gran's body felt so heavy. You don't realize how responsive the body is until it can't respond anymore. When we're alive, every little push and pull gets a response, gets acknowledged and countered in some minute way. This body that I held now gave me nothing back. She was completely gone. My gran. Gone.

Lucy filled a basin with warm, soapy water and together we washed Gran's frail body. Her thighs were skinny, white, and so vulnerable-looking that my heart clenched. The men from the funeral home arrived just as we finished dressing her in a fresh hospital gown, then I ran a comb through the cotton candy puff of her hair.

As they zipped her into the big black plastic bag that would shield her from curious eyes as they wheeled her from the hospital, my throat closed. It was too much like all those horrible Edgar Allan Poe movies. How would she breathe? Oh, yeah. She didn't need to breathe anymore.

Lucy put her arm around me. "You need to go home now, Chloe."

It was so hard to focus. I knew she was right, though. I nodded.

"Do you want me to call someone? Is there someone who could come get you?"

I wondered how many times had someone asked me that, and I had answered that they should call my grandmother.

CHAPTER FIFTEEN

Chloe's Guide for the Runaway Bride

If planning your wedding feels just like planning a funeral, buy a vowel and get a clue, baby. That relationship is doomed.

The first casserole arrived at eight a.m. the next morning. It was a Mexican one with ground beef and a corn bread topping. By nine-thirty, I had a lasagna, a plate of brownies, and a fruit basket. I was amazed that people already knew Gran was dead, much less knew and had time to cook. I felt like time had stopped, but everything around me was moving so fast that it blurred into a kind of surreal fast-forward movie.

Rafe and Lily and I went to the funeral home and made the necessary choices of casket and lining and timing. Well, Rafe and I made the decisions. Lily did nothing but weep.

The funeral director, a man in his late fifties with a slight New York accent, put his hand over Lily's and said, "You must have been very close."

I excused myself and went to the bathroom. I couldn't bear to hear Lily's response.

We went from the funeral home to the temple to meet

with the rabbi in his office. Lily wept harder. We chose readings and psalms. I went to Gran's empty house and found her address book and then went home. While we were gone, a tuna casserole, a pot of chicken noodle soup, a pasta salad, and a strawberry pie had arrived. I threw out the last of the wedding leftovers, except for the frozen salmon loaf that Gran had made me, called the newspapers in Davis and Winters, and then began to call any friend who hadn't already delivered food.

At some point, Rafe and Clarissa both arrived and took over the phone calls while I went to sit on the porch. Jesse sat next to me, his head in my lap, while we watched the sunlight rake over the hills, throwing everything into relief.

"Have you eaten? Lucy said it was important to make sure you ate." Clarissa stood next to me. I hadn't even heard her come out.

"I think I ate." I honestly wasn't sure, although I thought I remembered something chocolate. It must have been the brownies. "Lucy?"

"From the hospital. The nurse. She and I chatted for quite a while."

I shook my head. "Clarissa, I think she's straight."

"You're wrong." Clarissa grinned. "Queer as a three dollar bill and, for the record, she kissed me. You have absolutely no gaydar."

"Seriously? Oh, Clarissa, I'm so happy for you." I should have noticed; her face was literally beaming.

"Are the phone calls all done?"

"I think so." She sat down on the chair next to me. "Wanna talk?"

I shook my head.

"Get drunk?"

That had momentary appeal, but only momentary. I shook my head again.

"Wanna just sit?" She put her hand on my shoulder.

"Yeah. I think so." I tried to focus on the lengthening shadows, to watch their progress across the yellow hills without thinking or feeling. There would be plenty of time for thinking and feeling later, I suspected. More than enough.

Clarissa sat down next to me. Aziza gave her toes a snuffle, but seemed to understand it was no time to try to bite them. Rafe came out a few minutes later with wedges of pie and beer for everyone, and we all sat and watched the shadows until darkness fell and shadows were all there were.

I got up the next morning, fed the dogs, showered, and threw on jeans and a tank top. Jesse and Aziza started barking so I looked out the window. Dear Lord, it was Til and another woman and some kids in a beat-up station wagon that had an inch of road dust on it. I headed down the drive.

The driver's door opened and a woman who looked like a slightly younger version of Til with hair a slightly less garish red got out and walked very deliberately to the gate, staring at me all the while as if I were an alien that had landed right in front of her. She turned back to the car and said, "I'm sorry I didn't believe you, Til. It's just as bad as you said."

"It's just hair." I clenched my jaw.

Til got out of the car too. "Can you fix it, Susan?"

Susan craned her neck around to try to look at the rest of my head. "It'll take some time. Your grandmother, huh?"

"Yes. My grandmother."

She nodded. "We loved our nona very much. She practically raised us. I think I can make this right, but you're going to lose some length."

Forty minutes later, I had layers cut all around and it was short enough that my ears peeped through. Surprise of surprises, my hair actually curled when the length of it didn't weigh it down, so it waved around my face. It hadn't been this short since sometime in grade school.

They were just packing up to leave when Daniel arrived. I couldn't decide if it was an accident or if they were purposefully tag-teaming me so I wouldn't be alone. The second I stepped into Daniel's arms, I decided I didn't care.

"What do you think, green plates or clear?" Jen held two stacks of plastic plates out to me. We were standing in Party City, buying supplies for the reception that was to follow my grandmother's burial. "They don't have black. Besides, that seems . . . I don't know, unnecessarily gloomy."

"It's a funeral, Jen. Black is pretty much the theme color." The fluorescent lights threw everything into high relief, making everything look terribly sharp.

"Says who?"

I blinked. My eyes felt like they had sand embedded in them, or like I might have put my contact lenses in inside out. "I think it's one of those universal things. I don't think we get to choose."

"Well, I don't see any rule books out there telling us what we can and can't do, and the rabbi certainly didn't say that everything had to be black. I like green. It makes me think of growing things and flowers and gardens. Gran would have liked it. Besides, these green ones have matching napkins and they're nice and sturdy. We want ones that are stiff." Jen picked up two more stacks of the green plates.

"Lord knows, you want stiff at a funeral." I felt horrid laughter burbling in the back of my throat and fought like hell to tamp it down. It was no use, though. I began braying guffaws.

Jen's eyes got huge. "Chloe, what is the matter with you?"

I wished I could tell her. I wished I could make it stop. Instead, I pointed at the endcap where the Halloween supplies were all on sale. "Look, Jen, there are black plates there. Or do you think the little ghosts would just be too-too."

"Chloe, if you are not going to help me, maybe you should go wait in the car." Jen's lips had tightened into a hard straight little line. Funny, I hadn't really noticed before how much she looked like Gran until just that moment.

I wiped my eyes. "No, Jen. I'm sorry. I'll behave. I'm just . . . I mean, I'm so . . ." Overwhelmed by the absurdity of picking a theme color to decorate for the funeral of the woman I'd always thought of as my grandmother? I don't know why that would be it. Especially after the absurdities of arguing over the food.

I thought we should serve some of the ten thousand casseroles that had arrived. Jen thought we should have it catered. Rafe didn't care as long as there was enough booze. Lily just cried, although I suspected she agreed with Rafe. Oh, and then don't forget discussing what we were going to wear and what music would be played.

All in all, it really wasn't all that much different from planning my un-wedding, right down to the little lump of dread at the bottom of my stomach.

Jen shook her head and thrust the shopping basket filled with plates and napkins at me. "Fine. Take these. I'm going to look for some plastic wineglasses. I know they're tacky, but people will just have to understand that we're not up to doing dishes."

"No, of course we won't be." It came out sounding more sarcastic than I'd meant it to sound.

"Chloe," Jen repeated with a warning note in her voice.

I took my basket and headed toward the checkout stand.

I walked into the Green Creek that afternoon.

"What are you doing here?" Til asked.

I looked up at the clock. "It's time for my shift to start."

"Chloe, you don't have to be here today." Matt, Don, and Rob were watching baseball, but other than that, no one was there. She didn't really need me to be there.

I needed to be there. Everything at the bungalow made me think of Gran, and I wasn't ready for that yet. Jen and Stuart were going through her papers at her place and I couldn't stand to watch that, either. This was one place that had no association with my Gran at all. "Please, Til."

Her eyes misted up and for a second it looked like she might hug me again. I didn't think I could take that right now and still hold it together. I brushed past her and went to hang out with Matt and watch the Cubs get their asses beat by the Cardinals. Rob spent the next hour trying to explain to me why when a walk brings the tying run to the plate, it keeps them from pitching to the inside.

"He's just up and out," Rob said. "He needs to pitch outside, but this is getting out of hand."

I heard the door open and close, but didn't turn around. Til could deal with whoever the new customer was. Then I heard the creak and slap of the hinged part of the bar going up and down, and turned to see Karen. At least I thought it was Karen. Instead of her usual perky blond ponytail pulled through her baseball cap, however, her hair hung around her face in greasy locks. Red rimmed her puffy eyes and her nose looked positively swollen. "Karen?"

She waved a hand at me, dumped out the old coffee and started making a fresh pot.

"Are you okay?"

Again with the hand wave. Rob and Matt had lost all interest in baseball and were completely focused on her. Til came around too. Karen finished dumping the water in the coffeepot reservoir and turned around to find all of us staring at her. She took a big, deep, trembly breath and said, "Malcolm dumped me."

Til put her arms around Karen and Karen started to sob. "He said I was mean," she wailed. "Me! Mean!"

She sounded just like Troy, except not nearly so cute. Til patted her. "Poor baby," she murmured.

Poor baby? Poor baby snake in the grass, maybe.

"He said she never says he's stupid. He said she's nicer than me," Karen sniveled onto Til's shoulder.

"Who's nicer than you?" The words left my mouth and I realized it was kind of like asking who was younger than dirt, but there they were.

"Melanie," Karen wailed.

"Who's Melanie?"

"The girl. The one he was supposed to have the date with. The one we were supposed to laugh at. Now they're laughing at me." Karen pushed Til away and grabbed a bar napkin and blew her nose.

Striped Shirt? Malcolm had dumped Karen for Striped Shirt? It was too good to be true. "How did this happen?" I gasped.

"He showed up on Friday night!" Karen threw her hands in the air. "Can you believe it?"

With everything that had happened since then, I'd completely forgotten Malcolm showing up.

It was eleven-thirty. The service had started at eleven and was almost over. We'd made it through the eulogy and several readings and a little bit of singing. In a minute, we'd say kaddish and my grandmother's funeral would be over. Presto finito abracadabra voilà.

The rabbi asked if anyone else would like to speak. Mary Alice raised her hand and the rabbi motioned her forward. She came to the pulpit, pulled a crumpled piece of paper from her pocket, and cleared her throat. "I've written a poem in memory of my friend, Naomi."

Rafe's head swiveled very slowly in my direction. Our eyes met and then we both quickly looked away. I wasn't sure I could make it through a Mary Alice poem at that moment. I knew I wouldn't make it through if I looked at Rafe.

"I met Naomi one day in Winters," Mary Alice intoned.

I felt a mule bray of laughter gathering in the back of my throat, even worse than the one in Party City with Jen. I gritted my teeth hard.

Clarissa patted my hand and leaned over to whisper in my ear. "I'm so glad your grandmother didn't live in Nantucket."

I jerked forward and covered my face with a tissue, praying that everyone would think I was overcome with grief and crying. It wouldn't do for them to know that I was choking back a phenomenal case of the giggles.

"You did a beautiful job, Chloe. Very appropriate," Mary Alice told me as she shook my hand on her way out of the temple.

If she only knew how very inappropriate I'd been. Nobody except Clarissa knew, so I was hoping it didn't count. She was, however, about the fifteenth person to tell me that. "Thank you."

"Your grandmother would be very proud."

"I'm glad you think so." She was about the twentieth person to say that to me. I glanced over at Rafe, who stood next to me. Eric Godfrey had his hand on Rafe's shoulder and Rafe was nodding and agreeing with whatever Eric was saying. When Eric finally released him and he'd been hugged sufficiently by Mary Alice, he whispered to me, "I don't know how much more of this I can take."

I looked at the line of people waiting to pay their condolences to us and did a double take when I saw Officer Musciano. What on earth was he doing here? How had he even known my grandmother had died? On the other hand, should you really be surprised to see your stalker anywhere? "Maybe five more minutes, max," I said.

Lily was on the other side of Rafe from me, but I thought I could smell the alcohol on her breath from here. Enough people (can you really call them guests at a funeral?) recoiled from her hug to make me certain that it wasn't just my imagination. I wondered how much longer she'd last without either some food to shore her up or more alcohol to keep her from feeling any pain.

On the other side of me, Jen shifted from foot to foot. I looked down. She had on pointy-toed sling-backs. "What on earth possessed you to wear those shoes?" I asked.

"They go with the dress." Her mouth was a stubborn line.

"You're pregnant. No one cares about your shoes. You could have showed up in bunny slippers and no one would have thought badly of you."

"They go with the dress," she repeated.

I dropped it and let her shift back and forth. The whole day had been like this: everyone was raw and touchy and easy to bruise. I've heard that tragedies bring some families together.

Not ours.

"She left you the bungalow," Jen whispered.

"What?" I said out of the side of my mouth while trying to smile and look gracious while I shook hands with the pharmacist from the Winters drugstore where Gran always had her prescription filled. He'd probably known more about how bad her health was than I had.

"Gran. She left the bungalow to you." Jen rocked back on her heels and winced.

"You're kidding."

She scowled up at me. "In case you haven't noticed, I'm not exactly in a kidding around mood right now."

The bungalow was mine. Really mine. I'd been coming to feel like it was mine as it took shape around me, but now it was really true. How had Gran known? I couldn't wait to go back there.

I looked longingly to where the line of people headed into the room where the food was. Clarissa had gone ahead to make sure the caterer had set things up the way we'd asked.

"Officer Musciano, thank you so much for coming. I didn't know you knew my grandmother," I said when he came through the line.

"I saw you heading into town all dressed up. I figured something was up so I came to check it out. You know, in case you needed help again. I'm so sorry for your loss." His mustache quivered.

Everyone was very sorry for my loss. If one more person told me they were sorry for my loss, I was afraid I might lose it completely.

We all trooped into the other room. Except for Rafe, who practically sprinted.

"I want to find Til and Hunter," he said. "Tell me if this sounds crazy, Chloe. What if, in every situation, I chose to do the opposite of what Stuart or Dad would do? Do you think I'd end up being a good father?"

"It can't be a bad way to start."

"Okay. Good. Now, tell me if this sounds even crazier. What if by constantly doing the opposite of what Stuart or Dad would have done, I actually undo what they did somehow?"

"You mean like some kind of karmic undoing?"

"Yeah, maybe. Or maybe not even that deep. I just don't do the harm they did to one person who might be able to not harm the next one in the line. Stupid, huh?" He finally spotted Hunter, who had spotted him, too, and was waving frantically at him.

"No, Rafe. Not stupid at all." I thought about Spot and Jesse and Aziza and all the unwanted little creatures I had tried to make a home for. I didn't think it was stupid at all. Rafe left me standing by the door.

Then someone was shoving a plate of food in my hand. "Here. You look like you're going to fall over. Eat this."

It was Daniel, knowing just what I needed without me telling him. I started to thank him.

"Don't talk. Just eat."

I took a bite of pasta salad. My stomach growled and I swayed a bit. "I guess I was hungrier than I knew."

He put a hand under my elbow to steady me. "And probably more exhausted, too. How about I drive you home when this is all over?"

I thought for a second I was going to cry, but I was afraid if I started, I wouldn't stop. "Okay," I mumbled through the pasta.

"Do you want me to get you a drink?"

I nodded and looked around the room. A bunch of my friends were there. Besides Clarissa, who was having a very cozy chat with Nurse Lucy and Daniel, I saw Vicky over by the brownies. She was standing with . . . Officer Musciano? I started toward them.

"Run," Vicky mouthed at me from across the room.

It only took me a second to figure out why she was saying it: I recognized the smell of his cologne. I turned and said, "Hello, Mark, it's good to see you. Home from your honeymoon?"

He shut his eyes. "I'm sorry about that. I was hurt. I know it was childish, but I couldn't help myself."

He had a right to be angry. I knew that. "I'm sorry, too," I said and found I really meant it.

He pulled a chair out at the table we were standing next to. "Do you have a minute to sit down?"

I sat and he sat down next to me.

"So what's new?" I asked.

"It was my fault, Chloe. I knew you didn't want the big wedding. I knew you didn't want all the fuss, and I pushed you to do it. I didn't know it would push you right over the edge. I'm so sorry," he blurted.

Tears sprang to my eyes. I hadn't realized how much I'd wanted the responsibility for the fiasco to be shifted to other shoulders. I felt like a weight had literally been lifted off of them.

"I didn't know either, Mark. I thought . . . well, I thought it was just like a lot of other things. That I could make it through. I just couldn't, though."

"So you forgive me?" Mark reached over and tucked a strand of hair behind my ear. "You want to try again, too?"

I leaned back in shock. Try again? That thought hadn't occurred to me. "Mark, I don't know . . ."

He held up his hands to cut me off. "It wouldn't have to be like before, Chloe. It could be just you and me in front of a justice of the peace. No crowds. No muss. No fuss. This whole episode can be a funny story we tell our grandchildren."

Mark would have it planned right down to our future grandchildren. Everything would be set out neatly and logically, with a specific path to follow. I just had to mind and be reasonable. It would be easy in a lot of ways to go back with him. I knew everything I needed to know, and really, Mark wasn't a bad person. But he had a vision of how he wanted everything to be—me, included—and I wasn't sure that it was a vision that could ever be realized.

I wasn't sure that I ever *wanted* it to be realized.

"What about your new job?" I asked.

He leaned back, surprised. "You know about that?"

"I've heard rumors."

"I think you'd love New Hampshire. It's beautiful in the fall, Chloe." He leaned forward, straightened my skirt, and took my hands. "It would get you away from all this stuff that makes you so crazy." He cast a meaningful look at Clarissa and Rafe.

Did they make me crazy? The lot of them certainly were nearly certifiable. I didn't think they made me crazy, though. In fact, I suspected they were precisely what kept me from going completely nuts.

I drew my hands back. Leaving here would also get me away from my chance to go back for my Ph.D. and from the new life I was starting to build for myself.

Away from anyone and everything except him. I finally realized what else was bothering me about all this. "How long have
you known about New Hampshire?"

Mark's face grew red. "A few months."

"You knew before the wedding that you were going to move
away from here?"

He went redder. "I was waiting for the right time to tell
you. I knew you were stressed out about the wedding. I didn't
want to add to that." He picked a little piece of lint off my
blouse.

I brushed his hand away. "And when would that right time
have been, Mark? When you had my stuff packed into the moving van?" I felt like I'd been looking at everything Mark did
through a kaleidoscope, and suddenly it had whirled back into
the whole picture instead of little fragments. All the corrections
and criticisms, all the efforts to isolate me, all the work of keeping me in my place, came together into one big controlling
image.

Gran had been righter than she'd known when she said I was
just like Lily. I was an unwanted baby, just like my mother had
been, and until the voice told me to run, I'd been grasping at
every self-defeating, self-critical thing in my reach.

Maybe the craziest thing I'd ever done was actually the
sanest. Things aren't necessarily what they seem from the
outside.

I stood up. "No, Mark, I can't. I won't. Please leave."

"Chloe, listen to me, just for a minute." He grabbed my
hands and tried to pull me back into my seat.

I tried to pull my hands out of his grasp. He let go, but he
grabbed hold of my forearm instead.

"Let go of me, Mark. Right now."

"Not until you listen to me. Not until you see how reasonable I'm being about this. I'm willing to forget about these past few weeks."

"I'm not willing to forget about them." I pulled at his fingers to try to get loose.

Then Daniel was there, setting a sparkling water down on the table next to me. "I think you need to let Chloe go."

Mark stood, still not letting loose of me. He was two or three inches taller than Daniel and he made sure to pull himself to his full height. "I'm Chloe's fiancé. Who are you?"

Daniel didn't budge. "I'm Chloe's boyfriend, and I'm pretty sure she doesn't have a fiancé anymore. I'm equally sure that she'd appreciate your letting go of her. She's certainly let go of you."

The entire room had gone silent, and every eye was on us.

Mark must have felt it too. He dropped my arm. "This is it, Chloe. This is your last chance. Come with me now, or it's over."

"It's been over for a while, Mark," I said quietly.

He turned and left, and it was as if the entire room took a collective breath and sighed.

I turned to Daniel. "You're my boyfriend?"

"Too juvenile? I know it sounds kind of high school, but lover didn't sound right since we haven't, uh, you know. . . ." He stammered to a stop, then forged on. "Friend of the family didn't seem to cut it either, and veterinarian sounded wrong for a whole other set of reasons."

I put my finger to his lips. "Boyfriend is good. Really, really good."

He swallowed hard. "Feel like getting out of here?"

I looked around the room. There would be a lot to do when everyone was done eating and drinking, but maybe someone else could take care of it for once. I was sure Til could marshall the forces.

"Yeah. I do. I just want to take a quick trip to the ladies' room first."

I pushed open the swinging door in the restroom and stumbled directly into Jen and Lily. Lily had draped her arm across Jen's shoulder, and Jen was supporting Lily with an arm around her waist.

"What are you doing?" I grabbed Lily from Jen and shifted her weight onto my shoulder. She smelled of booze and vomit. "You're going to hurt yourself," I told Jen.

"I'm trying to get her to the back door. Daddy's pulling the car around," Jen gasped. "I didn't know what else to do."

"Stop. I'll do it. Come on, Lily."

"Chloe!" Lily said as if she'd just noticed me standing there even though I was supporting most of her weight. "There you are."

"Yes, Lily, I'm here. At Gran's funeral. Where you're so drunk, you can't even walk." We headed off toward the door with Jen hovering around us like a very fat bumblebee.

"Glad she's gone," Lily muttered.

"Mom!" Jen looked around us to see if anyone was around to hear.

I guess expressing happiness that your mother has just died doesn't put you in the "normal" family range. Or maybe it was just the falling down drunk thing that was bothering Jen.

"She ruined everything. Everything. She even ruined you for me," Lily slurred. "I'd come to pick you up from her place, and you'd cling to her leg like she was your mother and I was some interloper."

I knew what she meant. I remembered those times.

"You never wanted me anyway," I replied under my breath.

"What do you mean, I never wanted you? What's that supposed to mean? Did she tell you that I didn't want you?" Lily stopped cooperating in our progress toward the door.

I stared at her, amazed. "You told me you didn't want me. You told me you tried to shake me loose. Dad told me about you throwing yourself down the stairs so you would miscarry."

"Bastard," Lily hissed.

"Don't blame him for being honest. All he did was confirm what you'd been telling me my whole life. That I was a burden, a pain, an extra unwanted responsibility."

"That's simply not true, Chloe. My children are my whole life." Lily could be *soooo* melodramatic when she was drunk. Tears coursed down her face. "You don't understand, Chloe. You weren't raised by that woman—with her constant criticism, her steady reproaches about everything I did and said and wore and was. You don't know."

"Of course I know. The same woman raised me, Lily." I managed to half drag and half carry her to the back door, and open it. Stuart waited outside with the car.

"Chloe," he said. "I was expecting Jen."

"Yeah, well, I thought it might be nice if someone who wasn't massively pregnant dragged their drunken mother to the door."

Stuart at least had the decency to flush. "Someone had to bring the car around."

"And sit in the air-conditioning while the pregnant girl carried your wife around?" I snapped.

He clenched his jaw, but didn't say anything more as he

belted Lily into the passenger seat. I watched them drive away before I went back in. Jennifer leaned up against the wall, completely overcome with tears.

"Poor Mom," Jennifer gasped out between half-strangled sobs.

My face felt like a mask, incapable of moving. "Why poor Mom?" My lips felt numb. It surprised me that I could even get them to say three words.

Jen's face was a swollen blotchy mess. Mascara ringed her eyes. "Now she'll never be able to make peace with Gran. She'll never get closure. And poor us. We're all stuck now too."

If I thought my face would obey, I would have rolled my eyes. What closure could those two have? Besides, if closure was going to help, they'd had sixty years to make it happen. "She had plenty of chances," I said, unsure of which "she" I was speaking about.

"That's what's so sad." Jen blew her nose hard. "They had all those opportunities. They thought they'd always have more, and now they don't. Now Mom will always have to wonder what would have happened if one of them had said something at just the right time. Or had hugged the other one at a moment when comfort was needed. Or had forgiven a thoughtless remark. Mom will never know what might have happened. All her chances are gone."

David came around the corner, carrying a sleeping Troy against his shoulder. "Where have you been, honey? I've been worried." He looked from her to me and back to her again.

"Lily got drunk and Jen was trying to help her to the car," I said, not feeling like dressing things up for David at this point. "Jen needs to go home."

He nodded. "So does Troy."

"I'll go say good-bye to everyone," Jen said, and went back to the reception with David following.

I stared after them. Closure. It was a stupid, overused term, but maybe Jen had a point. Hadn't closure been why I'd been so dogged in my pursuit of the truth about Lily's birth? Now that I knew, what was I going to do about it?

I followed Jen and David back into the reception. Daniel was over talking to Rafe, Til, Clarissa, and Nurse Lucy.

"We killed her. We killed Gran," Rafe was saying.

A chill went over me. "What the hell are you talking about, Rafe?"

"All that morphine. We killed her. We're talking physician-assisted suicide."

I looked to Nurse Lucy for help. "Did we kill her? Did we kill my grandmother?"

Lucy looked distinctly uncomfortable. "Define 'kill.' "

I shut my eyes and counted to ten and then spoke very slowly. "How much longer would my grandmother have lived if we hadn't given her morphine?"

She shrugged. "Ten hours. Maybe twelve."

"And what would those hours have been like?"

"Terrible. She would have been gasping for every breath. Every second would have been a struggle."

I turned and looked at Rafe, who said, "I didn't mean that we killed Gran in a bad way."

What was with these people? Were they all nuts?

Of course they were. They were my family.

David came up behind me, Troy still on his hip, and tapped me on the shoulder. "Chloe, Jen's . . . uh . . . well, she's . . . um . . . spilled her tulips."

"Tulips? What tulips?" I remembered lots of lilies, orchids, and roses, but no tulips.

David blushed harder. "I mean, she . . ."

Jen came up then, clutching her stomach. "Chloe, my water broke. I need to go to the hospital."

"Who's watching Troy?" I asked.

Jen's face crumpled. "Mom's supposed to."

"Give him to me," I said, and held out my arms.

CHAPTER SIXTEEN

Chloe's Guide for the Runaway Bride

We create rituals to mark the important turning points in our lives and to imbue them with the significance that they deserve. We need rituals to force us to stop and contemplate the magnitude of births and deaths, beginnings and endings. It simplifies things when they happen all at once, though.

I don't think babysitting a three-year-old was precisely what Daniel had had in mind when he'd suggested leaving the funeral. I had a very strong sense he had been suggesting something entirely different, but really, what could be more life-affirming than taking care of the next generation? Okay, sex might be more life-affirming, but it would simply have to wait.

Troy hadn't been terribly thrilled with the plan either. He didn't much like the idea of his mommy going in one car and him in another one, even after we transferred his car seat with the special steering wheel toy on it into my truck.

So far, I'd tried to distract him with a stop at the bungalow to feed the dogs who had been beyond thrilled to play fetch with him. Then we tried a trip to McDonalds. Jen would know who to blame if he grew breasts, but the happy half hour in the ball pit was more than worth it, as far as I was concerned.

"Where's Daddy car?" Troy asked for the twenty-seventh time at least.

"Daddy's car is taking Mommy to the hospital so she can have the baby that's been growing inside her," I explained. Again.

Daniel glanced over at me. I'd let him drive so I could concentrate on Troy. He smiled.

"How will baby get out?" Troy asked.

Daniel's eyebrows climbed an inch or two. After a moment of utter panic, I said, "That's an excellent question, Troy. We'll have to ask her when she gets home."

Troy looked at me with his eyes slightly narrowed. He wasn't stupid and I had a feeling he knew I was shining him on, but apparently the rocking motion of the truck after a long day was more than his little three-year-old body could handle, and he fell asleep.

"So what now?" Daniel asked.

"Take him home and tuck him into bed, I guess. Do you want to go get your truck before I go?"

"Trying to get rid of me?" he asked with a smile.

"Absolutely not."

"Then tell me how to get to your sister's house." I leaned back in my seat. Daniel took my hand and held it all the way to Concord.

Troy hadn't woken up when I'd carried him in from the truck or even blinked as I'd put him in a dry diaper and then tucked him into his sweet little bed. I thought his body relaxed just a little bit more as it hit the familiar Thomas the Tank Engine sheets. He was home, and he knew it. I kissed his forehead and his mouth made its funny little round pucker.

When I came out into the family room Daniel had the base-ball game on. The Diamondbacks were up three to two over the Pirates. It was a full count with two outs and a runner on sec-ond. I cuddled in next to Daniel on the couch. It was only seven o'clock, but I was exhausted—physically, mentally, and emotionally. I fell into a deep, dreamless sleep before the inning was up.

I think Daniel must have fallen asleep as well, because when David came in at ten-thirty, the door made its triple-beep and we both jumped and clunked heads.

David sank down into the armchair with a tired grin. "What do you guys do for your next act? Throw pies at each other?"

"Well?" I said.

He leaned his head back. "A little girl. A beautiful baby girl with a cloud of black hair and the most amazingly long fingers I've ever seen on a baby. I have a daughter."

He looked so dazed and amazed, my eyes filled with tears. "Wow."

"Yeah. Wow." He sat up a little straighter. "It was the weird-est thing. The nurse handed her to me, all wrapped up, and she looked into my eyes and . . . I don't know how to describe it, but it was as if she already knew me. Almost like she knew a lot of things. Like she was . . ."

"An old soul?" Daniel asked.

"Exactly." David looked over at him. "That was exactly what it was like. Like she was an old soul."

"And Jen?" I asked.

"A total trooper." He rubbed his face with his hands. "It isn't easy to push something that size out and still be worried about what your hair looks like. She's amazing."

"When can I see her?"

"Jen says no one's allowed to visit until I bring her makeup bag and some decent clothes. She had a bag all packed, but it was here and not in the car, and stubborn me refused to come here before I took her to the hospital. She's still a little pissed about that." He yawned. "Good thing I didn't listen, though. She was already at eight centimeters when we walked in. I'll take it to her tomorrow morning when I take Troy to see her. You can probably all go to-morrow afternoon. Will you call Rafe and Lily for me?"

"Of course. Do you want us to stay tonight?"

He shook his head. "Nah. I got it covered."

I called Rafe from the truck while Daniel drove. He answered on the first ring. "She had a girl, Rafe. A beautiful healthy girl."

"Hold on," he said and I heard him relaying the information and then I heard Til squeal. "How big?"

"Seven pounds, two ounces. Eighteen inches. And you're not allowed to go visit tomorrow until after David brings Jen her makeup bag."

"Got it."

I called Lily next. Stuart answered. "David asked me to call. Jennifer had a baby girl."

"Thank you," Stuart said. "I appreciate your letting me know." He sounded about as excited as if I'd just reported that Jen had gotten her hair done.

"Can I talk to Lily?"

"She's tired, Chloe. Can't it wait until tomorrow?"

Ah, yes, I'd forgotten. Lily was very, very tired.

Daniel drove back to his truck and promised to meet me back home a little later.

Home. It had a very nice ring to it.

I drove in, looking at it all with fresh eyes. There was still a lot of construction debris lying around, but it was coming along.

The dogs were waiting for me, uncharacteristically quiet and calm. I got them food and fresh water. The notebook of Jesse's letters sat on the table among the piles of cakes and cookies that various neighbors had delivered. The notebook was surprisingly heavy—all that paper, all that sentiment. I wondered how different it all would have been if Jesse had made it home to his Laura. Who would my mother have been if she'd been raised by him and her real mother?

I thought about the last conversation I'd had with Gran before her collapse. What had she said? That people make mistakes? She'd thought of my mother as a mistake that needed to be corrected her whole life, and that had colored the way she'd seen her and treated her.

Who would Lily have been if she'd known that unconditional mother-love that Gran had simply not been able to give her, but had somehow been able to give to Rafe and me? Who would I be if I'd been raised by a mother who didn't see a child as something that always needed to be corrected?

I put my head down on the notebook, wishing that all that love trapped in those brittle pages and fading words could somehow seep into my body.

None of it really mattered now. Everyone was dead. Laura, Jesse, Granda, and Gran. All gone.

Well, maybe not *all* gone. There was a new little Naomi in the world.

Maybe Rafe was right. Maybe we *did* have an opportunity to undo all the damage that had been done.

Maybe Lily did have another chance. Not a chance to really make things right with Gran, but she could at least know that her mother had truly loved her.

That would be a closure worth having, wouldn't it?

*   *   *

I called Daniel and asked him to give me a couple hours. It would take me close to an hour to get to Stuart and Lily's house in Walnut Creek.

There were lights on in the house when I got there, though. I pushed the bell and waited, and then pushed again. And again.

Stuart flung open the door. "Who the hell . . . Oh, it's you, Chloe." He didn't invite me in.

"I need to see Lily."

"Now's not exactly a good time," he said, bracing one arm against the door frame and blocking my entrance.

"Sorry about that, but I need to talk to her now." I clutched the notebook to my chest and tried to duck past him, but he shifted to stop me again.

"You should have called first, Chloe. I would have told you to wait and come in the morning."

I took a deep breath to try and focus myself. "Look, Stuart, I don't care how drunk she is; I need to tell her about something. Something to do with her and Gran."

He just stood there with his arms crossed. "Nothing about your gran could possibly be urgent anymore, Chloe. Go home."

"Stuart?" Lily's voice wavered out of the interior of the house. "Stuart, who's there?"

Before he could stop me, I yelled back. "It's me, Mom. It's Chloe. I need to talk to you."

"Then come in and talk, for Pete's sake. Stop hanging around at the door."

I looked up at Stuart and he dropped his arm, but gave me that blank-faced, bland stare that had struck terror in me ever since I was eight years old and understood how cruel he could be. I swallowed hard and brushed past him, intent on doing what I needed to do before my courage failed me.

Lily was in the family room, tipped back in a recliner chair, a glass of clear liquid nearby on an end table. Judging by the trouble she had getting her eyes to focus on me, it probably wasn't water.

I turned the TV off and pulled a chair up next to her. "Mom, I need to show you something."

I showed her most of it, but I especially wanted her to see Jesse's letters about baby Corazon. I wanted her to understand how much Laura loved the baby, how you could see that in Jesse's replies to her.

Then I showed her the birth certificate.

"Do you know what this means, Mom? Gran was not your mother," I said, pointing to the dates.

Lily looked up at me, eyes bleary and unfocused. "So?"

"So? So?" I took her hands in mine. "Gran was *not* your mother. Aunt Laura was your mother. Your father died after the D-Day invasion. Somewhere in Germany, a place called Wiesbaden. Jesse and Laura never got a chance to get married. Gran raised you so Aunt Laura could avoid the shame of having an illegitimate child."

Lily stared at me, her mouth slightly agape.

"Don't you see? Gran never forgave Jesse Hernandez for getting her sister pregnant and then abandoning her, even though he hadn't wanted to do that. You were the product of that relationship. She thought you had ruined her sister's life. That's why she always treated you the way she did. It wasn't you; it was your father that she hated. Every time she looked at you, she saw Jesse. She couldn't help it."

"I was just a kid," Lily slurred.

"Yeah. You were. A kid without a mother. Don't you see, Lily? You weren't rejected by your mother. Aunt Laura loved you."

Lily pulled her hands out of mine and waved one of them in

the air. "Ancient history, Chloe. I don't even know why you're bringing it up."

I needed her to understand. I needed her to see. "Because it changes everything, Mom. Don't you see that? Knowing this changes everything."

Lily handed the notebook back to me. "It doesn't change anything, Chloe. Besides, I've known this for years."

I sat there, stunned. "You knew?"

"Since I was sixteen." Lily picked up her glass and took a long sip.

"How did you find out?"

She spit an ice cube back into the glass. "Laura told me. The bitch."

"When? Why?" I gasped.

Lily set her glass down. "I was dating some boy. Can't remember his name right now. Timmy? Tony? Something like that. Your precious Gran caught us in the orchard one day. Must have told Laura all about it. She came to give me some big speech about the evils of sex. How it was going to ruin my life, just like it had ruined hers."

"And she told you then? She told you that you were her daughter?"

Lily snorted. "Yeah. Didn't want me to get pregnant and ruin my life like I had ruined hers. Wanted to be a real mother to me and show me the error of my ways. Told me that she loved me so much, she gave me up so I could have a real life. Not just be somebody's bastard."

I couldn't believe it. Lily had known all long about Laura. And nothing had changed.

Or had it? "And then what happened? What did you do, Lily?"

Lily's head moved so slowly that at first, I didn't realize that she was shaking it "no." "Didn't matter. What does it matter if some other relative loved me? The woman I called mother never loved me. How worthless do you have to be for your own mother to not love you?"

She wasn't even crying, which made it worse. Maybe it would have been better if Lily had done her usual Drama Queen thing and tossed herself around in hysterics. Instead, she just sat there dull-eyed, staring at me. "And what kind of mother would stand by and watch that? If she really loved me, she wouldn't have let that old bitch treat me like that."

I stared back.

I stared back at this woman I almost never called mother, and saw myself reflected in the glaze that covered her eyes.

I didn't know the answer to her question. How worthless *did* you have to be for your own mother to not love you? How low do you have to be for not a single, solitary other soul to offer you unconditional love? Even your own child.

Lily said Gran had ruined me for her, and looking back now, I could see all the little ways that Gran had put Lily down in front of me, had shown her disapproval and disappointment. And I'd eaten it up with a spoon.

I put my arms around my mother's neck and hugged her close. "I'm so sorry, Mom," I said. "I just thought you should know. Can I help you get to bed?"

Lily nodded. I steadied her as we walked down the hall, then helped her out of her clothes. Her eyelids were drooping as I pulled her nightgown over her head. I tucked her under the covers.

"Good night, Mom. I love you." I smoothed her hair back off her forehead.

She grabbed my hand and gave it a kiss. " 'Night, baby. Love you too."

I was almost out the door when she stopped me. "Chloe?"

"Yeah, Mom?"

"I like your new haircut. It suits you."

"Thanks. Go to sleep now."

"Okay."

Stuart was waiting as I left the bedroom, a looming shadow in the dim hallway. "You know she's probably not going to remember a word of this conversation tomorrow."

"She already knew anyway," I said, brushing past him. "I guess it wasn't as important as I thought."

CHAPTER SEVENTEEN

Chloe's Guide for the Runaway Bride

So, you didn't get married. Maybe that will turn out to be
the best thing that could have happened to you.

I stumbled from the truck to open my gate; fatigue washed over
me in waves. When I collapsed at the table, Jesse whimpered a
little. "Hush, boy," I muttered and patted his head.

Aziza shoved her nose in for a pat as well, poor, unwanted
baby that she was. Just like Mom. Just like me.

"Don't you worry. You're a good girl." Aziza whined in return.

Except Mom hadn't really been an unwanted baby. Laura
had wanted her. Jesse had wanted her. She'd known that. Or at
least she'd known since she was sixteen and Laura had spilled her
guts, only to be rejected by her own daughter. Mom had had the
chance to be loved, but she'd shoved it away.

Instead, Lily had clung to the thing she'd come to think
of as love: Gran's disapproval. And she'd passed that disapproval down like the legacy it was. The legacy of the unwanted child.

I'd been about to keep the legacy going myself until that
voice in my head said, "Run." Mark had been clever and subtle

about how he'd put me down and tried to keep me down, but not so clever and subtle that other people hadn't noticed. When would I have noticed it myself?

I unwrapped a piece of candy from one of the bowls that had been delivered and popped it into my mouth. Mmmm. Green apple. My favorite Jolly Rancher flavor.

So Lily had known who her mother really was since 1962. Suddenly, the math came clear in my head. Laura had died when my mother was sixteen. The year she'd told my mother whose daughter she really was. What if her death hadn't been an accident?

I gasped at what that might mean, and suddenly I couldn't breathe—I'd gasped the Jolly Rancher right down into my windpipe. I tried to gulp, but nothing could get past the Jolly Rancher. Was this it? Was I really going to die just like my grandmother—my real grandmother—alone in her house, that was now my house?

Panic gripped me. I couldn't think of anything except air, and I couldn't get any of that. A giant fist was squeezing my heart and I couldn't think straight. The edges of the kitchen started to go gray. My vision narrowed down to a pinpoint tunnel. Then a voice inside my head said, "Run."

So I did.

I ran out of the room and down the hall. I didn't know where or why I was going. Jesse flung himself in front of me, tripping me. I went flying, my arms stretched in front of me like Superman. After what seemed like an interminable slow motion flight down the hall, I slammed flat on my chest onto the newly refinished hardwood floor, and the Jolly Rancher popped out like a cork from underchilled champagne.

Oxygen rushed in. Within seconds, my field of vision returned. I gulped and gulped and gulped at the air. Jesse licked my face. Aziza ran a series of circles around us.

We were still on the floor when Daniel came in and found us.

We sat on the couch eating tuna casserole with crushed potato chips on top from the Hilberts, two farms over. Nothing says comfort like something made with cream of mushroom soup.

"So you self-Heimliched?" Daniel asked.

I took a long drink of water. My throat was still scratchy from the Jolly Rancher's expulsion. "No. Jesse Heimliched it out of me."

"Jesse's a dog. He has no thumbs. He can't Heimlich." Daniel took another big bite of his casserole and chewed. "Tripping you doesn't count as a first aid procedure."

"All I know is that I heard that voice telling me to run, and when I did, Jesse tripped me in just the right way to have that Jolly Rancher shoot out of my throat. Jesse never trips me. Aziza does it about fifty times a day, but Jesse never does."

I patted my sweet dog's head, then patted the head of my whiny nuisance dog. They both licked me, then turned back to pay attention to Daniel. After all, he was waving his fork wildly around and was much more likely to drop something edible.

"And have you heard a voice like that before?" he asked.

"Mmm hmm," I said quietly.

Daniel stopped waving and chewing. "When?"

"When the glass didn't break at my un-wedding."

I scanned his face for his reaction. I really wouldn't blame him if he made some excuse and left. We'd only known each other for a few weeks. Hearing voices could easily be a relationship deal breaker for some people.

"Well, then, it must be okay." He took another big bite of

casserole, and I took a big, deep breath as if I was surfacing from being underwater for a very long time.

After we finished eating, we put our dirty plates and glasses in the sink. As I started to fill it up with hot water, Daniel came up behind me and put his arms around my waist and kissed my neck. I relaxed back into him, feeling like a bowl full of caramels just starting to melt. He turned me around and kissed my mouth, his arms pulling me close against him.

I reached behind me and turned the water off. Daniel took my hand and led me back to my bedroom.

I left the dishes in the sink. They'd still be there in the morning. I'd still be here in the morning. This was home, after all.

Up Close and Personal with the Author

WHERE DID YOUR IDEA/INSPIRATION FOR *UN-BRIDALED* COME FROM?

Both of my last two books, *Do Me, Do My Roots* and *Balancing in High Heels*, were in large part about the healing abilities of family. This is a natural subject for me because I'm lucky to come from a supportive and loving family who is also slightly insane and thus provides a lot of great material. I started thinking, however, about what happens if you don't have that base of support. How does that impact your life? I began to focus on mothers—also a natural topic for me because I'm a mom and consider that to be pretty much my most important job—and what happens if you don't have that base of mother love in your life.

I had also been thinking quite a bit about how to break out of destructive behavior patterns. While I do believe that our early experiences are extremely important and influence how we behave later, I also very firmly believe that at a certain point, we must take responsibility for our own behavior. Chloe's mother was an unwanted baby, the illegitimate offspring of a relationship that was frowned on. In turn, Chloe's self-destructive mother never really wanted her. Chloe could choose to continue to hand that legacy down or she could choose to understand it and end it. Her mother wasn't strong enough to do that, but Chloe is.

ARE THOSE YOUR DOGS? I THOUGHT YOU ONLY HAD CATS!

The dogs are based on my sister's dogs, Jesse and Aziza. Jesse has almost eerily human reactions to things and often looks really embarrassed if he does something too doggie. He is extremely attached to my sister, to the point of sometimes being jealous of her husband. On one memorable occasion, he bit my brother-in-law on the butt when he was dancing with my sister. One day, while sitting in my sister's kitchen and watching Jesse follow her every move, I asked him if he had been my sister's lover in a previous life and the dog looked at me and winked. Of course, that could be coincidence, but it didn't look or feel that way to me! Aziza, on the other hand, is a total goofball and is clearly quite content that she's a dog.

DOES THE GLASS EVER REALLY NOT BREAK?

At my first wedding (and anytime a sentence starts that way it should be a clue that the marriage didn't go exactly smoothly), the glass didn't break. It did what I described in the opening sequence of this book. It flew a few feet, hit a wall, rolled, and didn't even get a crack in it. When that marriage was falling apart, I often wondered if that had been a bad omen and what would have happened if I'd just turned tail and run at that point. It took years for me to realize that I'd known at that point everything that I needed to know to realize that that relationship wasn't going to work out. I didn't know all of it on a conscious level, but I knew it deep down. I kept wondering what would have happened if everything I knew on a subconscious level had come to a head when the glass didn't break and I had picked up my skirts and run, and suddenly I was writing a runaway bride book.

ARE THE LOVE LETTERS FROM A WAR HERO REAL?

Jesse Hernandez's letters are based on letters that my second husband's father sent to his family during World War II. After my husband died, there were several boxes that I couldn't bring myself to go through. A few years later I was possessed by an odd fit of spring cleaning (and trust me, that doesn't happen often) and went through a few of the boxes. One of the things I found was a manila envelope stuffed full of letters. My children, who were nine and eleven at the time, were fascinated and so was I. I decided to put the letters in protective sleeves and put them all in chronological order, along with various official documents that I'd found in the boxes. It was a fascinating glimpse into his character (and into my late husband's in some ways too!) to read those letters. It was also a fascinating glimpse into history. When I read the letter about how he had been training in the ocean in seven-man boats, the hair on my arms stood up on end. I knew he'd been part of the D-Day Invasion, and to hear first hand how they prepared the troops for that day was both fascinating and horrifying.

WHAT IS IT WITH THE JOLLY RANCHERS?

Jolly Ranchers are my favorite non-chocolate candy and green apple is my favorite flavor. One of my best exercise buddies here in California has taken to carrying Jolly Ranchers in her fanny pack when we're out on long bike rides and whipping them out to give us a little sugar buzz when we're flagging. There's actually a bend in the road about six miles or so from home that we now refer to as Jolly Rancher Corner since we stop there so often. This exercise buddy is also a writer and has helped me work out countless plot and characterization problems on those bike rides. This same friend almost choked to death on a hard candy when she was in high school just like Aunt Laura did and like Chloe almost does at the end of the book. It seemed appropriate to have the final leg of the book's journey come from a Jolly Rancher episode inspired by my friend, since she and the candies have helped me literally and figuratively make it home so many times.